YESHIVA GIRL

A Novel
by
Rachel Mankowitz

Chapter 1

THE ARRAIGNMENT

I was fifteen and a half years old when my father was arrested. It was only October, and I wouldn't have thought he'd had time to get into trouble yet, what with all the Jewish holidays early in the school year. But, clearly, I was wrong. He was a middle school math teacher, with a history of "misconduct" with his female students. But this was the first time the police had gotten involved.

He spent the night in jail after his rabbi went with him to surrender to the police, on advice of counsel. I imagined him sitting on the grimy floor in his black suit and wondered if he was allowed to wear his smooth black hat and if it would matter to his fellow prisoners that he was supposedly orthodox and righteous. Would they be fooled? Would he have to pee in front of them?

Mom looked so small that morning in court; her clothes floated around her without weight. She was like one of those Yorkshire Terriers - as tiny as a Chihuahua underneath but blow-dried to look almost like a real dog. She'd asked me to come with her to court because that's what my father wanted, for the judge to see that he had a family who supported him and depended on him. But I agreed to go for mom's sake, so she wouldn't have to be alone in the courtroom with all of those eyes on her, telling her it was her fault.

I hadn't wanted to miss school. My father had switched me to an orthodox school in September, and I was just starting to get used to it, and didn't want anyone to ask where I'd been. The change in schools was supposedly for my benefit, because I didn't have friends at my old school, and because orthodoxy would transform me the way it had transformed my father. Ahem. Mom didn't like the idea of switching schools, but when she wasn't sure what to do she deferred to my father. She thought, or hoped, he knew what was best.

Mom used to let me stay home from school when I was barely sick as a kid, when she only worked part time. She never told my father about it, because he would have disapproved. She made toasted English muffins with strawberry jam and then opened cans of matzoh ball soup for lunch. She wanted to spend time with me but felt guilty about it, so while I was watching soap operas or children's shows, she would clean the house. She would start to do the vacuuming in the living room and find a shelf of books that was too dusty and out of order, and then she'd spend the whole afternoon pulling all of the books off the shelves and dusting the built-in bookshelves. She never had time to put all of the books back, and she'd forget about it, until weeks later when the books were in dusty piles on the floor and on the couch and my father was screaming that he couldn't sit anywhere, and no one would want to come over and visit a house this disgusting.

On those afternoons when I was a kid I would come downstairs in my pajamas, holding my bowl of salty, metallic soup, and I'd sit on the bottom step of the stairs and watch her reach far back into the shelves, sweeping the edges of her long black hair through the dust. I kept waiting for her to turn around and notice me but she couldn't look away from the dust.

The courtroom was filled. We sat on the benches in the back and waited for my father's turn in front of the judge. A young black man was being arraigned and a large black woman, I assumed she was his mother, stood with all of her weight leaned against the small woman next to her and she wept, so loud that I couldn't hear what her son had been accused of. He looked back at her, blank eyed, as she called his name, "Jamie, Jamie," as if he were still a little boy and she was calling down every street in the neighborhood looking for him.

The woman was a deep purple black, not chocolate brown. Her skin shined as if it had been oiled along her forearms where the fabric of her dark suit jacket came up short. The way she cried, with her whole body collapsing into each sob, made me think of Lot's wife in Genesis, when she looks back at her lost city and is turned into a pillar of salt. I could understand a woman like that, feeling so much grief that the tears consume her.

I looked at my mother, with her hair pulled back in a ponytail at the nape of her neck, staring at the floor as if her head was too heavy for her to hold it up straight. She would never cry like the boy's mother, in public, with her whole body.

My father's rabbi was sitting in the row in front of us, wearing a grey tweed hat over his black suede Kippah, keeping God in mind, but out of view. I wondered if he'd told his wife why my father had been arrested, or if he was worried about his own daughter. I wondered if he thought my father was innocent.

My father walked in from the other side of the courtroom in his ill-fitting, slept-in black suit, a large black Kippah on his head, but no hat. He was handcuffed. I noticed other people noticing him. He looked like a rabbi. Even more like a rabbi than his real rabbi. He smiled at the room, but not specifically at me and Mom.

I couldn't hear what the judge said. I could only see the look of disgust on his face as he looked down at my father, now uncuffed and holding his blue bible in both hands.

3

I stared at the wrinkles in the back of his suit and the gray tinge it had picked up overnight. He stood up straight and relaxed. I would have been fidgeting or stooping my shoulders, trying to get away from the words said about me. I glanced at his rabbi. He was leaned forward in his seat, trying to follow the action. Mom sat back against our bench, eyes on the floor. She knew how to find a blank space in her mind and crawl into it.

The arraignment went quickly. I only knew it was over because my father was being led out of the courtroom and then the rabbi turned in his seat to talk to Mom. I thought he might offer her words of comfort. That maybe he was there as much for us as for my father and he would realize how scared Mom was and how much she needed someone to tell her she hadn't done anything to cause this.

But he was my father's rabbi, not ours. My father had found him and chosen him for a reason and my father was, in his way, an astute judge of character.

"He'll be hungry," was all the rabbi said to Mom. "They don't serve kosher food in the holding area downstairs."

"I brought sandwiches," my mother said.

The rabbi wasn't impressed. He'd probably expected her to roast a chicken for her newly arrested husband. I glared at the side of his head and the suede Kippah dangling towards his ear from under the hat.

"I'll go speak to his lawyer," he said, whispering as the next case was called. "You should bring your car around and be ready to take him home as soon as he's been processed."

My mother kept nodding her head even after the rabbi left. When we walked out of the courtroom the black woman was still in the hall, crying more quietly now, leaning her back against the wall for support.

"I didn't expect the handcuffs," Mom said as we walked out to the car. "You shouldn't have had to see your father that way."

We walked through the metal detectors and outside. The wind swirled orange and red leaves from one parked car to another, and I listened to Mom breathe in and out in time with the wind. She had a habit of blending in with her environment so completely that she was indistinguishable from it.

My mother's old green Mercedes was where we'd left it. Her father had bought the car for her when I was born, because he wanted me to be safe. My father called it the tank. I took my place in the back seat.

"What happens next?" I asked, leaning forward.

She let her hands rest on her knees. She was wearing one of her skirt suits, in Burgundy, with the hem down at mid-calf. I hated her clothes.

"They'll keep him out of the classroom and he'll work at the Board of Education offices for a while."

"And if he's convicted?"

She turned away from me and stared at the steps of the building. "I don't know."

There was a bag of sandwiches in the front seat. The salami one was starting to smell, despite the two layers of aluminum foil around it. I saw my father walk out on the steps and shake the rabbi's hand and then he came towards us. I hugged my book bag and looked out the other window.

He sat down in the passenger seat next to my mother and draped his arm over into the back. "Hey Jezebel, how you doin' back there?"

He liked to call me Jezebel, instead of Isabel, most of the time. There are, I assume, some good arguments to be made against insinuating that your daughter is an idol-worshipping femme fatale, but I was used to it.

I shrugged

"How about we all go out for lunch?" He reached back and tugged the hem of my skirt, brushing my leg.

"I have to go to school," I said, curling my legs under me.

"No, you don't," he said.

My mother started the car and pulled out into the street.

"How about pizza?" he asked, turning to look only at her, as if I hadn't said anything.

"I brought sandwiches," she said.

He took the salami on rye from the bag and unwrapped the aluminum foil and with the sandwich in one hand he dug out the thermos of coffee with the other. "Open this," he said and handed it back to me. I unscrewed the top and poured coffee into his cup, careful not to drip any. I had to hold the cup in the air until he finished chewing the first huge bite of salami and mustard and rye bread. Between chews he started to outline his plan for religious improve-ments. We would never drive to shul on the Sabbath again. We were going to walk all the way there and back every Saturday. We'd have to wear skirts every day, no more pants for the women in his family. And the dog food would be kept in the laundry room, not in the kitchen spreading its unkosherness into the air.

I sat forward. "But the dog likes to bring a mouthful of food over to the table so she can eat dinner with us. She shouldn't have to eat alone, should she?"

He didn't answer me, just kept on with his list of new rules, and made no mention of his night in jail or why he needed to upgrade his religious obligations.

Instead of dropping me off at school, as Mom had promised, I had to sit in the car while they did errands, shopping for things I didn't know we needed, like more Jewish books, a new bookcase, a new microwave that would represent the start of a new level of *Kashrut*, and on and on. By the time we got home I just traipsed up to my bedroom with the dog, dropped my book bag on the floor, and fell onto my bed waiting for the whole world to go black, and after a few face licks, the world obliged.

Chapter Two

THE SANDWICH

My father drove me to school the next morning so he could catch morning prayers with the boys, because he'd missed early services at all the local synagogues, too busy ranting at mom about the lack of moral support from his union representative and fellow teachers while she sipped at her cooling coffee.

The drive across the Island was silent except for one of my father's fifteen Jewish History tapes, a man's voice droning on about the establishment of the state of Israel. I was always surprised by the things he needed to learn through his audiotapes.

My father was lost. We were in an industrial park that I didn't recognize and the roads turned us in circles. So much of Long Island is housing developments and strip malls and industrial parks and fast food restaurants in gaudy yellows and blues, but the dominant color is green. There are trees and healthy green grass between each store and along each parkway and right up to the sand on every side. The leaves had been swept up as soon as they'd hit the ground, so they barely changed the color palette. My father suddenly slammed on the brakes in the middle of traffic and backed up onto the grassy lawn of one of the commercial buildings and turned around, again. He'd driven to the school before, and I'd been riding on the school bus for a month, but neither one of us was thinking clearly that morning.

He smacked the glove compartment until it popped open. "Find the map!"

I dodged the used deli napkins as they fell to the floor and pulled out the car's registration, then business cards from various Judaica stores in Brooklyn and Queens, a tall plastic cup that smelled like pee, and his blue bible with a map of ancient Israel glued to the inside cover.

"We don't have a map of Long Island," I said.

He crossed oncoming traffic as he turned into the lane he wanted to be in and I didn't cringe. I was proud of myself for staying so calm. In the past I would have screamed, but then he would've told me that I was taunting him and overreacting and making it worse – so I'd learned to grit my teeth and hold onto the door handle unobtrusively.

"Now, which street am I supposed to turn on?" He asked.

"We could stop at a gas station and ask."

"You think a man who pumps gas for a living knows what a Yeshiva is?"

I wanted to say that, yes, it was possible that someone who worked near the school might know where to find the place better than we did, but then he banged on the steering wheel with both fists and screamed, "Where the fuck is it?" So I kept my mouth shut.

He made a sudden left turn at a red light, driving over the concrete divider in the middle of the road, and for one second I pictured myself jumping out of the car, rolling across the asphalt, and scraping off the skin on my legs in a bid for safety. But by then he'd started to breathe normally again and even used his turn signal before shifting into the right lane and easing into the Yeshiva's parking lot.

The building was red brick and three stories high. It looked like a factory. Add girl and stir.

I was relieved when my father disappeared into the gym with the boys and I was able to get lost in the crowd of girls by the lockers. He wouldn't come to check on me before he left, because, after all, I wasn't the reason he was there. I went to morning prayers with the other tenth grade girls and then hid out in the classroom until I was sure he'd be gone.

During first period bible class, the little Rabbi droned on about the book of Beresheit, Genesis in English, but it really means "In the beginning." There was a monotonous, bored quality to his voice that made me think he didn't care whether we listened or not. And I started to think about the words. About how there was a difference between an event being the genesis of every other event, or just being the first event in a long list. My birth didn't cause my father's anger and bad behavior. but he kept pointing to me as the source of his problems. Because I came first, he said.

During the break between classes, Shira, the girl who sat next to me, leaned across the aisle to my desk. She'd been sucking on clumps of her blond hair so it looked like she had sheets of undercooked spaghetti resting on her shoulder.

"I'd rather be watching cartoons, what about you?"

"Little House on the Prairie," I said.

"Really?" She looked surprised.

"No."

She kicked my leg with the toe of her shoe, and it hurt, but I didn't flinch.

"Don't laugh at me," she whispered. "Please?"

"I won't."

She was my new best friend, not that I'd ever had one before. She wanted to know everything about my old school, about being allowed to wear pants in front of boys, and if it was weird to do bible studies with boys, and was there a lot of sex going on and drugs and parties with boys? I kept the notes she wrote to me during class. The only notes I'd gotten from the girls at my old school were things like, "Your bra strap is showing," or, "you need to shave your legs." I'd kept those too. I could still see those girls doing the Cooty dance in first grade, hands in claws, feet flat on the ground as they stomped in a circle around me. They'd always known there was something wrong with me: my sandals were not up to code; my mother didn't know how often to wash my hair; I stared too long at nothing.

I was wearing my yellow cotton dress with the long gored skirt that morning for the school-wide Rosh Chodesh breakfast. It was a monthly event, after the first two periods, to celebrate the first day of the new Hebrew month, on the lunar calendar. We'd never had first day of the month parties at my old, less religious, but still Jewish day school. There is something reassuringly isolationist about keeping up a whole separate calendar while living in a largely Christian country. The fact that the Jewish calendar is so wonky that it needs a whole leap month every few years to even things out is just part of its charm.

The party was an excuse to get out of the rest of our morning classes and eat bagels and dance and have awards given out to the best students. The best kiss-ups, Shira said, though she'd won a certificate herself the year before and it was still taped to her bedroom wall, or so she told me.

I'd hoped the yellow dress would make me feel clean and cheery, but every other girl wore some variation on a black and white theme and I just wanted to hide under our table.

Shira, in a fitted black dress that belonged to her taller, thinner, older sister, picked the doughy guts out of her bagel, but I couldn't eat. I felt icky in my clingy dress, too aware of my breasts and hips. The band started to play on the small stage in the gym and

YESHIVA GIRL

I pushed my untouched bagel into the center of our table. One of the more heavily bearded rabbis stood at the microphone and began to sing an amalgam of klezmer folk tunes, Hebrew prayers, and rock and roll. Boys stood up on the other side of the room, pushing their tables aside with a group heave-ho to clear the floor.

Shira turned herself around on our bench to watch. I followed, trying not to pull my dress up too high during the maneuver. She gawked at the boys as they started to dance and made her best attempt to wink at me, which turned into a blink and an eye rub when her eyelash landed on her contact lens.

Four big, tall senior boys linked arms and squatted low to the ground then sprang up, again and again, lifting off and flying a few feet to the side each time. Rabbi Gottlieb, the principal of the school, chose the smallest boy in the room and swung him in a circle, a makeshift jump rope for the other boys to hurdle over.

The Rosh Chodesh music pulsed and shook the gymnasium walls and I noticed Jake standing on the outskirts. He was wearing dress pants for the party, and a white shirt, even a tie, like a nice orthodox boy, instead of his usual flannel shirt over a t-shirt. I noticed him the first day of school, when Tova Keifer gave him her best seductress glance and he made a point of ignoring her. For that alone, he had my attention. He sat behind me in all of our secular classes in the afternoons, Jake Hirsch, behind Isabel Halpern, with Tova Keifer in the next aisle over, resenting me. I liked the flannel shirt too, because it made him less like everyone else in the room; it made him an outsider, like me.

Early in the semester, while the social studies teacher was giving a monotonous lecture on the Spanish Inquisition, Jake, who had to borrow loose-leaf paper from me because he hadn't bothered to bring any, leaned forward and whispered in my ear.

"I'm an atheist. They'd have burned me at the stake for sure."

12

YESHIVA GIRL

The soft low sound of his voice made my ears burn. I didn't have the nerve to risk talking and being caught by the teacher, so I wrote to him on a clean sheet of paper.

"I don't want to believe in a God who would let any random man become a rabbi instead of me. But I believe in God anyway. I'm in conflict."

I handed the note over my shoulder and listened as Jake unfolded the paper, said "Ha," and then crumpled the note. The sound of crinkling paper bothered me, until he whispered to me again.

"Conflict makes life interesting, don't you think?"

Tova noticed the whispers, but so did the teacher and we kept to ourselves for the rest of the class.

I had to lend him paper the next day too, but it wasn't clear what he was doing with it, certainly not taking notes. I was curious about what he was doing back there, but I didn't have the nerve to turn around and ask.

A few minutes later, I thought I'd caught my hair between my chair back and his desk. But then Jake breathed on my neck.

"My little sister wants me to braid her hair," he'd said. "Can I practice on you?"

I sat through class, dutifully taking notes on various methods of torture, while my scalp tingled and tiny braids appeared and disappeared behind me.

He was scanning the gym now, squinting as if he was really trying to see something. Or someone. He stared in my direction for a long minute and I wanted to believe he was looking at me, but then he turned to watch the dancing and took his jacket off and joined the boys on the floor. I wasn't sure what was going on between us. One day he'd write me a long letter about French philosophers, and the

13

next day it was as if I didn't exist. Having a crush on Jake was humiliating, but I couldn't shake it off.

In a small corner of the room, our nineteen-year old frizzy blond teacher who sat with us for morning prayers was trying to pull girls onto the floor. Her ankle length green skirt, with a modest kick pleat, only allowed her the freedom to move one step in any direction. But she gamely lurched and skipped and urged her little circle into motion.

For one crazy moment I wanted to dance, not off in the girls' corner but out in the middle of the floor. I would spin until my skirt flew out and swirled around me. I closed my eyes and imagined running to Jake, grabbing his hands, and dancing him in circles until the only thing he could see in the whole world would be me. But I couldn't do that. So I followed Shira over to the grateful green-skirted teacher to dance with the girls and try not to step on anyone's feet.

At lunch, over baked potatoes in the cafeteria/gym/auditorium, Shira pulled on her ears and looked over at Tova Keifer sitting at the next table, not eating. Tova was beautiful in the same way as the girls at my old school; the ones who lived in mansions with elevators and custom designed swimming pools. She had bright white teeth and long curly black hair and gold hoops in her ears and the black fabric of her skirt shimmered.

"My mother won't let me pierce my ears or wear makeup. So I'm bitter. I admit it," Shira said.

I peeled the skin off my potato with a plastic fork, to keep my hands busy. "I had my ears pierced before my Bat Mitzvah," I told her. "They take this gun and put it up to your ear like they're gonna shoot you in the head. But I let the holes close."

Shira pointed her fork at me, her mouth full. "Why would you do that?"

14

I pushed my hair back and felt the little scarred bumps on my ear lobes. "I found out that Jewish indentured servants had their ears pierced by their masters, to show that they were owned." Shira was silent for a while after that but then came back to life with a discussion of the difficulties of shopping at the mall where they never had enough modest skirts and the food smells were so tempting but nothing was kosher.

I asked Shira if she would be my orthodoxy tutor and she thought that was hilarious. But she jumped right in, explaining the hierarchy of head coverings. Boys who wore crocheted kippot in bright colors were modern orthodox. Boys who wore leather or suede kippot were a little more religious, like Shira. Her older brother wore a black leather kippah because he thought it looked cool with his heavy metal t-shirts. I asked her about the oversized cloth kippot the rabbis tended to wear.

"To cover bald spots?"

"No," she said. "The larger the kippah the further to the right they are, religiously. And a lot of the rabbis at our school aren't modern orthodox. They don't watch TV or go to movies or want to mix with the outside world much at all."

"That explains why some of the rabbis look at girls like we have a bad smell."

She nodded.

"There was a woman at my old synagogue who wore a kippah she crocheted for herself," I said, but Shira didn't believe me. She gave me a rundown on how you could tell the religiosity of girls by the length of the skirt, length of sleeves, and if they wore tights or had bare legs.

She was still talking when she dropped me off at my English class. Something about a dress her older sister had made in Home Ec., and how one of the side seams fell apart one day when she was

15

praying a little too vigorously. There was some relief in knowing that Shira was not in most of my afternoon classes.

I wanted to talk to my mother when I got home, but she wasn't there. And my father was out somewhere too. There was a message from Mom on the answering machine telling me about the leftover spaghetti in the fridge, and the frozen peas I could add for my green vegetable.

I avoided the saran-wrapped plate of pasta and took an orange upstairs, but I didn't want to eat it, I wanted to throw it at my parents' bedroom door. I wanted the fruit to splatter and the door to crack open, but I threw it like a girl. The orange barely thumped the wood before rolling calmly to the carpet below. My part Labrador retriever part something unknown shelter dog ran over and picked the orange up from the floor as if it were one of her dusty drool-covered tennis balls. She inched her skinny, black-haired body past me with her nose down and the treasure in her mouth and ran down the stairs. I went to my room to watch TV and consider homework and to see how long I could go without eating anything at all.

By lunch time the next day, the gym was back to normal, but I could hear the echoes of the pounding feet from the party; maybe because the boys were playing basketball on the other side of the room.

Shira was at a far table, studying for a math test with one of the girls from her class. We were in different tracks for the afternoon classes, which she pointed out any number of times, waiting for me to reassure her about the meaningless-ness of grades at determining intelligence. I obliged every time, but it's possible that I didn't give the speech with enough conviction to convince her.

I sat alone at a table near the wall, staring at the peanut butter and jelly sandwich Mom had made for me. I worried for a moment about the Kashrut of my sandwich, because my mother had a habit of switching the meat utensils with the dairy ones just to piss my father off, but then I got distracted watching Jake bounce-pass the basketball to a boy with white tzitzis fringes hanging out from an untucked button down shirt. The fringes swung from side to side as the boy lumbered up the court to try to make a basket.

Before the arraignment, before I even knew for sure that my father would be arrested, I'd written to Jake about how my father became religious to hide his real self. And Jake wrote back that his parents "probably became religious to hide, or change, who I really am too. They've got me in long hours of school, with strict teachers, and religious peers, instead of actually spending time with me."

"Where's your sidekick?" Jake asked, suddenly in front of me in the gym, wiping sweaty hands on his rumpled flannel shirt.

I pointed to Shira with her face down in her notebook. "I'm alone today," I said, swallowing the bit of sandwich that stuck to the roof of my mouth.

He sat down across from me and I didn't know how to handle that. I wasn't used to looking him in the eye. And the public display of possible potential coupledom would be embarrassing when people realized he had no real interest in me. He reached across the table and took half of my sandwich - the half I'd already taken bites from - not even bothering to ritually wash his hands like he was supposed to.

"Aren't you worried it might not be kosher?" I asked, caught off guard.

"I don't care," he said, and took a big bite.

But I cared, suddenly. A switch went off in my head. He really bothered me, the way he just took what he wanted, did what he wanted, and didn't care what effect his behavior would have on

17

other people. That sandwich belonged to me. I crossed my arms in front of my chest like a shield.

"My father told me a story once," I said. "About how a boy in his elementary school tried to steal his lunch one day."

"Yeah, what happened?" Jake stopped for a moment with his mouth open.

"My father took the metal fork he'd brought from home," I said, "and stuck it through the top of the other boy's hand." I flattened my left hand on the table and then slammed it with my balled right fist. The sound of it, and the pain, shocked me.

Jake put my sandwich down and stared at my hands. I turned away and pretended to watch the basketball game, my heart thumping with each bounce of the ball.

"You remind me of my older sister," he said, finally. "The way she changes into somebody else, someone I don't recognize."

"Does she change back?"

"Yes, eventually."

"How?"

"I don't know."

"You change a lot too, Jake."

"Do I?"

"Yes. And I'm not your sister," I said, rubbing my left hand, trying to erase the red mark.

"No, you're not."

"What am I?" I asked, hoping he could answer the question for me, not just, *what am I to you*, but *what the hell am I*, period.

He shrugged.

"Are we friends?" I asked. My legs were shaking, but I always found multiple choice and yes or no questions comforting in their simplicity.

"I think that's up to you, Isabel," Jake said.

"Is it?"

He nodded.

I handed him the untouched half of the sandwich and picked up the piece he'd returned to me. We chewed to the uneven beat of the basketball hitting the gym floor.

Rabbi Gottlieb, the principal, called me into his office the next morning for a check in. He'd promised to keep an eye on me, but I'd thought he meant from a distance, like God. I was afraid he knew about my father's arrest, or that one of the teachers had complained about me. I wasn't used to being summoned to the principal's office.

Rabbi Gottlieb was thin with coarse black hair cut close to his head, and a hint of grey so light it could have been scalp. He stood up from behind the desk by the window and smiled at me. He was clean-shaven, around my father's age, and wore a dark blue suit with blue and white sneakers.

"Hello, Isabel," he said, still standing.

"Hi," I said, staring at the eight by ten photograph of a Chihuahua in a frame on his desk.

"Would you like a cookie?" he asked, holding up a flat white box with the lid open.

"I think I'm going to throw up," I said.

"No cookies then."

I nodded and sat down in the black leather chair he pointed to.

"Am I that scary?" he asked.

"I'm not sure why I'm here."

"And you think you're in trouble?"

"Yes?"

"Did you do something wrong?" he asked with a grin.

"I'm sure I did. It's inevitable, isn't it?" I sat there, strangling my fingers in my lap, waiting for him to tell me that the police were on their way to get me. But he didn't know his lines.

19

"I'll try to make this as painless as possible, okay?"

"Okay." There was a window behind him and a baseball diamond and soccer fields. I'd been hoping that one of the benefits of orthodoxy would be no more team sports. I was usually picked last for softball. I don't know if the slight came first, or if I just naturally stood in the outfield with my hands at my sides and my mind on other things, so the girls knew not to choose me.

"I've been concerned," he said, sitting down in his swivel chair, "ever since you came in for your entrance interview. It was obvious that while your father was enthusiastic about having you come to school here, you were...not."

I sat as still as possible, waiting.

"You're not breathing, Isabel. I need for you to breathe."

"I'm trying."

"That's all I can ask of you," he said, with a smile. But he looked concerned, and, maybe, confused.

"Your father said something the other day when he was here."

I flinched and he noticed.

"You knew he came in for morning prayers on Rosh Chodesh, yes?"

I nodded.

"He said that you were 'adapting,' that's the word he used."

"Oh," I said, deflating suddenly. "That's all he said?"

"It wasn't a long conversation," Rabbi Gottlieb said. "Was there something else he should have told me?"

I shook my head.

He turned his chair to look out the window. There was an empty pool in the yard next to a small brick building that looked abandoned, and the lawns were a patchy green, but he surveyed it all with his head tilted back and a deep satisfied sigh.

He swiveled his chair back in my direction. "So, have you been 'adapting'?" he asked. "Because I wouldn't want you to do much of that."

"I don't want to play softball." I said, suddenly.

"Is there anything else you don't want to do?"

"Many, many things."

He grinned.

I liked him. I liked that he asked me questions and waited to hear the answers. I wasn't used to that.

"Can you promise me that you will come to me if you need anything: cookies, an oxygen tank, anything?

I nodded.

"You may even learn to like it here," he said.

I gave him a look.

He tilted his head at me, in imitation of the Chihuahua in the photograph. "Can you believe that I want things to work out well for you?"

"I guess so," I said.

When I left, I reached out to shake his hand before I remembered I wasn't supposed to do that. I hoped he didn't notice, but just in case, I walked out into the hallway swinging my right arm as if I'd meant to do that all along, as if I didn't want to cut the damned thing off.

Shira and I sat together on the gym floor a few hours later while some of the other girls, including a suddenly animated Tova Keifer, played basketball in their long skirts. The gym teacher was the only one in shorts. Participation, she said, was optional.

"At my old school we had to change into shorts and t-shirts for gym and run laps to the theme song from *Rocky*," I said, trying to find a comfortable position on the hardwood floor.

"With boys?" Shira asked, eyes wide.

"Yeah." She didn't know better. She'd never played dodge ball with boys who wanted to kill each other and couldn't see very well. I wondered if I should ask her what she knew about Jake. I just wanted to say his name to someone. But she was back on the subject of clothes and the wonders of the flea market.

"My mom buys my clothes," I said.

The shock on her face was real. "You trust your mother to choose your clothes?"

"Not trust, exactly," I said, thinking about the orange skirt with black zigzag trim and the white sweater with a silver and blue unicorn across the front. "But when I try to go shopping I can survive about ten minutes of looking through the racks of *stuff* before the dizziness sets in and I start to feel an inexplicable desire to throw things as hard as I can, at people."

"Huh." Shira examined my face carefully. "Are you sure you're a girl?" She pinched my arm to show me she was, sort of, kidding. I couldn't sit still anymore. I stood up and started to walk the perimeter of the gym. And she followed me.

My father picked me up from school that afternoon, as a surprise. He took me to the kosher butcher store, because, he said, we needed a reward for our difficult ordeal. He liked to think of us as a team. The smell of raw meat hit me first, then the bloody apron on the man who came to greet him. They walked to the back of the store together to confer over exactly how to cut the half a cow's worth of steaks my father would try to stuff into our freezer.

"Get a wagon!" he shouted at me over the other customers' heads. "We'll buy whatever you want!"

A middle aged woman, wearing a kerchief over her hair and a long denim skirt down to her shoes looked up from examining a cellophane wrapped chicken thigh and stared at me, from my knotted hair to my ill-fitting skirt and down to my dirty sneakers.

I grabbed a wagon and it clanged against the others in its row. For one short second I thought about plowing through the lady, knocking her into the packages of raw chicken livers. But I wheeled around in the opposite direction, through the bakery section of the store to the packaged foods where the stale blood smell was less prominent.

Marzipan fruit. There was a perfect red strawberry with a green plastic stem, and a tiny banana nestled in next to it. My mother would never let me buy such a thing. She already thought real strawberries were too much of an extravagance. But I was with my father and he said I could have anything I wanted.

I pushed my tiny basket up and down the skinny aisles, dodging an elderly couple who seemed to know where I was headed at each turn and lodged themselves there first. I didn't want Israeli pickles or giant matzoh balls or bright red packages of brisket large enough to feed a whole community. I especially didn't want to get any closer to the back of the store and glimpse the butcher and his chopping arm at work.

There were veal sausages and the good chopped liver in the freezer section so I headed there, and loaded my wagon with cherry blintzes and potato pierogen and chocolate tofutti even though I hated the taste of the fake ice cream we had to eat after meat meals ever since my father decided we'd be kosher. They had fake shrimp too, and I missed the real stuff, so I picked up three packages of those and frozen gefilte fish and once I hit the dessert aisle again I think I just lost my mind. There were chocolate covered apricots, cinnamon raisin rugelach, a huge box of hazelnut truffles that would make even my mother's silent disapproval turn to screaming. I filled the basket to the top with kosher cheeses and Israeli yogurt and chummus with whole chickpeas and even gave in and took two cans of Israeli pickles because they fit neatly next to the quarts of non-dairy chocolate milk.

I could barely breathe when I reached the register where my father and his pile of steaks were waiting. He handed his credit card to the cashier, opened the bag of challah rolls I forgot I'd thrown in and took a deep whiff of the sweet egg bread. When we got to the car he kept that bag out of the trunk, ripped a roll in half and handed it to me. We ate the whole bag together the rest of the way home.

My mother, dressed for her secretarial job at an accountant's office in her ten dollar black pantsuit from the consignment shop, stood on the porch when we pulled into the driveway. She looked like shattering glass, as if she was in a constant state of falling into a thousand pieces.

I rolled down the window and yelled, "We have groceries!" But Mom just stood there next to our front door, looking as empty as the house itself. When she was still painting, she used to wear these long batik skirts with leather sandals and plain white t-shirts. She used to wear clothes that fit her instead of these suits that still looked like they belonged to someone else.

I opened the car door and put a sneakered foot on the driveway, and as soon as I stood up she disappeared into the house. She's just trying to keep the dog from running out, I told myself. I carried the shopping bags into the kitchen with my father's help and then Mom started to prepare a few of the steaks while I put the rest of the groceries away. She didn't complain about the $500 we'd just spent at the butcher. She just bent forward to open the oven door and prick the steaks with a long fork and said nothing.

I wanted to hide behind her skinny legs the way I used to. I wanted her to hug me and not let go. She used to have a smell, like caramelized onions, and I would lean in close to her and feel safe and warm. I couldn't remember when she'd lost her smell.

Chapter Three

Home

The dog stayed in my room, stretched out on the denim skirt I'd dropped on the floor earlier. I couldn't fall asleep. My bedroom door was closed, because I had long since given up on my mother's ideal of a family with open doors. When I was little and couldn't sleep, I would tip toe down the hall to my parents' bedroom and, if their door wasn't locked the way it sometimes was, I would drag my bare feet across the worn spot on the carpet and make my way to my mother's side of the bed, careful to keep an eye on my father's rising and falling belly. She barely woke up when I tapped her shoulder with my fingertips and whispered, "Mommy, I don't feel good." Sometimes she would shift over on the bed and leave room for me. After a while, I stopped waking my mother up and just stayed in bed each night staring at the swirls in the ceiling tiles, trying to hypnotize myself to sleep.

I crawled to the floor to seek comfort from my warm dog, but she was busy chasing squirrels in her sleep. Even she scared me sometimes, in her willingness to chase after small creatures, to bare her teeth at a bird flying too close. One more predator who I loved and protected, and identified with. One more sign of the monster living inside of me, the one who would take over one day, no matter how hard I tried to resist.

"We really need a second dishwasher," my father said Friday afternoon, while I was chopping carrots on the cutting board next to the stove, and he was sautéing mushrooms to pour over his steak. My classes let out at 1:30 p.m. on Fridays, so we could all be home in plenty of time to help our mothers prepare the Shabbos meal (girls), or to shower (boys). My father was a rarity for wanting to cook his own Shabbos dinner, and he was also bored enough to do it because he was still home from work.

His happy mood was not a great sign, though. The day he threw my mother's easel out of our attic window, he was so happy he bought me three different kinds of ice cream.

Jake had skipped school for the day. He had a habit of skipping, just stepping off the school bus in the morning and walking to the mall, then getting back in time to take the bus home. He'd told me once that his older sister had a theory about it. Their parents were the children of holocaust survivors, and his sister believed that, even generations later, the family was still trying to escape, but, without the concentration camp, they didn't know what to escape from.

"Are you really using the holocaust to excuse ditching school?" I wrote back, and he just laughed, folded the note, and stuffed it in his pocket without answering.

Thinking about Jake was my escape. But it didn't work for long.

My parents had had our kitchen redone when I was eight or nine, before the first accusations surfaced. The counters were white Formica, alternating with thick butcher block cutting boards that my father liked to stab with his cleaver every once in a while just to see the knife balance on its tip. Grease and dust and dog hair stuck to the cabinet fronts and the black and white floor tiles, but my father was more concerned with the questionable Kashrut of the leaky dishwasher.

"At least keep the dairy utensils on one side and the meat things on the other," he said, pulling a silverware drawer open and ignoring the way the blonde wood rim came free of the drawer front. He pressed it back in place with the handle of the cleaver and grabbed a fork.

"There's only one bucket for the utensils, Dad."

"Your point?"

"There's no space for a second bucket, so your suggestion would leave half the forks unwashed. Isn't cleanliness next to godliness?"

"You watch too much goyishe television."

He watched TV almost from the moment he came home until his regular bedtime, around eight o'clock, and he left the TV on all night just in case. But I didn't want to argue with him about which one of us had more non-Jewish influences flowing through our brains. He sent me to Jewish schools because he didn't get the chance to go; he'd said so many times.

We were home because he was trying out the idea of not going to shul for Friday night services. He didn't want to drive on Shabbos anymore, and he really didn't want the other congregants to see his car parked in its hiding spot three blocks away from the building.

I made the challahs myself, the two braided egg breads. We'd had a special baking class early in the school year to learn about yeast and kneading and burning a portion of the dough for the priests, a meaningless gesture now that there were no priests, but it was an old ritual, to commemorate the double portion of Manna God sent the Jews in the desert to prepare for the Sabbath. It should have annoyed me, like everything else, but Shira was there too and she taught me how to make a six part braid with the dough and made me feel, for a moment, as if God would try to provide for me too. My hands felt safe in the dough, and I felt hopeful, in class. Not so much when I was at home.

"Where's Mom?" I asked my father, as I collected carrot peels from the floor to throw into the garbage. I wanted Mom to see the braids before he could devour them.

"Her mother wanted her, so of course she ran right over there," my father said. He and my grandmother had a tense relationship. She didn't approve of him. Because he was poor, he said. But I could think of other reasons. She was used to my grandfather, the gentleman and caretaker. And she didn't like the way my father dominated his wife, that was supposed to be Grandma's job.

My father wanted me to light the Shabbos candles, as we got closer to the candle lighting deadline. I'd done it before, on occasion, when my mother was busy getting dressed, or was rebelling in some other small way against the encroaching religiosity. But I wanted to wait, just a few more minutes, in case she came home in time. I didn't want to be the woman of the house. And this was one of the rituals Mom actually liked: the flame, the smell of the wax, the particular look of the thick fingers of opaque white candle, welcoming in the holiness of the coming day.

"In two minutes it will be too late to light the candles at all, Jezebel," my father said, his hair still wet from the shower he took while I was setting the table and retrieving a bottle of red wine from the case in the basement. He had a special relationship with the wine. He called it an investment, but he never let the bottles age enough to accrue a financial value, he used them to consecrate the Sabbath and make it holy and get God on his side. It had to be kosher wine, watched wine, to make sure no one had pre-consecrated it for some other purpose.

I stood in front of the mini-candelabra in my school clothes and dirty white socks and waited until the last possible second, watching out the window for my mother to arrive. There were four stubby white candles, two for my parents, one for me, and, in my mind, one for the dog. I had to melt the bottoms of the candles and stick them into their holders, still holding off lighting them, waiting for Mom to arrive.

At ten seconds to the deadline, my father struck the wooden match against the box, shoved it between my thumb and forefinger, and held my left hand over each wick until they were all lit. I closed my eyes, waved my hands over the flames three times on automatic pilot and mumbled the blessing to welcome the Sabbath.

He patted my upper arm, said "Gut Shabbos," and walked over to the table.

"Good Shabbos," I said, because I couldn't manage the Yiddish pronunciation.

Cabernet and *Sauvignon* were the only French words he chose to pronounce correctly. He said the French didn't deserve his respect, but the grapes did. He poured the wine into his silver Kiddush cup and I thought he might wait for my mother before saying the blessing, but he sailed right through, blessing the grapes, ritually washing his hands, coddling the breads under their special embroidered challah cover, ripping off sections for each of us, salting them, and finally sitting down to chew.

So much money went into sanctifying the Sabbath in our house. The challah was dressed better than I was, in its fancy velvet cover with fringes all around. And the bread knife had Hebrew lettering etched into the handle and was only used one day a week. Not to mention the silver Kiddush cup, a goblet really, and the special bottles of wine reserved for just this purpose.

When my mother walked in, she went straight to the stove and began to ladle out the soup. I jumped up to help. I wanted my mother to look at me, to smile, to hug me. Her arms were so skinny.

"Mommy," I whispered as we passed each other in front of the fridge. "I don't feel good."

30

She put the bowls of soup down on the counter and felt my forehead with the back of her hand; her thick veins were like soft cushions on my skin.

"You're not warm," she said. "Is it your stomach?"

I wanted her to read my mind, to bring me presents so I wouldn't feel so jealous of the Kiddush cup anymore. But she glanced down at the chicken soup and the dog's nose inching closer and closer to it.

"Maybe you're just hungry," she said and asked me to serve out another bowl of soup, for her. When she sat down at her end of the table my father let her listen to his list of complaints and things were back to normal.

We had a chocolate layer cake for dessert and I automatically scraped the frosting off my piece with a fork and passed the naked cake over to my father. We always did this. It took me a second, and a look from my mother, to remember that I wasn't supposed to eat the frosting any more than I was supposed to eat the cake. But then we started singing some Shabbat songs that made me feel like my old self and I felt the same surge of energy as at my Bat Mitzvah, when I stood at the podium at my old synagogue and led the prayers and read from the Torah and felt like a super hero. Super Jew. That was back when I thought I could be a rabbi one day, or a cantor, or maybe a movie star.

I felt, for a moment, powerful. Then my father switched keys. His voice strained up an octave further than I could follow. He couldn't reach the notes either, but that didn't stop him from trying. Finally the dog joined in, he was singing her kind of song.

Chapter Four

DAVID

Shira told me that she had decided that I was a good replacement for her older sister, Dahlia, who was spending the year studying in Israel and sending letters home about lessons in how to wear a gas mask. Shira planned a get together at her house, for school friends and for her brother's school friends, on a Saturday afternoon, and in order for me to go, and as her new best friend I had to go, she said I could sleep over and borrow Dahlia's bed in their shared room.

I had stared at the note on which this invitation was written, filling in the last free space on the ripped piece of paper, snaking around the sides of a previous note about the coolness factor of polka dots. I liked having Shira as my school friend. She kept me distracted. She wrote to me during her afternoon classes and passed me exquisitely folded pieces of paper in the hallway like a spy. But I was afraid to go to her house.

I wasn't sure I wanted her to see me with my guard down. I wasn't exactly sure there was more to me than my guard, at that point. But my other option was to hurt her feelings, and I couldn't do that. One day at lunch I had declined the offer of a sour cream and onion potato chip and she looked just like my mother did sometimes, as if all the bones holding up her face just sagged and started to break apart.

Shira's little brothers were everywhere. Like overgrown mice crawling out from behind the corduroy sofa in the living room. One little boy with long blond curls and a leather Kippah dangling from his bobby pin ran through the dining area and skewed his path to avoid me and then hit hard against his mother's legs before he could escape up the stairs. Her dress seemed to be made from the leftover sofa material, navy blue and full length down to her black suede clogs. She was enormous. Another boy hid behind her, waiting to catch the runner, but she held them apart, one hand on each head. Her head was covered with a black scarf and for one moment I just wanted to push it back to see her hair. Why didn't the rabbis know that hiding a thing could make it more alluring? But maybe everyone else respected the modesty of married women covering their hair, and I was the only freak. I held tight to my book bag so she wouldn't see my grabby fingers.

Shira came out of the kitchen with an open jar of peanut butter and a spoon already in her mouth. "Mwah some?"

Her mother looked at me and raised an eyebrow. "Can you believe what my daughter eats?" But she sounded almost proud.

After we had dropped our things off in Shira's room we were set to work in the kitchen, chopping carrots and celery for the chicken soup, emptying the dishwasher and putting the meat dishes away into the cabinets marked with red tape.

I pretended to be blind and deaf when Shira's older brother walked in with two friends from school and stole a bag of pretzels off the counter next to me. I didn't realize I was holding my breath until

33

Shira waved her hands in front of my face and whispered "You're turning blue," in her very not quiet voice.

Panic set in again later when I realized I would have to sleep upstairs on the same hallway with the boys. All sharing one bathroom. I sat on Shira's sister's bed, dressed for Shabbos in basically the same clothes I'd worn to school with just a different shirt swapped in, one that didn't smell from boiled chicken, and I told myself that I did not need to pee. I could wait. I watched Shira run in and out of the room, first to shower, then to brush her teeth, then to borrow a lipstick from her mother's dresser, and I did not move.

By candle lighting, Shira's mother had changed into a long sleeved black cotton dress that swirled around her ankles and she had shoulder length auburn hair. Shira, handing me dinner forks out of the meat utensil drawer, told me that there was a shorter blond wig for work. "That one's easier to clean," Shira whispered as the soup spoons clashed in her hands. "You wouldn't believe what muck old sick people can spew on a person. I don't ever wanna be a nurse. No way." I took a handful of salad forks and followed her to the dining room table but I glanced back through the doorway to see how a real orthodox woman would light the candles. She drew the flames towards her heart with her cupped hands and then covered her eyes and swayed with the rhythm of the blessing.

There were pieces of red Lego lodged between the wall and the carpet in the dining room. And in the glass breakfront, where the showpieces no one was supposed to touch were kept, there was a miniature cowboy dangling from a polished silver Kiddush cup. The house was quiet because Shira's father and all the boys who were old enough were at shul for Friday night services. And the youngest boys were napping, or sitting in their room planning more mischief. Their whole house felt warmer than mine, especially after Shabbos started, and I thought the heat came from Shira's mother – from the easy way she moved through space, as if she had nothing to apologize for and no reason to feel awkward with anyone. But maybe it was just from the stove top, which was covered with a sheet of metal and kept at low heat through the holy day to keep the food warm.

I liked the smell of the house too: roasted chicken with a hint of Play-Doh in the background. We sat at the kitchen table and waited for the men to return, Shira and her mother sneaking bites of noodle kugel from under the aluminum foil. At home I felt like I was always, just a little bit, in the way. But here, with all of the extra people, there was room for me.

As soon as the men and boys returned from shul, Shira's tall, thin father stood at the front of the table and held each of the heads of his children in his hands one at a time and a blessing over each of them. I'd seen the special children's prayer in my *Artscroll Siddur* – the pocket sized prayer book my father bought me to use at school – but I thought it was just one of those extra prayers that no one actually said, like the one for using the bathroom.

The three-year old boy ran up for his blessing and even he was stunned for a moment, as if the grace with which his father held his small face was a drug that calmed him. I wondered if Shira's father said the prayers as written each time or if he added individual thoughts along the way; that the little guy would stay away from the tantalizing red Lego bricks in case he might swallow one, again; that the eldest boy would get a good night's sleep despite the presence of his friends; that Shira would enjoy her party and not be too worried about who liked her enough. He could think small, because he knew he could offer them more blessings the next day, or the next week, when he would love them just as much as he did now.

The boys were loud. I couldn't make friends with the little ones no matter how often they crawled under the table and tried to pull off my shoes. And the older boys were discussing some complicated Talmudic argument about women's hats without ever asking any of the females at the table what they thought.

I ate chicken soup and left the potatoes and pieces of chicken at the bottom of my bowl. There was no dog to sneak my food to. Shira's mother watched me carefully as I failed to eat the noodle kugel and the two pieces of brisket I had dutifully taken from the serving dishes. Her stare was unnerving and I took the opportunity to escape to the upstairs bathroom.

There was a pair of tiny blue and white underpants next to the toilet and a sign in Shira's handwriting with an arrow pointing down to exactly where the little brothers were supposed to aim. She'd warned me to bring my hand towel with me to and from the bathroom to keep it out of the line of fire. But I'd forgotten. I stood in front of the sink with wet hands and I couldn't figure out what to do.

Shira slept late Saturday morning. I sat on the second bed in her room, fully dressed, and waited for the noise in the hall to die down before attempting the bathroom again. I was on alert, holding my hand towel, wishing I'd brought a book to read that wasn't written by Kafka. Shira's house was Shabbos-proofed as well as child-proofed: with plastic covers on the light switches so I'd remember not to turn the lights on, a tissue box on the back of the toilet so I wouldn't be tempted to rip toilet paper, and the dials on the stove were covered so no one would be tempted to start or stop a fire. The boundaries were so clear, and practiced, as if their world had been exactly this way since day one, instead of constantly changing, like at my house. Shira knew what was expected of her and didn't even have to think about it anymore. I was worried that, even with all of the safe guards in place, I was going to screw something up.

I'd asked Jake's advice about the weekend, because he had a lot more experience staying at orthodox houses than I did. The religious boys in his class were always willing to invite him over and proselytize. I'd brought his response with me as a bookmark for Kafka.

Izzy,

I find the minute rules for every behavior in orthodoxy reassuring. There's no time to think on your own, because you're so busy mumbling prayers over food and trips to the bathroom, and making sure you don't touch a light switch or rip toilet paper, you don't have time to get caught up in the meaninglessness of it all. And you don't have to believe in anything, you just do all of the behaviors and that makes you one of them.

When I asked him why he would want to be one of them if he thought everything they did was meaningless, he wrote back, "I get lonely. Don't you?"

By the time Shira woke up, the rest of the house was empty and I'd been sitting in her room, silent and shaking for what felt like days. I had just come up with my own primitive form of meditation – humming to myself on one monotonous note – when Shira turned her head towards me.

"What's that noise?"

"Stray cat?"

She giggled and then checked her bedside clock. "Ooh good, we're too late to go to services." She kicked her blanket up like a tent. "Only guys have to watch each other pray to make sure they're really doing it." She yawned and smiled at me and then sat up suddenly. "I hope they didn't eat all the cereal!"

I watched her eat two bowls of cookie crisp mixed with shredded wheat while I picked through my cheerios. She had plenty to say, between slurps of the chocolate colored milk in her bowl, about the girls she'd invited to the party after lunch. I got the feeling she expected me to be a draw: the new girl. Something for her to show off to the girl who used to play dress up with her in kindergarten and now couldn't be bothered.

I asked why she stayed at our school, instead of switching to a single sex school in seventh grade, the way her brother did.

"I didn't wanna be on a bus for two hours every day," she said, and licked her spoon before putting it down, and searching through the cabinets aimlessly. "And I'm used to the kids at our school. Who wants to start over and be rejected by new people?"

I raised an eyebrow at that and she blushed and opened the fridge for cover. The light didn't go on inside, because they'd disabled it for Shabbos. One more strange little thing that made Shira more religiously correct than me. She grabbed an apple from the crisper and came back to the table, shining it with her hands to put off eating it.

"And no boys," she said, still blushing.

"A tragedy," I said, and she giggled and then looked away.

"But I think I was just scared," she said, staring at the table. "At the school I visited, they expected all the girls to be smart. They didn't believe in separating us out into different tiers and accepting that some people are slower to learn than others. I just, I didn't want to spend six years feeling like a moron."

I didn't know what to say. She kept telling me things I wouldn't have dared say to her, or to anyone. I smiled my weak smile and she rolled the apple across the table to me.

"You can have it," she said. "I'm really not a fruit and vegetable person." And she stood back up to search the cabinets again.

38

When David arrived late in the afternoon with a group of other boys from the neighborhood I only noticed him in particular because his name was crocheted in white letters on his blue Kippah and Shira elbowed me to tell me she'd made it for him. She didn't introduce me to him, just told me he went to school with her older brother and lived two blocks away and he was practically a member of the family.

His dark blond hair was perfectly straight and his navy blue suit hung from his neck and shoulders as if he were a human hanger.

I sat alone on a soft leather chair next to the coffee table, at a little bit of a distance from every other group. I was exhausted by the effort of having to be a person for so long. I craved my TV and the chance to let the information just wash over me.

David was in a circle on the floor with a couple of other boys I didn't know and I had to look over his head to stare lovingly at the chocolate covered crumb cake Shira's mother had set out for us on the dining room table. I wanted the whole cake, anything to kill the grasshoppers in my stomach. But I couldn't stand up and risk walking past the boys; they would hear the swish of the too shiny stockings Shira had forced me to wear instead of the white socks and loafers I'd started out with.

David pushed bangs away from his glasses. "My rabbi says the lesson *isn't* that you should be willing to give up your most precious possessions to a cruel God."

One of the other boys tried to interrupt with a "who are we to question God," argument, but David was on a roll.

"The point of the Binding of Isaac story is that everybody was sacrificing their children back then, to any and every god. You want a better harvest, throw the little boy on the fire. A better sex life? How many kids you got?"

39

I was inching, carefully, so as to avoid swishy sounds, closer to the conversation. I was curious, wondering if the boys were given a more sophisticated version of the Abraham-goes-to-kill-his-son-to-show-his-devotion-to-God story. The idea had always bothered me, that it was seen as Abraham's sacrifice, and Abraham's test, rather than Isaac's. David caught my eye, just for a moment, and then continued talking at a slightly slower pace

"The lesson here is that God, as opposed to the multiple imposters Abraham had grown up with, would abhor such a murder and rejection of his gift. When Abraham hears the voice telling him to kill the ram instead, that's Abraham turning a corner, starting to see God through the fog of other voices in his head."

This was new and I couldn't keep quiet. "So Abraham was mentally ill?"

"In a way," David said, more seriously than I'd expected. "In a way we're all a little bit crazy, hearing voices telling us what to do. We follow Halacha, we walk the righteous path, as a way of not falling into the craziness in our heads."

He directed all of this towards me, not to the boys who were already turning around to join a less interesting conversation about their school's pale imitation of a basketball team.

"Do I have to agree with you," I asked David, "or can I have my own opinion?"

He smiled, all tilted lips and sparkly blue eyes. I took that as permission and moved down to the floor.

"I don't think everyone is crazy, or even potentially crazy," I said. "For example, Sarah would *never* have sacrificed her son to God. If she had known what Abraham was planning, she would have killed her husband, in order to protect her son."

"What makes you think Sarah didn't know exactly what her husband was doing?"

I stopped short. I remembered something about Sarah supposedly being kept in the dark, but he was right, a mother would know; especially a mother like Sarah who waited so long for her one child.

"I would have killed Abraham," I said.

David brushed his hand up and down the corduroy ribs of the couch. "So you believe women are fundamentally superior to men, based on how you see yourself?"

"No. It's not that," I said, clasping my hands firmly together. "I don't think every father would kill his own child. Isaac and Jacob didn't go homicidal on their kids. They had other problems: favoritism, blindness, an unseemly need for extra wives. But they wouldn't need God to tell them not to kill their kids."

We were sitting too close at this point, because mid-rant I had scooted closer to him on the floor, getting rug burns on my knees. He wasn't moving away or moving towards me, just listening.

"Then men aren't uniformly evil?" he asked.

"No, men are evil in all different sorts of ways," I said.

He didn't know how to answer that and I was annoyed with myself. I wanted more than anything for the conversation to continue. I wanted to talk about Isaac, about God stepping in to save Isaac from his father, and how I didn't believe God would make a spectacular gesture like that for me. I never got the chance to talk this way in the girls only classes at school, where the limit of our class discussions was whether Rabbi such and such would translate a word the same way as Rabbi so and so. But the basketball conversation took over and absorbed David and I was too afraid to reach out and touch him to get his attention back. It would be wrong to touch him. He wouldn't want that. I ended up playing Trivial Pursuit with Shira and a couple of girls I didn't know. I thought David looked over at me every once in a while. But I wasn't sure.

41

When David left with the other boys to go to shul for late afternoon services he barely, just barely, glanced in my direction before walking out the front door. I stood up after sitting on the floor for too long and almost blacked out. I had to hold on to the arm of the couch to avoid falling head first into the coffee table.

"Are you okay?" Shira grabbed my arm, the one holding me up, and I fell onto the couch.

I sat there, dazed. "I don't know."

She ran into the kitchen to get her mother. The other guests were long gone.

"I'm okay," I called after her but she ignored me. I'd been having little dizzy spells and blackouts ever since I stopped eating regular meals. It made me feel just a little bit virtuous.

Shira's mother came into the living room still wiping her hands on a dish towel. She was back in her clogs and house-dress. "Isabel just needs to eat more. A body needs more cushioning if it's going to protect the vulnerable parts inside."

She took my hand and pulled me up from the couch and I followed her into the kitchen. The three of us sat at the kitchen table and ate the rest of the chocolate covered crumb cake as if it were the medicine we needed to live. For the first time in months, I felt full.

I called home as soon as Shabbos was over and got the answering machine. At first, I pictured my mother already in her car racing toward me, realizing how lonely she was without me. But after Shira's brother and his friends drove off with David for pizza, and her parents left us to babysit the younger boys while they went to visit neighbors, I started to wonder if my mother could have forgotten about me. Or if, somehow, she knew about the illicit cake-eating event and had decided to punish me.

Shira rambled on about how David had asked her brother to ask her about me, but she wasn't sure what it meant, but David had always been kind to her, like a big brother.

Then Shira's little brothers started having a wrestling tournament in front of us in the TV room that involved the couch and my legs braced against it as safe zones. I called home again after the booboo count reached time out proportions but still got the machine. Another part of my brain kicked in, very calm, telling me that my mother was dead.

When the youngest boy grabbed onto my left breast for ballast during the second half of the tournament, I decided that babysitting wasn't for me and took a bathroom break. The upstairs hall was quiet without all of the boys. Even the bathroom seemed like a safe place. I stood in front of the sink and held my fingers under the cold water. I think I meant to wash my face, or dab my eyes, but I forgot to move on from the stream of water on my skin, until I heard the doorbell ring. I crept to the top of the stairs to see who was there, ready to race back into the bathroom, but then I heard Mom's voice. I grabbed my things form Shira's room and ran down the stairs, tripping over my own feet on the way down so that I landed with a bang against the hallway closet door.

"Ready to go, sweetheart?" Mom asked, with a look of concern. I nodded and dropped to the floor to find my own shoes among the crowd of them by the closet.

"Your Dad is waiting in the car," she said. I wasn't sure if she was warning me, or just offering a piece of neutral information, but I suddenly had trouble remembering how shoes worked. Shira helped me up from the floor and gave me a hug before I followed Mom outside and did my best to black out.

Jake was sitting cross-legged on top of his wobbly desk when I walked into English class on Monday. When he squinted in my direction, I felt prettier, more important. And then he looked past me, and I felt the tiniest bit humiliated. The inconsistency of his interest in me, or in anything, reminded me too much of my family, the way reality seemed to keep shifting under my feet.

Shira had said something about Jake that morning, about rumors she'd heard, about how he'd hurt me, and David wouldn't. As if David was an option for someone like me.

"Why don't you wear your glasses?" I asked Jake as I crossed the room to my seat, trying to shake off the hopeless thoughts that pretty much made up the whole of my brain.

"Girls like it when I squint," Jake said. "I'm rebelling against the 20/20 ideal."

"Shah," Yitzchak Steinberg said, smacking his index finger against his lips. He was our class crackpot, railing against the presence of girls in his classes. He was reading one of the oversized sacred books girls like me weren't allowed to touch, let alone study. He rocked back and forth so hard he lifted his chair off the ground an inch or two.

I sat in my alphabetically assigned seat in front of Jake and whispered, partly as an excuse to lean close, "Why doesn't Yitzchak go to an all boys school if he's so offended by girls?" I was thinking about David, just a little bit, and it felt wrong with Jake's breath on my hair.

"Why are you whispering?" Jake asked, full voice. "Yitz doesn't really know we're here, he was just warding off the voices in his head. Right Yitz?"

Yitzchak's rocking increased in fervency until he knocked his whole desk to the floor. He was a pitiful figure, the uncouth face of orthodox manhood, but I wondered sometimes if he was just more

44

honest about his fear of women than the other men. They were able to hide it behind charm better than he could.

Mrs. Sturman walked into the room in the same knee length black skirt and brown turtleneck sweater she wore every day, and the odor of old flowers and sweat followed her in.

"Jake, get off the desk, before you fall on Isabel and she sues you for sexual harassment." She dropped her heavy canvas bag on the floor for emphasis.

"Izzy wouldn't do that," Jake dropped into his seat, banging his desk into the back of my chair.

I pushed back, harder than I expected to.

"Okay, maybe she would," he said.

The classroom filled up while I sat there feeling like an idiot and thinking about how much safer I felt in the morning classes, without the boys, where the teachers kept a fierce eye on skirt lengths and hallway interactions. It was insulting and lonely, yes, but at least the rules were clear. Mrs. Sturman and the other afternoon teachers couldn't care less what we wore or who we touched, accidentally or otherwise.

"Everyone sit down so I can give you your test and get back to my reading," Mrs. Sturman said, and passed Xeroxed sheets to each row.

"Did we know about this?" Jake leaned so close to me that each word blew strands of my hair forward.

"You can't copy from Isabel, Jake. This is an essay test."

I tried to block out the noise and focus on the essay topic, "Hell is other people, give examples."

"Can we cite from Jewish history?" Yitzchak asked.

"No, and not from your paltry, inconsequential little lives either. Try quoting Sartre, as a lark," Mrs. Sturman said. "Start now."

Tova Keifer took a folded sheet of paper out of the pocket of her black skirt and began copying the contents onto her test sheet. I tried to ignore her and focus on why Sartre might think being around certain people forever would be hell.

When I stood up to hand in my test, Jake was walking by, and my hand brushed his leg.

"You should keep your hands to yourself, Izzy, or I'll be able to sue *you* for sexual harassment," he said. It was a joke, but it made me feel like a criminal and I pulled my hand behind my back.

Tova reached out and grazed his arm with her pinky. "I'm not scared of you," she said. And he turned towards her.

I wiped my hand on the side of my long denim skirt, dropped my paper on the teacher's desk, and took the long way around to my seat.

Chapter Five

THE WALK

My father woke me up at seven o'clock on Saturday morning. "Why aren't you dressed yet?" He asked, standing over my bed. He had on his black suit and black sneakers. I was wearing an old t-shirt and my only pair of shorts, no bra, with my blanket pulled up to cover me.

"Too early," I mumbled, stretching the blanket over my head, leaving myself an eyehole so I could keep track of him.

He yanked the blanket and a few strands of hair off my head. "Let's go. The rabbi's waiting." My father smiled at me. "It's a long walk."

"The rabbi isn't waiting, he's sleeping."

"Get up right now," my father said, in a different tone of voice. "Or don't ask me for anything ever again."

I thought about how infrequently I'd asked him for anything, but he probably meant that he would refuse to pay the phone bill, or the mortgage, if he felt under-appreciated which he'd done before. And that would lead to sulking from Mom, and lectures from my grandmother over my head about how he shouldn't be allowed to get away with such behavior.

"You have five minutes," my father said, and then left the room with the door wide open.

I pulled my long black corduroy skirt off its hanger and dragged it over my shorts before I remembered that I hadn't been to the bathroom yet or brushed my teeth. Then there was the question of what to do with my all-over-the-place hair. In the end I wet my whole head in the sink and raked my hair into a high ponytail. Then I threw on a blue sweater over my t-shirt, stepped into my loafers, and ran down the stairs, because my five minutes were up.

My loafers were already rubbing against my heels when I reached the kitchen, but it was too late to switch shoes, because my father was handing me a piece of buttered challah and aiming me at the front door. I noticed my mother standing in front of the sink in her thin yellow nightgown, the one that showed her protruding hipbones, and I wondered why she wasn't even looking up at me or saying goodbye.

I stopped. The coffee maker was on its side and dripping coffee into the open dairy silverware drawer. And our big serving dish – the one I'd put in the dishwasher myself after its short, but fulfilling, relationship with roasted asparagus had come to an end – was sparkling white but broken into a dozen pieces and scattered on the floor next to my mother's bare feet.

"Mom? What happened?"

She didn't make eye contact with me but she did look at my father. She didn't glare at him; she didn't have any expression at all.

"We don't use the dishwasher on Shabbos any more," my father said as he opened the front door and nodded for me to walk through.

My shoe scraped against my left heel as we walked past the local Rec Center where my Mom used to teach art to the seniors.

"I hated it there," I said as we passed the jungle gym and the swingset where I used to play while Mom gave her classes.

I didn't want to be talking to him. I wanted to show my righteous indignation and be silent for an hour and a half to punish him. But already, five minutes into the walk, I was too lonely to keep quiet. This desperate need to be connected to my father had been around for as long as I could remember. I needed to hear his voice and see his face or else I didn't really exist. But then I thought of Mom and the times we'd sit on the floor in the attic and make paper dolls together, cutting out dresses, coloring ribbons and shoes. I wanted to be home with her and draw her some warm clothes to wear over her nightgown.

"Were you jealous of the time Mommy spent teaching?" My father asked me, with that you're-so-interesting tone of voice that always drew me in.

"No. I wasn't jealous of anyone," I said, lying, because I didn't want to give him anything to use against Mom.

"I just thought she should have spent more time looking after you," he said, "that's all. We used to argue about that all the time."

I turned away from him and then I saw the hole in the fence, tall enough for an adult to walk through from the wooded area behind it.

"They should fix that fucking hole already," I said, because I couldn't stop myself. This kept happening to me, not being able to shut up, or control my own behavior. I wanted to at least be in control of myself and I couldn't even to that.

"Language, Izzy."

"That's where I saw the Pink Man."

I was such a good girl those days when Mom was teaching her classes. I played by myself. I didn't even ask for cookies or

49

lemonade, even though the seniors always had some. I only ran into the middle of the class once, because of the Pink Man. He had stood in that break in the fence, his big black coat held open, with white tube socks up his calves and brown lace-up shoes and the rest of him was pink.

My father's only comment when I'd repeated my story to him at dinner way back when was *that the man was stupid, to risk sunburn like that.*

We passed the Rec Center building and continued up the road, my father humming one of the tunes from the Yom Kippur services as if it were a light little ditty, ignoring what I'd just said.

"Do you remember the man who flashed me?" I asked him.

"I remember you told a story about something like that," he said, and then he started to sing, no real words, just a tune. My head felt like it was going to explode and he walked so slowly that even the exercise wasn't helping to calm me down.

"Why did they arrest you for touching this girl, and with the other ones they just sent you to a new school?" I asked.

He stopped singing.

"The climate is different now. They're looking for people to hang."

I started to swing my arms, the way I used to do as a little kid, until they felt like stretched out pieces of dough. "What did you actually do to her?"

I purposely walked through the dried leaves on the side of the road for the crunch crunch sound.

"Supposedly, I touched her breast," my father said, walking closer to the middle of the street. Not many cars passed us on the small side road, but when they did, they had to drive around him. "She needed a hug. She has a very difficult home life."

"You stopped hugging me a long time ago and I have a very difficult home life too," I said. "My rabbis told me not to touch you."

I thought about that, about which rabbi he spoke to about that, and what they thought he meant by "touch."

"Why is it okay for you to touch someone else's daughter?"

He shrugged.

We rounded the corner to the duck pond but stayed on the far side of the street to avoid the lumps of green goose shit.

"Do you remember that piano teacher you had?" he asked, touching my elbow to navigate me around more green lumps on the side of the road.

"Which one?" I spent years on piano lessons, but I never got better, partly because when I tried to practice at home my father would complain about the "cacophony."

"That first teacher, the man who came to our house."

I remembered that piano teacher, an older man. He wore cologne and a tweedy sports jacket and he always managed to reach around me to write in my music book and scratch my arm with his jacket. I always felt sort of nauseous when he was nearby, because of the smell of his cologne, and the way he was always leaning against me as if my six year old body could hold him up.

"When you complained to your mother about the way he touched you, I realized that you were extra sensitive to that sort of thing, so I kept my distance from then on," my father said, and continued walking.

The red leaves looked like velvet and I hated how beautiful they were. Nothing in my world could just be bland and serene. For one second a flash of penis flashed through my mind; the time I walked in on my father in the bathroom, and he just stood there. No, he turned towards me, he must have, or I wouldn't have seen it so clearly.

The shaded part of the trip was over and we crossed over to the expressway service road, both of us staying to the side because the traffic was heavier here. The sun was hot on my hair even though the air over all was cool. We passed the police station in silence.

"Do you think the piano teacher or the pink man should have gone to jail?" I asked him.

"My honest opinion?" He paused. "I think those men have a sickness and they can't control it. Maybe they can't change who they are, so is it really fair to hold them responsible for their actions? How much harm did they really do?"

I wanted to rip those red leaves into long strips and dice them like a bell pepper and then scrape each piece with the edge of my knife until it was as close to dirt as it could get. I had to stop walking and lean down to adjust the sock on my left foot where the fabric was gathering under the heel.

"Did you know that causing someone embarrassment is equal to killing them in Jewish law?" I said. It was something I'd learned at my old school that I'd never forgotten, because it made more sense than I was used to. There were so many laws that seemed to break life down into meaningless compartments, but some laws were there to protect me. To help me protect myself.

My father just laughed. "Then the Board of Education should be paying me a shitload of money any day now." He wiped sweat off his forehead with his handkerchief and I wondered if that was legal, because you're not supposed to carry things on Shabbos and once he took the handkerchief out of his pocket he was, technically, carrying it.

"But don't you think you embarrassed the girl you touched?" I asked.

"I can't help how other people interpret my actions. I'm not responsible for how she feels."

I wanted to stand in the middle of the road and let one of the speeding cars hit me. I didn't think of it as being suicidal. I just wanted confirmation that I was still a solid object and not flimsy, like my mother.

He kept walking, jaunty and happy as if all the exercise was doing him good. I focused on the pain in my left heel until I felt like I was an inch from the ground staring at the blister as it formed and broke and oozed pus on my socks.

The large room next to the sanctuary at the synagogue was filled with gossip and perfume and shrieking children I didn't recognize – except for the Rabbi's five year old daughter. She and I had become friends, or, at least, I bothered her less than the elderly women who insisted on kissing her cheeks with their sticky red lips.

I had to sit in the sanctuary with the serious folk and pretend to pray, because every time the congregation stood up, my father could see me over the curtain that divided the men from the women. I could still see into the other room, and I resented that they were allowed to hang out while I had to pray. I hated being one of the only people on the women's side of the sanctuary. Even on the rare times when Mom came with me to shul, she'd find any excuse to leave early.

Mom told me once that she didn't believe in God. We were taking one of our nature walks at Grandma and Grandpa's summer house, back when they had the summer house upstate. I was learning small prayers then, for when I ate an apple, or washed my hands, or saw something new for the first time, and I said a prayer in my marble mouthed Hebrew when Mom introduced me to a ladybug.

"I wish I could believe the way you do," she'd said, in her wistful voice.

I was seven years old at the time and I did believe in God. I was pretty sure he looked like Grandpa and had butterflies flitting around his head, whispering secrets about all the people he needed to help. Mom went back to telling me the official names for the trees we passed, and I made up prayers for each tree, and gave them new names that were easier for me to say, like Betsy and Jim. But she never asked to learn the prayers, or make up any of her own.

I leaned against the sanctuary wall at the synagogue and talked quietly to myself, because I couldn't focus on the Hebrew words in the prayer book anymore. On the men's side, the rabbi was rubbing his eyes and muttering the prayers with a yawn. My father was a few rows behind him, shuckling back and forth, and praying with great intensity, as if he were trying to force God to listen to him.

I could picture Mom at home, cleaning. It's what she always did to feel better. Even when I was little I used to sneak down to the kitchen after she and my father'd had a fight, and we'd scrub the floor together. I taught her about sliding across the floor in clean white socks and banging into the cabinets, and she taught me the joy of removing dirt with every tool imaginable.

My father and I stayed through all of the morning services at shul, and the women gradually came in to fill up the empty spaces on my side of the sanctuary. After a quick blessing over the wine with the rest of the congregation, the rabbi invited us back to his house for lunch, and the rest of the afternoon, so we wouldn't have to make the trek home. He'd invited a whole group of people and we all walked down the sidewalk together in a loose clump. The rabbi's daughter, Rivky, held my hand as we walked. Her skin was soft and cool and I was pretty sure my hands were never like hers as a kid. They were always sweaty. I remember a line of black dirt along each palm.

"You're too tall," Rivky said, skipping along next to me.

"No, you're short," I said.

"I am short!" she said. She seemed to like that a lot for some reason. I wondered if people usually just went along with whatever she said.

We walked behind her grandmother and an elderly couple from shul discussing the planned renovations to the Synagogue building. Rivky kept kicking her grandmother's shoe and then turning away in a who-me gesture that never got boring for her.

My father and the rabbi walked ahead of us with a young man who'd just started teaching at the same school where the rabbi taught on the south shore. I could hear them every once in a while discussing their work. The young man taught Gemara, and he wanted advice from my father about how to make the kids pay attention.

I thought about one of Jake's scribbled notes to me, about how his Gemara teacher called him Yaakov, and it was like he had a second self in class, someone who could be taken over and brought to life by religion. I wished I could organize myself into two distinct selves like that. Most of the time I felt like ten different people, all struggling to live in one body, with none of them getting along. But most of all I wanted to be anywhere but listening to my father explaining to these men how to teach kids to listen to him, and to trust him.

The rabbi's house was a small box in the middle of a big lawn. Their Sukkah was still up from Sukkot. My father had helped build it for them so that it could be "easily" taken down after the holiday was over, but he'd been too busy to help them with that recently. Inside the house, the rabbi's wife and two little boys were waiting for us and the dining room table was set for a crowd.

Rivky pulled my hand so I had to bend down low and she cupped her hands over my ear and whisper, "My Imma is so fat." Which was true, because she was pregnant with baby number four. Maybe they could keep the Sukkah up all year, give it a more substantial roof, and put the extra kids in there.

But maybe I was jealous. I'd always wanted siblings. I didn't want to be the only one standing between my parents.

The adults finished two bottles of wine with lunch and then started on the Johnny Walker Black over dessert. I drank diet soda, and Rivky poured her glass of water onto her plate until the roasted red potatoes looked like islands.

The boys were insane; a one and a half year old and a three year old who both liked to scream. And then shriek. Rivky put her hands over her ears and stared hard at the boys as if her disapproval would bully them into submission. When that didn't work, she put her hands over *my* ears and said we would practice lip-reading. I couldn't make sense of anything she was trying to say to me, though, because she wasn't really speaking and her idea of mouthing the words involved molding her lips into unlikely shapes for any language I knew.

I offered to help her mother clean up afterwards but it turned out I didn't know the orthodox rules around washing dishes on Shabbos, so I was sent to play with Rivky and help her choose an outfit for the next day, which turned out to be an exhausting process during which I discovered that tights come in every possible color and design and must be matched carefully with the headband but not with the dress because that would be "too much."

I accepted Rivky's wisdom in her final choice of blue and red plaid tights with pink dress and brown cowboy boots – she knew the look she was going for and it did not involve dressing "boring" like me.

We only made our way back downstairs when Rivky realized that everyone upstairs was asleep and therefore uninteresting. My father was reading in the living room, looking a little sleepy himself, and I wanted to leave him alone, but the toys Rivky wanted were in the living room and she was in charge.

After a while, I couldn't find the energy to play anymore, and sat down in a chair across the room from my father and watched as

Rivky opened every container and collected a pool of toys around her that should have kept her busy for at least five or six minutes.

"No one reads to me," she whined instead. She picked up a stuffed alligator and slammed it against the floor. "Abba and Imma spend all their time with the baby."

"I'll read to you," my father said.

I stared at him.

"I don't want you to read to me like I'm a baby," Rivky said, crossing her arms and swinging her body from side to side. She had a plastic hammer in one hand and managed to hit herself with it on the back of her head.

"I have an ouchy!" she screamed, and then she stood still in the middle of the floor, on the edge of tears, as if she was waiting for me to figure out what to do. I would have gone for ice but I didn't want to leave her alone, there.

My father leaned forward. "Do you want me to look at that for you?"

She thought for a moment, and then stuck out her hammer in his direction. "No. I'm better." She came over and squashed in next to me on my chair, handing me a book to read. When my father left the room a few minutes later, I felt the little girl relax against me. I didn't want to think about it. I didn't want to think about anything.

Chapter Six

THANKSGIVING

A few days before Thanksgiving our regular Jewish Law teacher had a family emergency and one of the older rabbis had to substitute. There were rumors that he had been in a concentration camp, and other rumors that he was not supposed to teach girls because he always made someone cry. His name, Rabbi Wald, was written in spidery print on the chalkboard and he stood at the front of the room as we all sat down and waited for him to say something, or at least to stop staring at us with contempt.

"So what have you been learning?" the old rabbi finally asked, massaging his white beard, lowering himself into the desk chair at the front of the room.

Tova Keifer raised her hand and he nodded permission for her to speak. "What do you think about Thanksgiving?" she asked.

His eyes flashed and he pulled even harder on his grey beard. "Just because we live in America, that doesn't make us Americans. This is not our holiday."

58

"But most of us were born here," Tova said. The rest of us were too scared to agree with her. At least I was scared; maybe the other girls weren't actually paying attention.

"So what if you were born here?" He stood up and kicked his chair into the wall with a loud crack. "Do you think they'll call you Americans when the next Hitler arrives? No. You'll be Jews only, just as you are now."

He stood still suddenly, as if he'd just remembered where he was. "Don't cry," he said. "Please just don't cry."

He sat down again and sighed heavily and then he pounded his fist on the table. "They're drugging you with turkey so you won't fight back." His stare was frightening. "Even turkey sandwiches should be avoided."

He said it so seriously, with real conviction, and I started to laugh with spit flying out of my mouth and hitting my notebook. I had to cover my nose and breathe deep to make it stop. Shira looked at me with horror. But the old rabbi slowly turned to me, and winked.

At dinner, I told my parents about Rabbi Wald's class, because I couldn't stop thinking about it.

"He spent the rest of the period giving us his opinions on why we shouldn't watch television and the purpose of female modesty and the compromises of American Judaism in all areas."

"I've heard of him," my father said, pausing to cut through an inch thick piece of steak with his serrated knife, and then not bothering to follow through with his thought. My father would have survived very well in the wild; ripping a leg off a turkey would have been no problem, though he'd probably forget that he was supposed to kill the poor bird first.

"What have you heard about Rabbi Wald?" I asked, because I hate unfinished thoughts, and trying to focus on eating my spaghetti wasn't working, because each time I twirled the fork, tomato sauce splattered across the table.

"Rabbi Wald has a reputation."

"For what?" I couldn't stand the way he drew things out, like it was all some big mystery. Mom just sat on her side of the table, staring at her food and saying nothing.

"The rabbi has a unique way of seeing things," My father finally said.

"Controversial, you mean. Do you agree with him about Thanksgiving not being our holiday?"

My father put down his knife and fork, rubbed his mouth with a napkin and smiled at Mom. "I think Izzy has a point. We should skip Thanksgiving this year."

"That was not my thought at all. What are you talking about?" I couldn't figure out how he'd done that, how he'd turned things around like that. "I think Rabbi Wald is wrong. I know I'm a real American, whether I like turkey or not."

"You see, Robin? Isabel doesn't even like turkey," My father said, as if I'd just added weight to his argument.

My father tapped his knife against his plate and stared at my mother, waiting.

"We're going to my parents for Thanksgiving," Mom said, staring at a spot on the tablecloth, probably where my tomato splatter had landed.

"No," my father said with a smile. "I think you'll have to call and tell them we can't make it this year."

Mom placed her half full plate on the floor, and the dog rushed to dig in. "I ask you for so little, Martin. The least you can do is let us go to Thanksgiving dinner, for my parents' sake."

My father threw his steak knife and I watched it pass about a foot from Mom's head before glancing off the counter and doing a back flip onto the floor by the dog food.

"Why should I sit at your mother's table when I know that she spends her every free moment trying to turn my wife against me?"

"Because she's my mother and I'm asking you to," Mom said, quietly.

I could hear myself whimpering but they didn't notice.

"You spend too much time with her as it is. You need to be here taking care of *my* home and *my* family."

"Pop needs my help."

"No he doesn't. He just can't see through her any more than you can. The two of you are wrapped around her arthritic little finger." My father dropped his steak bone on the floor and the dog raced over to get it, leaving the spaghetti dangling off of Mom's plate.

It was all my fault. I should have just kept my mouth shut. Why couldn't I do that?

"We have non-dairy ice cream," my father said, calm again, his eyes twinkling at me. "Why don't you get it from the freezer, and a few bowls while you're at it?"

The chocolate-ish ice cream needed to soften before I could scoop it out, and I put it in the microwave and watched it turn on the glass plate inside.

After the microwave beeped, Mom turned towards me. "Would you like to go to Grandma and Grandpa's for Thanksgiving?"

I didn't look at my father. "Yes, I would."

I focused on scooping the non-dairy ice cream into bowls and placed a small serving in front of Mom.

"Thank you, sweetheart."

"You're welcome." I dropped the other two bowls onto the table and passed one down to my father, but I couldn't convince myself to actually eat the brown goop.

"Mom, can I be excused?"

"Yes, sweetheart. Of course."

I didn't wait for my father to disagree. I just turned and ran up the stairs with the dog at my heels. As soon as I was halfway up the stairs their fight restarted and it lasted two hours. By the end I was wrapped in my blanket and huddled in my bedroom closet, mumbling history notes out loud to try and block out the sound of Mom's almost keening tone of voice and Dad's booming yell. The dog was stretched out on my bed, perplexed but unwilling to sacrifice her comfort for a show of solidarity.

Jake wrote to me during social studies, with a piece of paper cadged from my notebook of course, that he was going to visit his older sister for Thanksgiving, while his parents took his little sister to visit friends in Canada. His older sister was going to put him up in her dorm room, and probably try to convince him to stop the orthodoxy madness, he said. She was the one who sent him to all of those foreign movies with subtitles, and recommended obscure French writers with hygiene issues. It was hard to know if he really enjoyed that stuff or just liked the pretentiousness of it, or the connection with his sister. She was already too old to be co-opted, he said, by the time their parents got religion and now she was studying comparative languages, including Hebrew, but for strictly cultural, rather than religious, purposes.

Jake went off on a tangent, along the side of the page, about his fantasy of what methods his sister would use to seduce him back to the dark side: one really long scenario involving the other girls on her floor in the dorm made me want to rip the paper to shreds and spit on it.

He ignored my lack of response, or maybe he noticed it and that's why he changed tacks and actually talked to me on our way out of class.

"My sister thinks I'm a turncoat for trying to be orthodox. She thinks I should bring ham sandwiches to school. But it's not like she's here to do it herself."

"What would she do, if she were here?" I asked, noticing his elbow brushing against my arm.

"Nothing, she's all talk," he said.

"Like you?"

"Just like me," he said and smiled, and then squinted at me for a second before walking ahead to catch up with the other boys on their way to gym.

Mom and I left our house early Thanksgiving morning to help with the cooking. My father had agreed to arrive in time for dinner, but he didn't promise to stay long.

Grandma and Grandpa's house was small and filled with the furniture that had survived their forty years of marriage, including the apartment in Manhattan, the house in Brooklyn, and the summer cottage in the mountains. Only the solid pieces remained: a blue and white embroidered sofa, a dining room table protected by pads, a plasticized cover, and a lacy white tablecloth that was washed with care once a month. I felt untested and impermanent compared to the leather covered chairs surrounding the table, and the dark stained hardwood floors. I didn't think I would last 40 years and therefore I didn't belong.

Some of my mother's old sketches were framed on the wall as we walked into the Living Room. My favorite was the one of a mommy bird feeding her baby bird in a nest – the worm was fat and the baby bird's mouth was wide open. The baby bird was supposed to be me. I guessed that even before I knew that my mother had a real name and that it was Robin.

Grandpa welcomed us with hugs and drew us into the kitchen. He loved to cook. Well, love is maybe the wrong word, because it implies images of passion, and knives dancing and bits of parsley flying into the air. He was more methodical. He mostly used the recipes my grandmother had written out for him when her arthritis and escalating asthma symptoms had pushed her out of the kitchen. Even on Thanksgiving, eating at their house meant chopped liver with chunks of hard-boiled egg, freshly baked bread, brisket, gefilte fish (from the can then re-cooked with carrots and onion to get rid of the goop and the metallic flavor), noodle/apple kugel, chicken soup with matzo balls, and, recently, salad.

Grandma stayed in her room all morning, so Mom and Grandpa had to take breaks from cooking with me to take turns sitting with her, to keep her from getting too grumpy. I stayed in the kitchen chopping vegetables. I even preferred dealing with celery to visiting Grandma, and I hate celery. I hate the smell of it. I hate the way the strings refuse to be cut so they dangle off an otherwise perfectly chopped piece of snot colored vegetable. I could only eat it when it had been cooked into the soup for so long that it had become a new thing, a conveyor of soup.

Grandpa was obsessed with using as much of each vegetable as possible. He wanted to leave the carrots unpeeled, for flavor, he said, but accepted that I saw things differently. I was used to my father's way of doing things, where half of each onion ended up in the garbage can, and all that was left was the most pristine white flesh. My grandfather would stand over an onion for as long as it would take to lift off the papery brown skin, leaving all bumps and discolorations intact. When he took his turn with Grandma, bringing her a plate of sharp cheddar and glazed apricots, I peeled potatoes with a paring knife and cut off the questionable parts, hiding them carefully under a thin sheet of paper towel in the garbage can under the sink so Grandpa wouldn't notice. If I'd used more than one section of paper towel at a time my grandfather would have been upset, as he had been in the past, and he would have taken the paper out of the garbage, flattened it with the palm of his hand and saved it for cleaning up the counters later. I didn't want to imagine how the discarded pieces of potato would have been re-used.

We walked into town for lunch, just Grandpa and me. Our mission was to pick up the special pumpernickel bread Grandma liked, and some fresh tomatoes, but first we stopped for ice cream. Wherever they lived, Grandpa always found the best local ice cream place and befriended the owner. He was skinny as a whippet but he could eat more mint chocolate chip than any human being I could think of.

"What should we try today?" Grandpa asked in his conspiratorial whisper as we stared over the glass counter top; ice cream clearly needed to be protected from the likes of us.

"Hazelnut?" I asked, like it was a test.

He stroked his chin. "Good choice. Do we want chocolate with that?"

I couldn't help smiling at him, but it was the good kind of smile, the one that warms your belly and makes your shoulders relax out of fight mode. We had to try spoonfuls of the other flavors first, of course; a little bit of peach, a dab of cheesecake, peanut butter and banana swirl, and, as a palate cleanser, lemon sorbet.

We walked home with our groceries and our cups of ice cream for later and we didn't talk about my father at all. We never had, as far back as I could remember. Even when I'd tried to tell him that something was wrong at home, Grandpa wouldn't pursue it. He told me stories about great philosophers, or the not so great students in his Western Civ. classes who made him laugh instead. He loved to laugh.

My father arrived with two full shopping bags just as my grandfather was slicing the brisket at the kitchen counter. He dropped his brown paper bags on the kitchen table and patted my grandfather on the back in passing.

Mom looked into the bags and started pulling out containers from a glatt kosher restaurant in Queens. "You were supposed to bring dessert," she said. "Why is there meatloaf?"

"Man cannot live on pumpkin pie alone," my father said and leaned against the refrigerator door.

I glanced around at the platters and pans full of food covering the countertops and the stove, with still more in the oven, and in the refrigerator. Grandpa stretched his shoulders a couple of times and hummed to himself and continued to slice the meat. He kept humming while my mother pointed out the plastic silverware and paper plates at the bottom of the second bag.

I wanted to put my head on Grandpa's shoulder, to let him know that I wasn't part of my father, but he wouldn't want me to do that I leaned against the counter and turned towards my father, who was taking a bottle of wine out of the fridge and, presumably, checking if it was kosher enough. Glatt kosher, as far as I knew, was a standard only applied to meat, but now everything in my grandfather's kitchen was being called into question, as if the less than perfect strictness of the brisket was a virus that would spread through the potatoes and into the fibers of the paper napkins.

"I'm still allowed to eat Grandpa's food, though. It's still kosher enough for a girl, right?"

66

"I'll leave that for you to decide," my father said, and winked at me. "And now I must say my hellos to the lady of the house." He left the room and Mom sat down in one of the wooden kitchen chairs, and stared out the window.

Grandma refused to come to the table for dinner, so I was sent to her room with a tray of food: a sloshy bowl of chicken broth strained clear especially for her, a plate of thinly sliced brisket and un-sauced asparagus spears, and a glass of opaque red wine. She had a book in her lap and a newspaper open beside her and the radio set to the local classical music station. I found the breakfast-in-bed table and placed the tray on top of it and slid the whole thing over her legs, locking her in place.

"Anything else?" I asked. It was the first time I'd seen her all day. I never spent much time with her, even when she was healthy. She'd always peered at me suspiciously from doorways when I was little, as if she'd never seen a child before. I couldn't acclimate to her recent interest in me after years of distance.

"Did that man really bring his own food?"

"Yes."

She patted the spot next to her on the bed and I carefully sat as far away as I could manage without falling off the bed.

"He thinks if he eats the most kosher food it will make *him* kosher. It doesn't work that way," she said and took a noisy slurp of her broth. "Your father is not a good man."

"I have to get back to the dining room. Do you need anything else?"

She put her spoon down in the bowl with a splash. "I need for just one of you people to listen to me. And I need a roll, no sesame seeds. And make sure it's still warm."

I ate salad for dinner. I didn't want to offend my grandfather by eating the bread pudding or stuffed cabbage my father had brought, and I didn't want my father to throw his plastic silverware at me if I dared to eat the brisket after he had deemed it not kosher enough. He gave us a ten-minute dissertation on how the *shochet* must check to make sure the lung of the animal is unperforated and clean in order for the meat to be truly kosher. We'd had a whole lecture on the ritual slaughter of animals in Jewish law class early in the year, with vivid imagery of the *shochet*'s long thumbnail used to slit the animal's throat. Somehow the kosher way of killing was supposed to be more humane, but they never took us on a field trip to see for ourselves, so I had to take it on faith.

I fished the cherry tomatoes out of my salad and built a tiny wall around my plate. The salad had been a lot of work for me, so at least eating three platefuls of it made that work seem worthwhile. I'd had to clean each lettuce leaf individually because the Jewish Law teacher had told us that bugs, who were not kosher on top of being disgusting, lived on the romaine lettuce we ate, and if we didn't clean off every speck of dirt then we couldn't be sure we were keeping our salad kosher.

I was used to Passover Seders at Grandpa's table, surrounded by his professor friends and the graduate students Grandma collected with her various degrees. For Thanksgiving we were alone, supposedly because of Grandma's questionable health, but I was pretty sure it had something to do with my father's current situation. I missed the noise. I missed the way I would fall asleep in the guestroom while the adults stayed up until all hours. And the way Grandpa used to carry me to the car when it was time to go home. Once, when I was six or seven, I asked if I could stay with him. I promised to be so quiet and do chores and not need anything, but Grandpa just laughed and snuggled my head closer to his shoulder and I didn't ask again.

Mom looked tense. She'd cut her brisket into tiny pieces and spread them around the plate. She left the table every five minutes to find something in the kitchen, or to check on Grandma. Grandpa tried to make the conversation with my father flow smoothly by changing the subject whenever a disagreement erupted, but they disagreed so frequently, on religious observance, politics, and especially teaching, that eventually, after a bottle of wine a piece, even Grandpa's voice became heated.

"You can't truly believe that the rabbis expected us to follow all of their decisions, unaltered, unadapted to our present circumstances and without question. You can't be that unthinking."

My father raised his eyebrows. This was as close to a criticism as Grandpa had ever launched at anyone, in my presence. "Unthinking" was his idea of a curse word. Before my father could reply, Grandpa excused himself from the table, probably shocked at his own temper.

"Are you enjoying your Thanksgiving, Jezebel?" My father asked. We were the only ones at the table: me, my father, and my wall of tomatoes.

"Is that a rhetorical question?"

"No. Why would you think that? Here we are at a lovely family dinner. Your Grandmother refuses to come out of her room. Your grandfather and your mother are at her beck and call." He paused for another dainty sip of red wine. "All is well with the world."

Mom decided to stay behind and help clean up from the meal. It made sense, because Grandpa looked very tired. I wanted to help too, but for the sake of peace in the family they sent me home with my father.

69

The car door creaked as he wrenched it open on the driver's side. I tried not to make noise on my side, as if pretending to be invisible might make him forget I was there, but he needed an audience.

"She acts like she's superior to me," he said as he backed out of the driveway.

"Who?"

"What right does she have to treat me like a criminal?"

"You *are* a criminal," I mumbled to myself.

"What was that?" He turned sharply to look at me, stopping the car at an angle in the middle of the road.

"I said that you *are* a criminal, Dad. You just don't think it should matter."

He gripped the wheel with his fists and aimed the car down the white line bisecting the two-lane road. "They're poisoning you against me. They're the ones who aren't rigorous enough with their Kashrut, who tried to convince me that Conservative Judaism was good enough, that you would learn everything you needed to know at that Day School. But look at what they did to Robin! They fucked up their own daughter, barely showed her any attention. That woman was so busy teaching piano prodigies and amusing her brilliant friends that she left your mother to raise herself!"

Mom rarely talked about her childhood, except to say that she didn't remember much, and that she wasn't anything special. So I knew he wasn't entirely wrong. I kept quiet as my father drove home, managing to miss three stop signs and swerve around imaginary obstacles.

"I'm the one who takes care of you, of both of you," he said as he finally pulled into our driveway. "You can't rely on your grandparents to be there when you need them. You can only rely on me."

He tagged my shoulder with a light punch and then opened his creaking car door. I wanted to wait for Mom to come home before going into the house, but it was so dark out, and the dog needed me inside.

Shira called the next day and I listened to her talk about how her Uncle Bernie ate too much turkey and had a bad reaction to the tryptophan and then started drinking in excess to cover the effect of the drug. It was great entertainment, she said.

She kept me on the phone forever, filling me in on gossip about our classmates that I may have missed, and then going on to tell me about every one of her weird family members, in details. I hmmed and wowed at all the right places, or at least I tried to, but I wished she would ask me questions, maybe ask me about my family, or ask me if I ever felt safe for even one moment in my life, but she didn't ask me, and I didn't know how to tell her anyway.

Chapter Seven

THE SHABBATON

My mother found the information sheet for the Shabbaton on the kitchen counter while I was doing my daily reconnaissance of the refrigerator early in December. Shira had invited me to stay at her house for the youth group sponsored weekend event, a brainwashing bonanza of orthodox outreach. It did not sound like a good thing.

"Go," my mother said, her eyes still scanning the paper.

"I'd rather stay home, where no one is judging my Jewishness and calling me a heretic."

She glanced up. "Does that really describe life in this house?" She took a pen from the jar on the kitchen counter and signed the parental consent line at the bottom of the form. "You should be with your friends."

David was going to be there. That was one of Shira's selling points, that and the fact that he'd been asking about me, and asking if I would be there too.

"Where's Dad?" I asked.

Mom shrugged and went back to stirring soup for dinner, and I went out to the back yard to watch the dog tear through the overgrown weeds, and sniff for week old pee. She was much better than I was at figuring out how to fill her time.

72

Shira called after dinner to give me the rundown on which kids from our school were coming to the event and whose houses they would be staying in. She told me that Jake would be there, and that the public school girl he'd had a crush on last year would be there too. She was trying to be off hand with the information, but I knew her opinion of Jake. She didn't believe his attempts at orthodoxy were genuine, and she didn't believe his attentions to me were genuine either.

"You need to come to the Shabbaton and focus on the important things."

"Like what?"

"Boys," she said. "All over the place."

"Don't we see enough boys at school every day?"

Shira snorted through the phone, struggling to find a suitable way to express her disgust with me. She'd told me that she needed me to be at the Shabbaton, and staying at her house, because I would be a good distraction for her mom. There was some drama going on with her father's job, and her mom was preoccupied and worried, but Shira didn't know the details.

"You need to dress up this weekend," she said.

"To look like what?"

"To look like a real girl. Let David know you're actually pretty."

"Doesn't he already know what I look like?"

"You'll have a good time at the Shabbaton, Izzy. I promise."

"You hope."

"I'll sneak the chocolate liqueur up to my room just in case."

David was dressed in a navy blue suit and white button down shirt on Friday night. He wasn't wearing his crocheted Kippah; instead he had one in black suede, and he looked like a modern orthodox rabbi in training. I couldn't figure out why he would want to be anywhere near me, but Shira said he did. She said I was the first girl he'd shown an interest in for a while, and we'd be good for each other. It was starting to feel like the hard sell and made me wonder what was wrong with him, or why she didn't want him for herself. It's not like she had a boyfriend already. But I didn't push her. She was my best friend, and I really needed one.

David sat across from me at our table in the basement of the shul, talking to Shira's brother, and occasionally checking on me and raising his eyebrows. The rabbi-in-charge had warned us that an evening lesson was coming soon, because shul is the Yiddish word for school and what would prayer be without study. He thought he was charming us, but even David had rolled his eyes at that, which was endearing.

Shira was sitting next to me and chatting up our school kissing coach, who was sitting on her other side. I didn't think Shira was the type to take him up on his services, but she sure did like to flirt. It made me wonder who she really was interested in, and why I didn't know.

Jake was across the room, near the windows, with the more religious boys from our class, listening carefully to their sales pitch. I kept looking in their direction, hoping that if I told myself I was really studying the shadows of the evergreens against the window, other people would believe that was what I was really doing, instead of staring at the side of Jake's face as he leaned in and squinted over someone's shoulder to look at the public school girl.

I couldn't eat the piece of roasted chicken on my plate. The wing, despite its deep tan, still looked like a useable appendage. I imagined the elbow lifting up and scooting through the air, trying to propel its flesh across the table to safety.

I had a deep desire to tear the paper tablecloth and break the Sabbath. Break anything. But then I would be a criminal. Father-like.

So instead I picked apart my challah roll until each crumb had its own place on my open napkin.

David leaned across the table and whispered, "Why are you destroying your food?"

"I'm setting the individual pieces free from the chains of conformity."

He sat back in his seat and watched me.

The evening talk was about the roots of the verb "prayer' in Hebrew and how similar it is to the word for "to judge." And prayer is our opportunity to judge ourselves each day, as well as to "serve God with your whole heart." Then there was a convoluted segue into the rules for the Sabbath, the long and detailed list of things we were not supposed to do, and my fingers were ripping the table cloth of their own accord, and I had to get out of there before I did something really noticeable.

I speed walked to the open doorway, and then ran down the hall towards the silence. In my head, the thirty nine categories of work you can't do on the Sabbath were swirling together with the look on Jake's face when he squinted at his crush girl, and I had to sit down to make the world stop spinning.

I didn't realize I was being followed until I saw a pair of men's dress shoes in front of me.

"You seem upset," David said, and I couldn't figure out if he was going for understatement or if that was just the way he talked.

"I needed some air."

He scanned the stuffy hallway and took a few trial breaths. "I see."

"It's just," I started and then couldn't stop myself. "There are all of these rules for the Sabbath. You can't make two pencil marks on a piece of paper because they did it while building the temple in the desert, and therefore you can't write at all, and you can't play piano because then you might be tempted to tune it, and you can't drive because it's like creating fire, and you can't turn on the light switch because it's completing a circuit, and it's all supposed to keep you from "working" on Shabbos so you will rest and be closer to God.

David watched me, and seemed to be listening, though I assumed he was just processing the reality that I was clearly a heretic, and crazy.

But I couldn't stop. "They start from this metaphor, that building a temple to God is work, and they make it into this concrete and tedious thing that ignores how it feels to not be able to play music or write a letter or drive a car or paint a picture on your supposed rest day. What if I don't find prayer services particularly restful? What if I think that wearing a pair of stockings, and socializing with strangers, and not being able to watch TV, or even turn on the goddamn light, is work? Shouldn't that trump the metaphor?"

And what did David say to all that, after I stopped hyper-ventilating?

He said, "So, you're thinking that if men had to wear stockings, we'd have a completely different set of laws?"

I was so surprised that I snorted, which was embarrassing, but at least there was no snot. I reached out and grabbed the leg of his pants before I realized what I was doing, and then let go.

"This is important to me," I said and he nodded.

"It really bothers me that all 613 commandments somehow weigh the same, and if I break the Sabbath I'm told that I've prevented the messiah from coming and I've ruined it for everyone. So then breaking the Sabbath weighs *more* than murder, as long as the murder isn't committed on Shabbos."

"I wouldn't go that far," he said. "We take murder pretty seriously.

I didn't argue with him on that one, even though I wanted to. He reached out a hand to help me stand up and I took it automatically, vaguely realizing that he was the kind of orthodox boy who didn't mind touching a girl's hand. He walked me back to the basement room, where the speechifying was finally over and everyone was standing around deciding who to walk home with. I ended up in a group with Shira and her older brother and David and the two boys staying at his house and I was okay with that, until I saw Jake walk off after the public school girl and follow her into the dark.

I slept well, for once. We even went to services the next morning, though we got there an hour late, which Shira said was way too early. There were plenty of seats in the women's section, which was up in a balcony looking over the men and the rabbi leading the service.

David waved to me from down in the men's section, and I smiled back, and then I scanned the sanctuary and caught Jake's eye. He was looking straight up at me, wearing his glasses. He glanced for a second at David, then back up at me.

I spent the rest of the morning services not praying at all, just speculating on what Jake was thinking. He was probably just looking for his crush, and not seeing her, he settled for me.

He sat at our table at lunch, with his group of religious boys from our school, and I noticed that he kept looking at me, and at David, squinting once in a while despite the glasses. When the conversation turned to school, and David was distracted com-paring test answers with Shira's brother, Jake leaned across the table towards me.

"Did you get the defenestration reference on the vocabulary test?"

David turned toward me for a moment, as if checking to see if I was okay, but I looked down at the piece of chicken on my plate, yellow fat congealing on the underside.

"Sturman thought she was being so cute," Jake continued, pressing his tie against the buttons of his shirt to keep it away from his cup of grape juice. "You know, Queen Jezebel was thrown out of a window to her death, and eaten by dogs, to fulfill a prophecy. Defenestrated. Fenestre, window."

"I'm not an idiot, Jake."

"I never said you were."

He went back to his buddies and their discussion of heavy metal music and its relevance to Talmudic study. I wondered why he wasn't sitting across the room with the public school girl and her friends, but I refused to ask.

The rabbi-in-charge and his minions kept us busy all afternoon, teaching us Hebrew songs and giving little lectures on the weekly torah portion and its relevance to our daily lives. They fed us again late in the afternoon: an un-tempting array of egg salad, tuna salad and some strange treatment of elbow macaroni. I ate an orange. I removed the rind, and the white pith, and separated the fruit into segments laid out in the center of my paper plate, and then I peeled the clear skin from each segment until the pits fell out and each kernel of pulp could be bitten into and popped like a blister.

"That is the scariest thing I've ever seen," Jake said, after I'd finished three segments of the orange. We were alone for the moment while David was deep in conversation with the rabbi-in-charge and Shira and her brother were table-hopping.

"Then you haven't seen anything, Jake, and I'm happy for you," I said.

"Don't take it out on me," he said.

"I don't know what you're talking about."

"Sure you do. They're getting under your skin."

For a second, I imagined my skin being peeled the way I was dismantling the orange, leaving me without anything to hold me together.

"I'm sorry, Izzy," Jake said, leaning closer to me. "I just think…" he stopped himself. "Forget it."

He sat back and deliberately looked away from me. I was too afraid to ask what he was thinking. Afraid he disapproved of me. But even worse, afraid that he was indifferent to what I did, or how I felt about anything.

We stared in opposite directions until Shira and David came back to the table.

After the meal, we were told to organize our folding chairs into a circle in the middle of the room to sing Shabbos songs. We all complied, except Jake, who whispered in my ear, "Don't let the music seduce you," and left the room.

I wanted so badly to give in to the groupthink in the room, and feel the togetherness they all seemed to be feeling. Yitzchak was rocking in his chair, singing with *kavanah* – deep belief, so that his voice cracked and he still kept on, eyes closed. I watched them all, and I couldn't see the wall between us, but I knew it was there, baffling the sound, and baffling me.

And then it was over: Havdallah, the walk back to Shira's house, Mom at the door to pick me up, the end.

Chapter Eight

THE NEXT STEP

On Monday morning, Shira dropped an envelope onto my desk before our first class, and then she bounced up and down in her seat across from me.

"You have to read it now, before I die," she said, eyes too bright for so early in the morning. "He gave it to my brother to give to me to give to you!"

Dear Isabel,

I've been thinking about something you said, or implied, the first time we met. Your assumption that I might want you to parrot my opinion disturbed me. I spoke to my Gemara teacher, a great man, and he said that whereas boys are encouraged, even required, to ask questions and debate and follow in the footsteps of the great rabbis, girls are more often expected to memorize and go along.

I can't imagine you in that type of environment. I keep listening to my teachers and being the good scholar, but really wishing I could hear what you would say to challenge them, and challenge me.

Sincerely,
David

I looked at Shira, after reading through the letter two more times.

"What does it mean?" I asked her.

She reached over and grabbed the letter, reading it to herself. "OK, this is guy speak. It means: I like you, I've been thinking about you, I hope you like me."

"No, it doesn't."

"You have to write back to him immediately," she said. "You don't want him to think you're not interested."

"I'm not sure what to say."

"Aren't you excited? Even a little?" She leaned across the aisle to hug me, and wrapped her arms around my shoulders so tight that I couldn't move. I was an ice sculpture, and I was afraid that if she held on any longer I would melt until there was nothing left of me.

In English class that afternoon, while we watched "My Fair lady," because Mrs. Sturman did not trust us to read "Pygmalion" for ourselves, I took the opportunity to try to write my letter.

Dear David,

Shira says your letter means that you like me. There is a whole subterranean world of dating etiquette that I do not yet understand. She has taken it upon herself to tutor me in the ways of normal people.

I crumpled that draft quietly so that Jake wouldn't try to read over my shoulder. But when I glanced back at him he didn't even have his glasses on. I couldn't imagine what the movie looked like to him.

Dear David,

81

I was flattered by your letter and by the idea that you spoke to your teacher about me. Horrified, but flattered. I am not Orthodox like you, nor do I intend to become Orthodox, so I figure I should warn you away before you are disappointed and I feel rejected and it all becomes a ridiculous mess.

No. Bad letter number two. I glanced back over my shoulder. Jake was facing the window, not watching the movie at all. I knew his feet were stretched out under my chair. If I let myself, I could touch his sneakers with my toes.

Dear David,

We are, sort of, doing "Pygmalion" in class now. Writing to you is my rebellion. I hate the idea of a man presuming to mold a girl into something more pleasant and acceptable to him. I worry that you'd want to do that with me. I really enjoyed our conversations, and felt like you were listening to me, but I'm afraid that, in time, you would start to steamroll me towards your way of seeing things. I sound more antagonistic than I mean to, but this is my third attempt at writing this letter and I'm running out of paper, and patience with myself.

Think what you will,

Izzy

I ripped that one up too. At the end of the day I tracked down Shira at her bus and told her to just tell her brother to tell David that I got his letter and liked it.

"That's all you want me to say?" Her bus was filling up and she was trying to whisper and scream over the din at the same time. "What if he thinks you're rejecting him or something?"

I shrugged. "I have to go before your bus starts moving and I end up at your house and have to try to walk home."

She didn't laugh.

82

I was already ten feet away when she called out through her open window. "Don't worry, I'll figure out what to say for you!" She hung her head out the window, like my dog, grinning.

I was eating a bowl of popcorn on my bed and watching TV when the phone rang that night. I've never been good with loud noises, or surprises, or telephones. I managed to drop the bowl of popcorn on the floor and the dog came over to clean up the mess for me.

I waited three rings before picking up, even though neither of my parents was home to answer the phone.

"Hello?"

"May I speak to Isabel please?"

I didn't recognize the voice and wondered, for a second, if it could be Jake. "Who's calling?"

"David."

I cursed Shira under my breath, or not so under.

"Isabel, is that you? Shira called me and said I could call you. Did I misunderstand the message?"

"My fault," I said, counting the popcorn kernels left on the floor as a way to help me calm down. "I wrote you three very stupid letters and ripped them up, so Shira took matters into her own devious hands."

"Is this a bad time?" he asked.

"I'm not sure how to answer that."

He laughed. "I'm asking if you would enjoy talking to me for a while or if you would rather paint your nails."

I could have given him a smart-ass answer, three of which were already forming in my mind, but then I didn't want to. The sensation in my body when I said, "I would rather talk to you," was like diving into a deep, cold lake without any confidence that I would be able to surface again.

He murmured, like the meow of a kitten.

"Do you ever wonder why orthodox men wear black hats, even though the good guys are supposed to wear white hats?" I asked him.

"That's only in westerns. And I don't wear a hat, I wear a kippah, remember?"

"How come men have to wear something on their head to remind them of God, and women don't?"

"If you asked my mom she'd say it's because men are forgetful creatures."

"Shira has holes in her fingers from her crocheting needle," I said. My conversational logic was disconcerting even to me.

"Can I ask you something?" He said, and then paused, and I realized that he was waiting for my permission.

"Go ahead."

"I've been orthodox all my life. In fact, if anything, I am more religious than my parents. I don't know any other life. Does that bother you?"

I sat on my bed and listened to him breathe on the other end of the phone. "Ignorance must be comforting."

"I didn't say I was ignorant," he said.

"What if you *are* ignorant, though? What if orthodoxy is a gloss, hiding the real stuff underneath?"

"Like what?" he asked.

But I didn't want to tell him. I wanted him to remain separate from my world, to be this clear space I could walk into and not feel all of the crappy feelings I was used to feeling.

"So," he said, because the silence had gone on too long. He seemed to want to rescue both of us from the quiet. "What do your parents do?"

He told me that his father was an architect, and his mother was a librarian, and I told him that my mother was a painter. I didn't

84

mean to lie. She'd started out as a painter. She went to art school. She'd taught senior citizens how to draw with pastels. But now she was a secretary and I didn't tell him that. I didn't mention my father. I told him about how my mother used to take me to museums and I could barely stand up straight to walk through the halls to look at the paintings. I would sit down on the hard stone floor while she stared at a painting and then I'd crawl along next to her with my hands over my ears to block out the echoes of all the footsteps. It was like a disease the way I hated art. I ripped up every watercolor I ever tried to do, and threw my little clay bowls with their warped lips against the red brick wall of the recreation center, just to hear the smash.

I was afraid he would see how much I was like my father, and would be more and more like him as time went on, because that's what my father told me would happen. But David stayed on the phone with me for three hours. He told me about the weekly study group his father had been going to for the past twenty years, and how he'd always wanted a more serious Jewish education for his sons.

"But he doesn't like my school, despite the great rabbis. He's disappointed by the less rigorous secular curriculum. He wants us to know about the outside world and be ready to make our own choices about how to live a Jewish life."

He kept talking and I didn't try to interrupt. The world David lived in sounded so much better than mine. He had dreams of backpacking through Europe, and working on a kibbutz, and learning to play guitar, and getting into one of the Ivy League schools, even if he ended up choosing to go to Yeshiva University after all. I couldn't think of anything like a future for myself, but for a little while, his pretty visions were calming the fiery beasts in my mind. By the end of the phone call he was reading whole passages from a psychology textbook, like a filibuster, just to keep me on the phone.

And then he asked me out. It was so fast, I almost didn't understand what he was saying. His mother came to his door to tell him that it was getting late to still be on the phone. She even sounded like a librarian, at least from a distance. After a few seconds, he whispered into the phone, "Well?"

And I said yes, even though I wasn't sure. He asked for directions to my house and we made a plan for Sunday.

"I'm looking forward to seeing you again, Izzy," he said, and then he hung up and I was left alone in my room, without the sound of his voice to reassure me.

During morning prayers the next day, the girls in my classroom were muttering and bowing as usual and I made a show of shuckling a bit, swaying back and forth, turning pages in my palm-sized prayer book. The lettering on the front cover was gold and chilly to the touch. The thin pages were scrunched and folded, not because I liked to mark favorite passages but because I kept dropping the book into my locker without looking and it got chewed up by the hard covers of my textbooks, because they didn't know that this book was supposed to be kept holy and sacred, or maybe they didn't know, and they were jealous.

I finished pretending to read all of the prayers in three minutes, instead of the half hour we were allotted, and then slipped out the door at the back of the room while our teacher was facing the windows. I wanted to see Jake. I needed to tell him about David and see if he was jealous, or see if he thought David would be good for me. But most of all, I just wanted to see Jake because he made me feel less like a stranger than I felt with everyone else. He was messy and conflicted and different at different times, just like me.

The boys had morning prayers altogether in the gym, with all of the grades and all of the rabbis, because they needed at least ten men to make a quorum and say all of the congregational prayers. For some reason, ten girls were just as hard for God to hear as one. I waited in the pay phone alcove outside the double doors of the gym and hoped Jake would step out early for a bathroom break. Given his professed atheism, I thought he might be bored or antagonistic enough to walk out, like I did.

After a few minutes, I finally gathered the courage to look in through one of the small windows in the door, and there he was wearing *tefillin,* the small black boxes with leather straps wound around his head and arm and down to his hand and fingers, another reminder of God. I wondered if it was meant as a comfort, to feel so strongly bound to God that it cut off the blood flow to your upper arm. Did it make him feel more alive, or more connected to the other men also wrapped in these leather straps and draped with prayer shawls?

Jake was standing next to one of the rabbis and they were swaying back and forth in the same rhythm. He looked like a believer. Even if he didn't believe in God, he believed in these men.

I walked back to my classroom and sat down, ignoring Shira's stare. I still had my prayer book in my hand. I'd carried it with me by mistake.

Chapter Nine

DELILAH

Mom was in the kitchen when I came downstairs Sunday morning. I padded across the floor in my comfy socks to where Mom was standing, her scrubber sponge temporarily dripping on the counter, while she contemplated the pieces of the broken serving platter from weeks earlier.

"I think I can fix it," she said.

I picked up one of the larger chunks and pressed my finger along the jagged edge. "With what?"

"I don't know yet." She kept staring at the jig-sawed platter as if she could manufacture the right glue from the sheer power of her will.

"He can buy you a new one," I said.

That broke her concentration. "Your father is helping the rabbi take their Sukkah down, so he won't be back until after."

She grinned at me.

"After what?"

"Your first date," she said, almost giggling.

"Why do you have to talk about my date and get so excited

about David as if you're the one going out with him?" I said in a rush, pacing across the kitchen floor, cleaning up some of the dirt with the bottom of my socks, the way I used to.

"I'm sorry, Izzy. I..." she paused and put the sponge down. "Was I really doing that?"

I had to walk faster to catch my heart beat racing ahead of me. "I don't know what you did or if you did anything. I think my head is going to explode, and I don't know what to wear, and the house is a mess, and he's gonna know how not kosher we are. He's going to smell it as soon as he walks in."

The dog tried to lick my knee below my pajama shorts, but I pushed her nose away with both hands. I should have said no to David. I should have pushed him away, too.

"Can you take a deep breath?" Mom asked.

"Of course I can't! I can't do anything I'm supposed to be able to do easily. I'm a freak and a mutant." I sat down on the dirty floor and began to hit the back of my head against the refrigerator in a soothing rhythm. Moments passed. Both my mother and my dog were at a loss for how to deal with me. I was never the kid who pounded her fists on the floor in the supermarket cereal aisle, or screamed bloody murder when the wrong presents arrived on my birthday. My head hurt at the spot where it made repeated contact with the refrigerator door.

"I need something to do," I said to the floor.

"Are you hungry?" Mom asked. "I could make you some oatmeal."

The last time I'd eaten was at three o'clock in the morning, when I raced downstairs for a green apple and a block of Swiss cheese and then ran back upstairs before I could run into my father.

"I hate oatmeal. He's the one who eats it."

She listed my other options: the leftover spaghetti, dry challah for French toast, iceberg lettuce, Swiss cheese.

"We don't have the cheese anymore," I said.

"Since when?"

I didn't bother to answer. She could pretend I had the power to see into the fridge through the back of my head, if that's what she wanted to believe.

"I don't think I'm hungry," I said, and stretched out on the warped kitchen tiles. My whole body ached, and I was nauseous, and I was thinking about Jake and how he would laugh at me for seeing David, and laugh at me for trying to be something I could never be.

"Don't rest your hair on the floor, Izzy."

"Why not?" I asked, unwilling to get up.

"Because it's dirty."

"My hair isn't dirty, I just washed it last night."

"The floor, Isabel. The floor is dirty."

I was not thinking well. Mom went back to sponging down the counter and I decided to attack the dirt along with her. There is something about cleaning; it acts as a mood stabilizer for me. I spent the next hour scrubbing the black and white floor tiles with wet paper towels, ignoring the pain in my bare knees. Then I cleaned out the dog's bowls and filled them with fresh food and water, to her utter dismay. Then I emptied the pantry and dusted the shelves, soaked the glass turntable from the microwave, and rinsed all of the dust-covered wine glasses we never used.

"Our house is almost clean," Mom said, after I'd changed into my date clothes. Long pants seemed more appropriate than the shorts.

"You sound surprised."

Mom didn't blink. "I still want to vacuum the living room carpet, in case you and David want to hang out there for a while," she said, hands now covered with yellow rubber gloves as she approached the refrigerator somewhat trepidatiously.

"David won't care if the egg shelf is sticky, Mom."

90

"I just want to make a good impression," she said, picking at the fingers of the gloves. "Will he expect you to wear a skirt?"

I squinted at her, Jake-like.

"I just wondered, because you said he was Orthodox, and I don't know what to expect. You've never been on a date before."

I growled, in an accurate imitation of the dog's voice when someone tried to share her food.

"I'm not trying to make you more self-conscious, Izzy. I just want things to go well for you. It would be nice for you to have someone of your own."

I heard a car door slam in front of the house and I jumped up and checked through the kitchen window to make sure it wasn't my father coming back from the rabbi's house early. It was David, climbing out of the driver's seat of a maroon minivan. I hid behind the counter, afraid he'd see me watching him through the window. My mother peeled off her gloves and went to open the door for him. She led him into the kitchen slowly enough that I had a chance to straighten up to my full height. He looked good. He wasn't wearing the suit he'd worn on Shabbos. He looked, almost, like a normal teenage boy in his khakis and an untucked button down shirt. He smiled at me, but I couldn't speak.

"Where are you going this afternoon?" my mother asked him, probably to cover the awkward silence.

"I was hoping Isabel would be in the mood for a walk." At the "W" word, my dog, the traitor, stampeded over to David.

"She doesn't speak for me," I said.

"You don't want to go for a..." here he whispered, quick mind, "walk?" But my dog heard him anyway and put her paws on his chest. "Should I take him out by myself?"

"Her name is Delilah, she's a girl, and no, I'll go with you."

91

I put the leash on the dog and pointed David out the door. As I walked past my mother she brushed my elbow with her hand and I flinched automatically. I don't know why.

David and I walked, in silence, for three blocks, though Delilah barked her way past three enemy dogs and nearly pulled my arm off trying to run across the street to meet the new white ball of fluff in the neighborhood.

"Who named your dog?" David asked, and I was sure he'd been thinking about it for all three blocks. I always thought of her as "the dog" for a reason.

"My father. He likes biblical names."

We walked past the library, and then the local Junior High School that I'd never set foot in.

"Why not Sarah or Rebecca?"

I shrugged. When we'd picked her out as a puppy at the animal shelter we were near the beginning of my father's religious escalation. I was allowed to pick the dog, and I chose the one who rubbed her nose on my fingers through the bars of the cage. I didn't think of it as snot, I thought of it as love. But my father lifted her up, once she was officially ours, and held her in the palm of his hand and kissed her stubby black nose and called her an enchantress. Which made my skin crawl. He named her Delilah, after the woman who betrayed Samson to the philistines. She was the traitor. The faithless one. I didn't like the way my father held her in one hand, as if he could drop her at any moment. She kept her eyes on his and never looked down at the pavement below her. But I looked down.

David took Delilah's leash from me and I let him.

"Did your father really mean to name you after Jezebel in the Bible?"

"I was named after his father, Isidor, who died before I was born."

"I'm sorry."

92

"Isidor was supposedly an asshole."

"Then why were you named after him?"

I shrugged again.

He touched my back with his free hand and I froze.

"Aren't there rules about touching girls?" I asked.

He laughed and took his hand away.

"I'm not as religious as all that," he said.

"How religious *are* you?"

"I don't know, it changes."

"How about right now?"

"I don't know."

He started walking again because Delilah strained at her leash, and I followed.

"My mom wears pants, and she only covers her hair in synagogue," he said. "And the fact is, my parents would probably be okay with me even if I ate cheeseburgers, as long as I was a good person. But, sometimes I wish I'd grown up as a Chasid, or in a time when Jews were more isolated. Then I wouldn't have so many choices about how to dress, whether or not to watch TV, how to deal with girls." He glanced my way on that last one. "I thought I wanted to be more strict, but now, I'm not as certain."

"Oh." I didn't want to be that important. I didn't want to be the reason he broke from his rabbis: just to touch a girl, to touch me. "Yeah," I said, walking faster now. "I feel just like you do. When I'm in Jewish history class and the teacher talks about the Spanish Inquisition, and all those fun times when Jews were burned at the stake or forced to convert, I just think, wow, I wish I could have been there."

He laughed, and I went on. "Our teacher told us stories about some of the Jews who converted, the Marranos. Generations later their descendants would light candles in a closet on Friday night, but they had no idea why they were doing it. Just that Mom had done it, and Grandma before her."

"I guess I wasn't thinking about that part of it," David said, sounding chastened.

"I didn't mean to criticize."

"Of course you did," he said, and laughed again.

"But I really think about this," I said, not looking at him, "about what I'd do if I had to choose between being Jewish and being dead. Would it be okay with me if I had to light candles in secret for the rest of my life in order to survive? What wouldn't I be willing to give up to save my own life?"

David thought for a second, and I could almost hear the gears in his brain whirring. "Well, the rabbis say you should choose death over praying to a false God, eating non-kosher food, and committing murder." His voice had fallen into the Talmudic drone, almost a chanting rhythm.

"I used to eat lobster. Should I throw myself over a cliff for that?"

He was about to answer when Delilah suddenly launched herself across the street after an overfed cat and we both had to run to keep up with her.

We were out walking for a long time, circling the library and the orderly rows of houses on the flat streets of my neighborhood, with bursts of conversation and then comfortable silences in between.

"I can see you as a prophet," David said, out of nowhere. "You have that kind of power about you. Like you could wake people up."

I flinched. "I don't have power. Please don't say that." I took Delilah's leash back and David touched my elbow through the bulky sweater and then his fingers traveled down my forearm to the open palm of my free hand, and stayed there.

94

We brought Delilah back to my house and then David politely asked my mother, who was standing in front of our empty refrigerator with the yellow rubber gloves and her sponge, if he could take me to a movie. She smiled at him and said yes before looking at me. And it didn't occur to me until later that neither one of them had asked me if I wanted to go. He opened the passenger-side door of his mother's burgundy minivan for me and I felt safe in the car with him. He seemed like an adult, like someone who would never back up off the highway or race through a red light to make a left turn.

He let me choose the movie and I restrained myself from tugging on his arm and asking if we could please see the new animated movie where all the cows learned how to moo in three-part harmony. The buddy comedy seemed like the safest choice, not too many kissing scenes to sit through. I thought I was getting through the date just fine, until David rested his arm on the back of my seat and I had to spend the next hour and a half crouched forward to avoid accidental contact.

When David dropped me off at home I found out that my father had put two new floor-to-ceiling bookcases outside my bedroom door, filled with a set of the books of the Talmud in English, and the twenty six volumes of the Encyclopedia Judaica. We now had more religious books than the rabbi, almost as if my father was building himself an army of texts to help him fight off the accusations. All the books were new and oversized and way more than we could afford, but I didn't risk asking him how we would pay for it all. Or why he had to set up his library right outside my door. I just huddled inside my bedroom, doing my homework, and trying to ignore the sound of his footsteps as he paced up and down the hallway.

YESHIVA GIRL

Chapter Ten

DATES

Jake seemed more distant at school for the next few days, and I assumed he was dating the public school girl, or someone else he'd never mentioned, and was preoccupied with her. I tried not to feel rejected. I had David, didn't I?

It was a relief, though, to get a note from Jake in Math class late in the week. He started back in as if we'd been talking all along:

Girls should have communal prayers in the library each afternoon, just like the boys. There's something about being stuffed in a room together in a haze of sweat and praying the same words out loud as a group. It's comforting. I think you're being cheated.

I wrote back that I probably wouldn't find communal sweat quite as comforting as he did. And he muttered as he read my note. He scribbled on the back of the paper and shoved it at me, *I guess you have your orthodox boyfriend for that kind of comfort.*

I couldn't catch my breath for a while after that.

David wanted to take me ice-skating. I'd mentioned the ice skates my grandfather had bought for me for Chanukah the year before, and how they just sat there in the back of my closet, taunting me.

"Do you even like to skate?" he asked me on the phone at eleven o'clock that night. He was barely awake but still unwilling to let me go.

"I like the way I felt in the rink during skating lessons as a kid," I said, "because I didn't have to look at myself in the mirror like in ballet class, or listen to the bad notes I hit on the piano."

"That sounds so sad."

I held the phone with both hands trying to read his tone of voice: sympathetic or sarcastic? I chose sympathetic.

"My favorite part was falling," I said, "because I was the first kid in my class to master standing back up. They'd all be on their hands and knees, tangled up in snow suits and untied laces, and I would fall down again and again, just to show them how to balance and get back up."

David laughed. "So, either you are a generous teacher, or you just like being superior to other people."

I did not like that. It sounded dangerously close to David saying I was just like my father. I should have stayed on the phone with Shira, listening to the adventures of the kissing coach who was reputed to have an "office" out by the empty swimming pool where he tutored girls in proper kissing technique. Or I could have been studying. I still had two chapters to read for social studies.

"Izzy?" David asked. "Are you still there?"

"Yes, barely."

He laughed. "Did I say the wrong thing?"

"I don't think I'm superior to you, David," I said, even though, in a way, I did feel superior to him. I believed that whatever fractured relationship I had with God and religion was at least my own, whereas his was a lesson he'd learned from his teachers.

"I wasn't criticizing you," he said, "I was just pointing out something we have in common."

He said good night a few minutes later, after reminding me, again, to bring gloves to the skating rink. "They keep those places pretty cold," is what he said, in a low voice that at first I thought of as sleepy, but after I hung up the phone, and stayed up for three hours trying to read the textbook, I realized he was flirting with me. He was trying to sound sexy.

The rink was cold and there were too many little kids in puffy jackets standing in line with David at the skate rental counter, screaming at their parents to bring back pretzels from the snack bar. One boy right in front of David kept slamming a locker door to see how far it would bounce back. I sat on a blue wooden bench and placed my skates next to me.

I had practiced shoving my feet into the white skates and lacing them up correctly, but I felt self-conscious suddenly, unwilling to show my socks to the world. I wanted to run out of the rink and leave David and my skates behind, but I sat still and waited for the feeling to pass. The skate guards in red jackets and hockey skates were on the ice, setting up the orange cones to mark the center circle. One of them looked like Jake, always pushing his hair out of his eyes.

David couldn't skate at all. His blue plastic rental skates looked like they were afraid of him and trying to skitter away in different directions and he had to hold on to the railing with both hands. I skimmed along next to him, occasionally taking a lap around the rink on my own, dodging fallen children as if they were orange cones, and coming back to where David had managed to move a couple of feet forward along the railing.

"This superiority thing is overrated," I said, but I had to repeat it three times before he could hear me over the noise of the other skaters and the blaring Madonna song on the loudspeaker. He had made it one full lap around the rink by then and was ready to take a break. We stomped up the bleachers to the very top where it was quieter.

"I'll get better at this," he said, "just give me a chance. It can't be that hard."

"And I'll memorize a full page of the Talmud for our next date and understand it perfectly."

"Sure you will," he said and looking back it's possible that he was being earnest, or didn't realize that he sounded patronizing, or he thought that with all of my sarcasm I'd take it as a joke and he'd earn my admiration. He was wrong.

"So just because I can skate it must be easy?" I said, seething.

"That's not what I meant."

"Bullshit." My legs were shaking and for some reason I couldn't explain, and I had to get away from him or else I was going to start kicking him with my toe picks. I ran down the wooden steps in my skates, probably dulling my blades with every step. When I stepped onto the ice this time I surprised myself with the curves I could take at speed. I felt like I was incapable of falling, and yet falling was all I really wanted to do. I saw David ahead of me, slowly stepping back onto the ice, holding onto the railing and leaning his body against the boards. I wanted to skate towards him and let him catch me, let him feel how fast I was going. I wanted him to know about all of the nights I'd spent with my face pressed to the cool bathroom tile, with the door locked, and the fear never going away... but I just kept going and passed him by.

100

My father was at the kitchen counter when I got home, and there was a bakery box in front of him.

"Where's Mom?" I asked, from the doorway.

"Out."

"But out where? Did she leave a note?"

He shrugged.

I cursed my mother in silence. She was supposed to be home. She should have known how much I would need her after the skating. She should have known that dating was too scary for me.

"I brought you a present," my father said, and pointed to the white box. I struggled with the red and white strings, because I couldn't remember where my mother kept her kitchen scissors, and he didn't bother to help me.

Inside the box there were cupcakes, three inches high, with blue and green frosting.

"What are these for?" I asked.

"I hate my daughter so much, I figured I'd poison her with sugar." He smiled.

I took a bite out of the green frosting and it tasted like Styrofoam. "Thank you."

"You're welcome. Are you up to some errands?"

I had homework in every class and I wanted to change into my pajamas and sit in my room with my books and a mindless TV show on in the background. I wanted my mother to be home – even if it meant she would stare at the cupcakes with disapproval.

"Where would we go?" I asked.

"Yes or no?" my father said, reclosing the bakery box and tucking the sides in carelessly so that the cardboard cut through the green frosting.

"What are the errands, though? How do I know if I want to go?"

"You'll just have to trust me."

I sat in the car while my father visited a Jewish bookstore and I read from the Hebrew language bible he kept in the glove compartment, even though it was the one he'd had with him over night in jail.

"You're lucky," he said, when he returned to the car and saw me holding the bible. "I can read the words, but I don't understand them."

He restarted the car but he still wouldn't say where we were going next. I wondered why he couldn't just ask me to explain the Hebrew words to him. He made such a point of how lucky I was: for having an expensive Jewish education, a TV in my room, the tallest cupcakes in the world, and all because Daddy bought them for her. She is such a lucky, undeserving girl.

When we ended up at the kosher Chinese restaurant, I put the bible back into the glove compartment. He held the glass door of the restaurant open for me and bent slightly at the waist, like a maitre d'.

"Look what your mother misses when she leaves us home alone," he said as he ushered me inside.

The restaurant was busy and so noisy that I worried that the fish in the tank along the wall should really have protective headgear, or Rivky's hands to cover their ears. I couldn't remember if fish had ears or not in real life, so I didn't mention the idea to my father. We passed through a skinny aisle between the closely packed tables and my father stopped three different times to wave at someone he recognized, but I followed the hostess directly to our table in the back corner, where I hoped I would not be seen by anyone I knew. The Jewish community on Long Island, however large it may be, still only had a few viable kosher restaurants where everyone you ever went to school with would eventually show up. I pressed my chair into the corner, against the wall, and waited for my father to meander through the crowd, keeping my eyes focused on the fried noodles on the table, and then the bowl of duck sauce, for variety.

But there was something exciting about eating out with my father. He never worried about money, or calories. He never felt guilty about wanting the best thing on the menu. It reminded me of the times when he took me to his school with him and I was suddenly special. I was the teacher's daughter, and his friends brought me art supplies and candy bars and the students thought I must be brilliant because I belonged to him.

We must have been thinking along the same lines, sitting there at our corner table devouring the vegetable dumplings.

"Do you remember my friend Nathan?" He asked between bites. "The music teacher?"

I did remember him, with his tweed jackets and too tight jeans.

"He moved in with that girl," my father said.

"Which girl?"

"The one who came to lunch with us, the violin player."

I stared at the disassembled dumplings on my plate, spilling their unidentifiable vegetable parts. "She was eleven," I said, and my father nodded and continued to eat.

I remembered her. She had an accent, Russian maybe, and her clothes were wrong, worse than mine: button down shirts that were too tight, and shapeless skirts, and clunky black shoes. By the time I met her I was getting overwhelmed by the attention from my father's students, and jealous of the way my father taught his students so carefully but then expected me to learn math by osmosis, just from living in his house. My head was blurry with too much information, and confused by all of the different faces and names.

Violin girl showed up just before lunch and she offered to take me out to get bagels. She was only a year older than me, but oddly self-assured, indifferent to the looks she got from the other kids we passed in the hall. She didn't have much to say, until we brought the bagels back to my father's classroom, and Nathan was there, and she started to chatter on about a piece of music she'd been practicing for him.

I didn't know what to think at the time, about how odd it was that she ate lunch with the teachers, and that Nathan kept touching her arm as he listened to her, and how he asked her questions as if he really cared what she would say next. I felt uneasy. I thought there was something wrong with the whole thing but I couldn't say what it was. Not then.

"Nathan left his wife and children to live with that girl in a tiny apartment in Brooklyn. The idiot," My father said, moving on to his Wonton soup.

"But how old is she now?" I asked, because I was sure she couldn't be more than sixteen.

"She might be seventeen?" My father said, and then shrugged.

I tried to catch a wonton with my spoon, but missed and hit the bowl instead. "Why are you telling me this?"

"I thought you'd be interested. Because you met her."

"But it's an awful story," I said. "I don't want to know that that's what happened to her."

"What would you rather hear?"

"I want her to have gone to Julliard and left skeevy Nathan behind and I want her to be safe."

"If it helps, Nathan is devoted to her. He would do anything to make her happy."

104

There was a message from David on the answering machine when we got back home. I waited until my father was in his room with his TV on full blast, then called David from the kitchen so I could keep watch on the door for when my mother came home.

"My father takes me on these dates," I said to David, when he asked how I was feeling.

"I'm not sure what you mean."

"We went to dinner. He takes me out alone sometimes. He buys me stuff."

"He's just being a nice dad, right?"

"You don't understand," I said.

"So explain it to me. I'm listening."

My mother walked in the door and the dog ran to greet her with loud shrieks. "I've gotta go, David," I said, and hung up before he'd finished saying goodbye, so it sounded as if the last thing he said to me was, "Good."

Chapter Eleven

FAMILY PURITY

At three o'clock Sunday morning, I knew that the monsters were hiding behind the walls and under the floor boards and waiting to eat me for an early breakfast. I told myself that I would be too crunchy, like a chicken bone, and I would get stuck in a monster's throat, but that was no comfort.

I shoved my rolling T.V. table up against my bedroom door and the fact that the wheels made it a useless blocking device didn't occur to me until much later.

I couldn't leave my room or sleep, so I watched *Roller Boogie* two times in a row, on the lowest volume possible, and huddled on my bed trying to lip-read. When it was officially time to wake up I changed out of my pajamas, scrunched down so no one could see me through the sliver of light between my heavy drapes. Then I brushed my teeth and combed my hair with my fingers and grabbed my winter jacket and ran out to the bus without breakfast because my parents had already left early to see the lawyer before court.

I didn't realize I'd forgotten to wear a bra until I woke from my nap in the little rabbi's class an hour and a half later.

The little rabbi moaned after hitting his head with a book, possibly a sacred one, though my eyes were still too bleary to tell. "Why don't you people listen?" he asked.

A girl in the back of the room called out. "Are you going to give us the answers to this test, too?"

"Yes. Damn it." The rabbi slammed his book on the desk. Then looked at it, sighed, and kissed it.

I felt sorry for him. He wouldn't want to abuse a sacred book. He usually let me nap, unhindered, with only an occasional snide comment about me to the class. I folded my arms, and noticed the missing bra. The worst part was that I was wearing the scratchy green sweater my mother had made for me, something I would have left in the closet if I'd been more awake. The material kept brushing against my breasts, reminding me, to my humiliation, that I had nipples.

Once the little rabbi's class was over we had a five-minute break to wait for our new Jewish Law teacher, hired especially to teach Family Purity. I kept my arms crossed.

"Why do we need a whole class on getting our periods?" Tova Kiefer asked no one in particular. "We already know how to do that."

"There's more to it," Shira said, under her breath, unwilling to confront Tova directly.

The new teacher walked in wearing a scarf over her hair, a heavy brown skirt, and scuffed brown flats, with tassels.

Tova stage whispered, "This lady has sex?"

Shira laughed. I was surprised that she would laugh at that.

The lecture started with a basic biology lesson. I tuned out. I'd had enough in ninth grade Bio and Advanced Bio. I didn't want to hear the religious version of where babies come from. I was sure a stork would be involved.

Towards the end of the class the teacher asked for our questions.

Tova raised her hand. "Can we ask anything we want?"

The teacher nodded and repositioned her scarf.

"Are blow jobs legal?"

I turned my face to the wall.

The teacher stayed calm. "Given that a man shouldn't waste his seed, unless he has permission from his rabbi, I'd say no," she said.

"What about hand jobs?" Tova couldn't shut up. It was like a disease. I knew she wasn't Shira-level religious, but I was surprised she even knew what a hand job might be. And angry at her for putting the image in my head.

"Why are you looking for ways to avoid intercourse with your future husband?" the teacher asked, tilting her head with mock concern.

And Tova blushed.

I'd never seen her blush before.

We'd had a few bomb threats, so the buzzing-in system was on at the entrance to the building and the other doors were chained shut, encouraging us to stay inside between classes. No one asked why terrorists would target a group of pimply, SAT-obsessed American kids; we just took it for granted. Shira went out for a walk to spy on her kissing coach during the afternoon prayer break and managed to get herself locked out of the building with him, so I had to walk up to the Advanced Biology lab alone.

Jake paced outside the door of the classroom.

"Don't go in," he said, a sheepish smile on his face.

"Why not?"

The door opened and the short, bangle infested biology teacher crooked her finger at me.

"Isabel, we're reading something you'll find fascinating."

I followed her into the room. Tova sneered at me, and so did some of the other kids who usually ignored my existence. The biology teacher proceeded to read from a piece of loose leaf paper.

"'I hate these useless idiots who make a show of being orthodox and eating the most kosher food and saying all the right prayers just to hide the steaming pile of,' ahem, 'they really are,'" the teacher paused. "I'll skip the profanities. But in the future, Isabel, I'd suggest leaving such incendiary thoughts where people like me will not discover them."

I stared at Jake's face through the small square of glass in the door. He mouthed, "Sorry," but I wasn't in the mood to answer. I shouldn't have written anything down. I'd written that letter so much earlier in the year, when I was still resenting the switch to yeshiva and willing myself to forget how awful the kids at my old school had treated me. I didn't want to be punished for things I'd forgotten saying to him, in confidence. And I didn't understand why he'd kept the note, or where the teacher had found it.

Jake sidestepped into the room while the teacher gave us our lab directions for the day and I tried to pretend I couldn't feel him breathing from across the room.

When the teacher was finished with her monologue she waved her bangles in the direction of the lab tables. "Choose your fetal pigs."

I kept my head down as I walked over, and ended up next to Tova Kiefer. "You need to wear a bra," she said. "Your breasts sag." She cupped her hands somewhere below her tiny waist.

I couldn't argue with her.

"He left the notes in the bottom drawer of one of the lab tables," Tova said in a stage whisper. I wasn't sure if Tova was saying that Jake had actually meant for my notes to be found and read by strangers, or if she was trying to say that he'd thrown them away wherever, like the trash they were, because I was meaningless to him.

I wanted Jake to have looked out for me, to take care of my notes and take care of me and not leave me standing next to Tova Keifer. But he didn't care about me. No one did. I was on the edge of tears, shoulders rolling forward, arms crossed so tight that I could barely breathe, and then I saw Jake watching me, studying my face.

He raised his hand and the teacher called on him.

"Is it really kosher for Jewish kids to cut open a baby pig?" he asked, and even Tova laughed as the teacher tilted her head on an angle to consider the question, or to imagine cutting Jake open.

He smiled at me as the teacher ranted about crazy rabbis and the difference between a baby and a fetus and by the time she was out of breath, Tova had forgotten about me, and so had everyone else. I didn't know what to make of what Jake had done, but I liked it. And I was very confused.

David came over that night before either of my parents came home. He'd called, ever his polite self, to ask if it would be okay and there was something almost desperate in his voice that made me say yes, but worry that I should have said no. I had time to change into jeans and put on a bra and a less scratchy sweater. We took Delilah out to walk in the dark and he stopped at a street light to look at me.

"Do you like me?" he asked. His voice was plaintive. His feelings scared me. I was hoping he wouldn't have any.

"Of course I like you."

He touched my wrist, really soft, like one of the earthworms in the Biology lab. Not the image he was going for, I'm sure. But I tried hard not to pull away.

He leaned close to me, until I was breathing his breath – he smelled like grape juice.

The kiss was fast. He might as well have stopped a centimeter away from my lips, though, because I couldn't feel anything. But he didn't seem to notice. He re-grasped my hand and walked me down the rest of the block with a smile on his face.

He'd been talking to someone at school, some boy in his class, about whether he should go to Israel for a year before college or not, and what would be stopping him. He said he realized that his reason to stay in the States would be me, but he wasn't sure if I felt the same way and it suddenly felt like an emergency situation, that he had to know.

This was a different David, almost breathless and not making the kind of sense I was used to from him. We barely knew each other and here he was, lusting after me or something, making plans for his life around me, and I was numb. I felt like I was stealing something from him, because I couldn't feel what he felt. Because I was broken.

He went home to get back to his homework and I went up to my room and slept until ten o'clock that night and woke up starving. No parents anywhere. I emptied the vegetable drawer in the fridge and chopped and cooked and covered all of it with a bottle of tomato sauce.

By eleven o'clock I was standing in front of the bathroom mirror with a pair of scissors aimed at the fatty center of my abdomen. After the vegetables, I'd moved on to pretzels (low fat) and a tuna sandwich (protein) and finally the pint of chocolate fudge ice cream from the back of the freezer (no excuse).

I stared at myself, pointing the scissors at my fat white thighs and droopy breasts. I wanted to cut through all the extra skin, like we'd done piece by piece with the fetal pig. Instead I grabbed my hair into a ponytail and cut it off.

111

I didn't hear my mother come home. I fell asleep on my bedroom floor with the dog curled up next to me as my bodyguard.

Tova caught me at my locker the next morning. "You're so brave, to cut off your best feature."

I stood back and admired her ability to hurl an insult

Shira arrived in time to see Tova walk regally away.

"My father wanted me to stay home today," Shira said, ignoring my hair. "He stood on the front lawn wearing an undershirt and drawstring pajama pants, giving me this hang dog look as the bus drove away."

"How long has he been out of work now?" I asked. I had trouble keeping track of other people's problems.

"Two weeks," she said. "He thought we could all stay home and play board games. Maybe bake a cake."

"You like to bake."

Shira stared at me. "You cut your hair."

I touched the uneven pieces at my neck and we walked to morning prayers together.

My nap lasted into the middle of Family Purity class when I woke up thinking bugs were crawling up my shoulder.

"You need to do your sleeping at night," Mrs. Lichtman said, her fingers tapping my sleeve. Her face was even with my desk and her skirt billowed over her knees like a parachute.

"I'm allergic to my bed," I whispered.

She wore a wig instead of the scarf this time and the orangey blond hair reminded me of a doll I once had, just before I cut the doll's hair down to the plastic nubs.

The teacher stood and straightened her skirt. "Shira, please summarize for your friend what we've discussed so far."

Shira blushed.

Tova took over. "It's a *mitzvah* to have intercourse with your husband on Shabbos, and you can't refuse." Mrs. Lichtman walked back to the front of the room nodding her head. Tova continued. "And you can't make fun of the size of his penis with your friends."

I thought the teacher would explode, but she just kept nodding her head.

Shira walked me to the Advanced Biology lab, and at the door of the classroom she peered through the little window.

"Jake doesn't seem to like anyone," she said. "What do you call a person like that?"

"Me?"

"There's an SAT word for it."

"Misanthrope."

She nodded, still staring into the classroom. "I think I'll go call my father," she said, and left me at the door.

Jake looked up when I opened the door and motioned me over to his desk. "I'm sorry about yesterday."

I leaned against the wall, arms crossed. "How'd she find my letter?" I asked.

"I left a pile of them in one of the drawers at my lab table."

My hands were sweating. "I always ripped yours up," I said. He winced, as if I'd caused him pain. "I didn't think you'd want anyone else to read them."

He stared at my dirty white canvas sneakers and said nothing.

The biology teacher walked in then, bracelets jangling across the room.

Jake opened his notebook and it was filled with actual notes. He even had his own pen.

I overheard my mother on the phone when I was sneaking down the stairs to make sure my father wasn't home. I didn't mean to spy on her.

"They were so small, like training bras," she said. I couldn't imagine who she was talking to but the word "bra" caught my attention.

"He hid them in the ceiling tiles in our room. I don't know what made me look there."

Mom's voice was loud, even indignant. I hadn't heard it like that in a long time. As if she were talking to someone she actually trusted. Maybe Grandpa. But I couldn't see her mentioning bras to Grandpa, in any context.

"Should I confront him? Because I don't know how long they've been up there."

I huddled on the stairs, holding onto the banister and waiting for the tornado to come and whip me up the stairs, out of the window, off the roof. It had never occurred to me that there was proof of anything my father had done.

Mom's voice rose over the storm in my head. "Izzy was never that size. I know for sure the bras aren't hers. Thank God."

There was quiet for a few moments, from the kitchen and inside of me.

"Do I tell the police? I don't think they'll take my word for it, now that the bras are gone."

I didn't hear the rest of Mom's side of the conversation because it didn't happen. My father came home, stomping through the front door with his usual aplomb and Mom said a rushed and quiet goodbye to the phone. But I spent hours thinking about who she could have been talking to. She didn't have friends of her own anymore. I'd seen pictures of her friends, some even holding me as a baby, looking like I was a firecracker about to go off. But my father had chased them away a long time ago.

When David called later, I didn't tell him what I'd overheard and I didn't tell him about my hair. I didn't want to give up on having a boy call me at home, but I couldn't think of anything safe to say to him. He told me he still wasn't sure which schools to apply to, or how far away. I knew he was hinting that I should answer the question for him, but I couldn't. And he switched topics pretty quickly after that.

The Family Purity teacher told us that if you're not sure that the menstrual bleeding is over you have to insert a tissue-covered finger into your vagina to "check." If the color on the tissue isn't red, but maybe green, you'd have to call a rabbi for a ruling to see if you can start counting down till you're clean for sex or if you still have to wait. Because for as long as you have your period, and for seven more days after that, you are unclean and your defilement is communicated to every object you come in contact with, especially your husband.

I headed for the shower as soon as I got home. My father was watching a loud gunfight on his TV and my mother wasn't home yet. The dog was blocking my bathroom door, resting her head on her paws, staring. I had to nudge her out of the way with my sneaker and then, once inside, push the flimsy gold chair my father's mother had left behind up against the door because the lock was broken. Then I closed the shutters and the drapes. But even with all of that, when I started to take off my clothes I felt like I was doing a scummy strip tease, as if someone was watching through the closed drapes or under the door. Maybe the dog.

"The Mikvah," our Family Purity teacher said the next morning, "isn't about being physically clean. You take a shower and remove all impediments, like band aids, nail polish, dirt under the fingernails, even scabs if you can, *before* you immerse."

Shira paled. She'd told me she planned to dunk in the Mikvah once a month after marriage. And she expected to get married as soon as possible after graduation, if she could. I should have asked David what he would expect from me, after changing his college plans for me, but I was afraid to find out.

"Men are required to go to the Mikvah as well," the teacher said, "when they've been ill, for example, but many don't do it." She rolled her eyes, as if men were such silly, harmless creatures.

I raised my hand.

"Isabel, you have a question?" The teacher was duly surprised.

"I don't understand. There are so many rules for orthodox women, about when they have to have sex, and when they can't even touch their husbands, for comfort, or a kiss on the cheek. Women are told they are unclean to such a degree that they have to scrub their bodies raw so they won't defile the holy water. If men can ignore the rules made for them as easily as you say, why can't the women?"

The teacher was silent except for a low hum that reminded me of a cat purring.

"Not every woman goes along with it. Do you want to know why I do?"

I nodded, embarrassed at how she looked only at me, and not at anyone else.

"Men have so much control over our lives, in Orthodoxy, but in the secular world too. Keeping separate in a physical way gives me back to myself. It gives me control over my body, and makes me feel sacred. My husband can't do that for me, but I can do that for myself."

"But what about all of the rules for not touching men in general, even when you are supposedly clean. Is that supposed to make you feel in control? That you can't even shake hands with men, as if you are molten lava and will burn them alive?"

"For me," the teacher said, "the rules about touch are a way of honoring the sexual undercurrent that exists between men and women. You can touch your spouse and he can touch you, when you're not otherwise forbidden from contact. And of course, you can touch your children and grandchildren."

She was turning away from me, trailing off that last part of the sentence, so she didn't see my face. I could feel the heat radiating from my skin and I thought about the shower I had taken with all of my clothes on and all of the time I spent watching strangers on TV, grateful to have a screen between us.

I spoke to the back of her head. "What if you keep yourself too separate?"

"Then you need professional help," Tova said. The teacher glared at her but looked relieved. She went on to tell us about the Mikvah lady who makes sure you immerse completely underwater and I tried to imagine what kind of woman would choose that job, checking under fingernails and behind ears, and who knew where else, to make sure each naked body was free of obstruction. Was she there to be of comfort? To act as a lifeguard? To offer proof to the rest of the Jewish community that these women were now officially clean?

I pictured Shira's mother, in her black dress and auburn wig, standing beside a small pool of water annunciating the blessing

117

along with a dripping wet naked girl with her head barely above the surface. The girl didn't look the way the teacher described her, confident and holy with a glowing yellow light around her hair. She looked scared. She looked like me.

Mrs. Lichtman decided to end the day's lecture with a soliloquy about how the two weeks of bodily separation heighten the sexual excitement in a marriage, leaving us to imagine the graphic details for ourselves.

Chapter Twelve

THE RUNAWAY

My father expected me to walk to shul with him again on the Saturday before Christmas, so when I woke up that morning to rain thudding onto the roof, my magical thinking kicked in. God was on my side and wanted to keep Rivky safe and everything was going to work out.

I padded downstairs in my makeshift pajamas – an old t-shirt from sleepaway camp and the oversized sweat pants that caught under my heels as I hopped down the last few steps. There was no shouting to warn me about the mood in the dining room.

"You knew it might rain," my father said in his *persuasive argument* voice. "We could have stayed near shul if you'd been home in time last night."

I couldn't see Mom, because she was learning to stand further and further away from him as his voice progressed from relatively harmless to wherever it ended up. I was still a little too happy and skippy for my own good and continued into the dining room.

"Mommy doesn't control the weather," I said as I grabbed a

piece of challah off the breadboard. Out of the two large braided loaves from the night before there were only a couple of small chunks left and my father slathered the last one with peanut butter and reclosed the jar without offering me any.

"Can I have some?"

"Only if you get me a glass of water with ice."

I could have done it. I could have taken his glass and filled it with ice cubes from inside the freezer without ever having to press the ice dispenser button – but I felt like making my own argument.

"Why is it okay for me to use the ice maker, or open the freezer so the automatic light turns on, just because you want cold water?"

I thought he might argue with me about how different rabbis interpret the do-and-not-do rules for the Sabbath, or he might laugh at me and say that girls are inferior creatures to whom the rules don't apply, but instead he exploded.

He pointed to my bare feet and yelled that I was an Aborigine, then he called me a heretic for daring to wear pants when a good Jewish girl would wear a skirt on Shabbos, and if you want the damn peanut butter so badly then take it, he screamed, and picked up the glass jar of natural peanut butter my mother bought instead of the good kind in the plastic bottle and he threw it at me. The jar landed and cracked open an inch away from the little toe on my right foot. Breaking glass on the Sabbath was a sin, even if throwing things at your daughter was acceptable. I didn't hear my brain click in until it whispered, "run."

The wet grass of my neighbor's lawn squelched under my bare feet and I had to work hard to avoid the piles of melted dog shit until I gave up and just ran on the sidewalk, through the puddles. I kept running until I reached the hill by the side of the expressway where there was a row of evergreens for shelter. The noise of the cars was a relief.

I used to run away a lot as a kid. I would be awake early in the morning, because I couldn't sleep, and I would sneak out the front door and find a place to hide: under the porch, behind a tree trunk, once, and I don't remember what triggered my nerve, I ran all the way to the rec center and climbed to the top of the jungle gym. There was a thoughtlessness to the running away; I never planned my future on the road; I didn't imagine myself as a tiny hobo with all of my worldly goods hanging off a stick.

I sat in my current, noisy hiding place by the Expressway and tried to think. My mother called these triggering events my father's "spells." As if they were a form of magic, the way he could transform from one person into another without warning; or without enough of a warning so you could get out of the way in time. And I felt stupid for not seeing it coming. I should have known. Nothing should have been able to surprise me about my father. I'd spent my whole life with him and I should have had him mapped out and under control and it was my own damn fault for still not knowing what to do.

But there were all of these blank spaces in my head, not steady ones that were always blank, but, like a kaleidoscope, the pieces of memory kept moving in and out. There were days when I remembered falling down the stairs in my white nightgown with the red polka dots, and then there were days when I could see myself at the top of the stairs, screaming, but the pictures wouldn't come together into a coherent movie. I'd wake up on my bedroom floor with a bad taste in my mouth. Was that blood? And then there I am in the hallway turning on every light switch I can, standing on my tippy toes to reach the tall lamp in the living room downstairs. And then I'm face down, suffocating in the dark, with the dusty velvet smell of my parents' blanket in my nose. And then I'm hiding under the porch where it smells just like the wet dirt of the hill next to the highway.

"I'm not crazy," I said to the tree trunk next to me. For one moment I can see myself at the bottom of the steps in my white nightgown with red polka dots and I'm screaming and Mom runs to me and I whisper in her ear, "He hurt me," but she can't hear me because she just keeps saying, "you're okay, you'll be fine, you'll be fine."

I knew I'd been trying to tell Mom, to tell everyone, for years. Hinting, maybe, because the kaleidoscope in my head kept moving and even when I was sure my father molested me, I couldn't *see* it. I could only see the dark because I closed my eyes as tight as I could. I couldn't prove it in court without evidence. I couldn't even convince *him* of what he did to me. And it felt like, if I couldn't convince him that what he did to me was real, and wrong, then I couldn't believe it either.

My damp sweat pants began to stick to my legs on the hill by the highway and I thought, "Mom." How could I have left her alone in the house with him in his current state? My toes were numb from cold and I couldn't feel the pebbles under my feet as much as I walked back, which made it easier to stay on the sidewalk and off the lawns of my neighbors where I'd be trespassing and risking more adult anger. I wondered what my father might throw at me once I got back. We had a whole drawer full of metal barbeque skewers for the one time each year he used the outdoor grill.

Delilah was sitting on the lawn, licking her paw. She must have followed me out the door when I ran. She jumped up and raced around me in endless circles. She licked my hand and her tongue was covered with peanut butter. She needed water. She followed me up onto the porch and waited with her tongue out while I tried to open the front door. I was thirsty too; running away was hard work.

But the front door of the house was locked. I stood there for a moment, confused. Then I went through the gate to the backyard to try the back door, which we generally left open in case the dog needed to pee at three o'clock in the morning. That was locked too. All of the windows on the first floor were locked. I checked each one, starting with the ones we usually left not just unlocked, but wide open. I didn't even know our windows *could* be locked.

Mom's car wasn't in the driveway or parked on the street in front of the house. Only my father's car was sitting there in front of the garage, going nowhere.

I sat down on the porch steps to rest and figure out what to do next. Delilah dog spread out next to me and quickly fell asleep while I tried to think. My father had locked me out of the house. My mother wasn't home. She could be with Grandma and Grandpa, or she could have run even further away. I would have, if I were her. Delilah whimpered next to me, mid-dream, and I smoothed the fur on her back.

I thought about how few people I knew in my own neighborhood. There was the lady who liked to report us to the village for not mowing the grass often enough – but I didn't know where she lived or whether or not she would spit on me if I found my way to her door. The girls who used to babysit for me had moved away long ago and I didn't remember their faces, let alone their last names or addresses.

Mom came running up the front steps. "Where were you? I drove around the whole neighborhood!"

She grabbed my forearms, hard.

"He locked me out of the house."

"I'm sure it was a mistake," she said as she unlocked the front door and Delilah ran past her and straight to her water bowl as if she'd spent days wandering in the desert.

"He locked the downstairs windows too."

She ignored me and refilled the dog's water bowl and then pulled a, hopefully, clean towel off the top of the dryer and wrapped it around my shoulders.

"You scared me," she said.

"He threw a glass jar at me, Mom. Was I supposed to just stay still?"

She rubbed the towel over my hair, vigorously, pulling me down to a manageable height, and then kissed my still wet forehead. "I'm just glad you're not an icicle." She rubbed my arms. "Delilah refused to get in the car or to come back inside without you."

I sat on the floor next to the dog and patted her back with the towel. She let me, but rested her nose in front of her water bowl, in case I should have designs on it.

Mom shook herself and then picked her keys up off the counter. "I'll be back before Shabbos is over."

"You're leaving?" I asked, unwilling to believe her.

"Pop has a study group this afternoon and I promised to stay with Grandma for a few hours. I won't be long."

"But how can you leave me here, with him?" In my mind, she'd heard everything I was thinking on the hill, and that should have changed something.

"He's probably asleep," she said, and left quickly before my dirty look could get any dirtier.

I curled up on the floor with my head on Delilah's skinny butt. "Why didn't you run away when you had the chance?" I asked her, but she didn't answer.

When she stretched her legs, and pushed my head to the floor in the process, I stole the towel back and stood up. I noticed in passing that the pieces of glass had been cleared from the dining room floor.

My father was sitting on the couch in the living room. He never sat there. He hated the cheap brown and white striped sofa my mother bought at St. Vincent De Paul. His head drooped forward like one of my worn out old dolls.

124

"Dad?" I thought he was dead. I thought, maybe, he knew what kind of damage he was doing to all of the women in his life and he'd swallowed rat poison or shot himself, in a discreet place, or overdosed on hypertension meds. He opened his eyes, not dead. I was relieved. And then angry at myself for being relieved.

"Is it still raining?" he asked.

My sweat pants were soaked and my hair was dripping on the living room carpet. "Yes, it's still raining."

He closed his eyes again. "Next time we'll walk to shul even if there's a foot of snow. I'll buy you a pair of snowshoes." He smiled to himself. "Or maybe we'll just stay at the rabbi's house overnight so we don't have to walk so far."

He sort of hummed himself to sleep and I stared. Why couldn't I throw a glass jar at him? Why was I so meek that I couldn't kill him when I had the chance?

Delilah came up next to me and licked water from my toes and I took that as a sign to go upstairs and change into dry clothes. Then I could hide out in my room until Mom came home, and maybe she'd have an extra dose of obliviousness she'd be willing to share.

Chapter Thirteen

WINTER BREAK

The rabbis wanted us to remember that we were Jewish boys and girls – just in case we were watching too many Santa movies on TV – so we had to go to school on Christmas Eve. Except, the school bus companies on Long Island were closed, and a lot of parents couldn't bring their kids in, or didn't bother. Shira was home with her father and her little brothers and I was supposed to call her during lunch and let her know who came in, and who didn't, and if her kissing coach had really found a new student and what did she look like.

My headache started during Jewish History class, but only because up until then I was asleep. I had to try and knock the ache out, so I picked up my loose-leaf and started tapping it on my head.

Tova leaned across the aisle, over Shira's abandoned seat. "You want me to do that for you?"

For a moment I wanted to say yes. I wanted her to pick up my hardcover loose-leaf and smash it against my skull with her aerobicized arms. But Tova had already looked away; she expected me to know she was only kidding.

The Jewish History teacher droned on without pause. I couldn't figure out why she'd become a teacher, given how little she

126

seemed to like teenagers, or public speaking, or any of the material she was attempting to cover. The rumor was that, at 25, she was the oldest of the unmarried teachers and desperate to change that. Her straight black hair was cut helmet style, presumably so that when she switched to a wig after marriage the transition would be less noticeable. She stood straight as a pole and held her breath for long stretches, as if she was afraid too much oxygen would make her fat.

I wondered what she would have been if she hadn't grown up orthodox; if she'd had more options than teacher, social worker or wife to choose from. I wondered if she longed to be a dancer and held her body so stiff in order to keep her dangerous self under control.

Tova and I walked out into the hall together after class, as if we were friends, and a woman in a navy blue pantsuit walked up to us. I was used to some of the female teachers wearing pants, but only in the afternoon, during general studies classes, never in the morning. The woman wore a slate grey cape around her shoulders, but the luxurious fabric kept slipping to show off her collar bones.

"I've been waiting in the principal's office," she said to Tova. "Aren't you smart yet?"

Tova stared at the floor.

"Is this your friend?" the woman asked, glancing at me in my flannel shirt, scrunching her red lips for a moment before forcing a practiced smile.

Tova turned towards me and for a moment her eyes were unguarded. She was embarrassed. "Stop staring," she said to me, and then swept past both of us.

"My daughter has no manners," the woman said and then re-draped her shawl and followed Tova down the hall.

I didn't want to pity Tova Kiefer. I wanted to hate her clean and clear. I also didn't want to go to my next class with a headache that was infinitely more complicated than before I'd started hitting myself with books.

By lunchtime most of the other kids had been whisked away, some in carloads with the smaller ones piled on top of the bigger ones. They were desperate to get home in a way I could not understand. A lot of the kids at my school lived in Shira and David's neighborhood and I wondered, for a moment, what kind of welcome I'd get if I stuffed myself into one of those cars and landed at David's house. I was surprised at myself for thinking like that, and imagining his house and his parents, welcoming me. They would be kind, but perplexed about what to do with me. Just like David.

Mom came for me right on time, and Rabbi Gottlieb practically locked the glass doors behind me.

"Grandma and Grandpa invited you to their house," she said, as she drove out of the parking lot.

"When?"

"Today. Now."

"Why?"

"Do they need a reason to ask their only granddaughter for a visit?"

"Yes," I said.

"I packed a bag for you and I can bring you anything I forgot at home." She was already turning to the left instead of the right, heading to Grandpa's house instead of ours.

"Are you staying too?" I turned to look in the backseat but there was only her pocket book, and a box of tissues and an extra cushion for the driver's seat in case she felt especially short.

"I can't leave your father alone," she said.

"Was this your idea? Are you mad at me?" I asked, turning towards her, holding my seatbelt out so I wouldn't lop off a breast in the process.

"I thought you needed a break, from everything. And Grandma needs more attention than I can give her with all of the extra hours I have to work through the holidays, and…" she sighed and gripped the steering wheel. "I thought, with your father home all day you'd be better off…"

"What?"

"You'll be fine with your grandparents. They can help you with your homework and actually be helpful, which is more than I could ever do for you."

"What about Delilah?" I asked. We were passing the ice cream place. I don't know why that made me think of the dog. She was much more of a Twizzlers girl.

"Grandma wasn't up to having two guests at once."

"Maybe she'd prefer the dog."

Mom laughed. "Nope. You actually trump dogs on her list of welcome visitors."

"But not by much?"

"By just enough."

I was surprised my father had okayed a week long stay with Grandma and Grandpa, given the lower level of Kashrut and religious observance I would be contaminated with during my visit. My grandfather only kept one set of dishes, instead of one for meat and one for milk, because, he said, if the dishwasher is powerful enough to eradicate germs, it should be trusted to remove the last traces of meatloaf from a plate that might later be used to serve macaroni and cheese.

But then I wondered if my father actually *had* okayed the visit. I was being whisked away at the last minute for a reason. I just didn't know which reason.

My grandmother was taking a nap when we arrived so we had to whisper our goodbyes at the front door. Mom kissed the hair near my right ear and patted my head the way she did to Delilah. I felt guilty leaving the dog at home. She was used to having me around, and she didn't like sleeping alone any more than I did.

I called Shira to tell her where I was staying, and to give her the phone number, and she said she'd let David know because his family was coming over for Friday night dinner. I couldn't ask for details because Shira was being attacked from all sides by little brothers and a boiling-over pot of chicken soup. She promised she would call and I promised I would answer.

My grandfather had already gone food shopping and defrosted the Kineret challah before I arrived, so after my mother left it was time to start making dinner.

"How are your cooking skills developing?" my grandfather asked with a twinkle in his blue eyes that made me think of David. I didn't want to think through the train of thoughts that came from being attracted to a boy who reminded me of my grandfather. I wanted to poke my eyes out.

"I still peel potatoes with a paring knife," I said.

He laughed. Grandpa loved me; I could hear it in his laugh.

"First lesson," he said, dumping the contents of his mug in the sink. "How to make good coffee."

"I don't drink coffee," I said.

"Yes, but your husband may, and your grandparents, who will be visiting you regularly, certainly drink the vile stuff."

He walked me through each step of the process until we had three pots of coffee steaming in a row of stainless steel bowls on the counter.

"Do we pour it out?" I asked.

He looked stricken at the idea. "Why would you even think that?"

"Because you poured the rest of your coffee in the sink before, and I just figured that was the protocol."

"That was yesterday's coffee. I gave it my best effort, but even I have my limits. This batch, we'll use. If we have to make ice cream with it, or chocolate cake, so be it."

He brought a cup of coffee in to my grandmother and then came back to the kitchen. "Roasted chicken and red potatoes. Are you ready?"

I chopped garlic and flat-leaf parsley and I actually shoved both, with a good dose of olive oil, under the skin of the poor defenseless chicken. I had a brief flashback to the fetal pigs in biology lab and told Grandpa about the rubbery texture of their skin. He asked the same question Jake did, about the moral implications of Jewish children dissecting the unborn progeny of an unkosher animal.

"We only allow ourselves to kill our fellow creatures out of necessity, for food," he said, tying the chicken's wings with twine. "It seems disrespectful to say that a pig isn't good enough to be eaten, but is good enough to be cut up and, presumably, tossed in the garbage can." He covered the seasoned chicken with aluminum foil and placed it carefully in the roasting pan. I was tempted to wave goodbye as the oven door closed, but I worried it would be an unfair gesture, since the chicken could not wave back.

Grandma dressed up for dinner, or rather, she draped a gauzy multi-colored scarf, with fringes, over her beige sweat suit. She lit the Shabbat candles with all due drama and Grandpa said the Hebrew blessing for her.

I ate a little of everything at dinner, even the non-dairy chocolate cake made with vile coffee and pureed prunes. But mostly I just watched the way my grandfather listened to my grandmother as if everything she said was worth hearing.

The next morning, Grandpa woke me at six AM to help make breakfast and I realized that I had actually slept all night, like a regular person. He taught me how to poach eggs, which sent me out of the kitchen for a moment when I thought I would vomit. I realized that we were cooking on a Saturday morning, Shabbat, and my father would be angry and call me an apostate, but my grandfather thought breakfast was too important to be deterred by long dead rabbis.

He liked to argue with rabbis whenever he could. He didn't want to be labeled as Orthodox or Conservative or Reform, even though the synagogue he went to was officially Conservative. Any talk of that would start him on a language rant about how inappropriate it was to use the word Conservative to describe a movement that actually embraced change.

We made blueberry pancakes and more coffee and quartered oranges and placed the whole meal on a tray, with a flower from the dining room centerpiece and a newspaper, for Grandma. My grandfather walked out of the kitchen in his baggy pajama pants and white t-shirt like a man wearing a three-piece suit.

When he came back we ate cereal at the dining room table, followed by mint chocolate chip ice cream, and then it was time to get ready for shul. Or synagogue. Or temple. Whatever we were supposed to call it.

We were early for services because Grandpa liked to help set up the table outside the sanctuary for the extra kippot and doilies (for married women who wanted to cover their hair), and he wanted to schmooze with the cantor for a few moments about a bar mitzvah student they had in common. He loved being Jewish and talking to other people who also grew up with a carp in the bathtub and matzoh balls in their soup. I sometimes wondered why he hadn't become a rabbi, or at least a Jewish Studies professor, instead of History and Economics, but he just said it wasn't an option at the time.

The main sanctuary in the synagogue was set up in a semi-circle around the bimah (the stage, sort of), and men and women sat together. I'd forgotten how good it felt to be allowed to sit in the main sanctuary, instead of off to the side or closed into a classroom. I thought about Shira and how she'd spent her whole life hidden away in the balcony. And David was fine with that; would be fine with that for my sake; if I were his wife.

I sang along with the congregation during the long Shabbat morning services and Grandpa smiled at me and sang too. For the first time in ages I felt Jewish. The Hebrew words passed through my brain without friction, like a warm chocolate sauce.

At the *Kiddush* afterwards, food and drinks were set out buffet style and the rabbi said the blessings quickly before the older folk could get too grumpy. Grandpa took me around to meet his fellow congregants and board members and I watched them smile at him and speak, waiting with respect to hear his responses. This was so different from the charm that oozed off my father and the way people either swarmed to him for his exclusive attention or stood at a wary distance.

I tried to eat a piece of herring in cream sauce, but had to spit it into my hand before I could locate a napkin. The tiny balls of gefilte fish were easier to manage with their individual tooth pick handles, but I still had to drink a plastic cup of grape juice as a palate cleanser before moving on to the chocolate frosted brownies. Grandpa drank a shot of the *Slivovitz*, plum brandy, but I abstained.

As he drove us back to his house though, he was quiet, and I wondered if he'd had more to drink than I'd realized.

"Do you know what I've been thinking about?" Grandpa asked as he parked safely in the garage.

I shook my head as the creaking garage door made its way down from the ceiling, patiently taking its time over the rusty spots.

"I was remembering your Bat Mitzvah," he said. "I was remembering how happy you were that day."

"Hmm." I stared at the side view mirror, the metal part, not the reflective glass.

"I was realizing today how infrequently I've seen you happy."

He put his hand over his eyes and then coughed. I wanted to ask him if he could tutor me, in anything, the way he sat with those pre-bar mitzvah kids and led them patiently through their Torah portions and the complicated differences between biblical and modern Hebrew. I imagined us sitting at the kitchen table studying Gemara and arguing over minute points of language that could explode even the most basic tenets of Judaism. I wanted him to teach me how to argue with my father. He coughed again and then wiped his eyes and smiled at me before getting out of the car. I couldn't believe he'd been crying about me. I didn't believe that. I believed he had allergies and chose to be clandestine about his snot.

We went into the house and spent the afternoon quietly playing cards at the kitchen table. We played Gin Rummy and Casino and Spit and finally Go Fish until my grandmother came out of her room. Dinner was canned soup and toast because that's what she requested. Even Grandpa sneered at it, but only when she wasn't looking.

When Shira didn't call me Saturday night, I called her, but she couldn't talk long. She told me that Jake had been in town for the weekend and that David and her older brother were helping babysit and she put David on the phone before I could think.

"We were supposed to go out for pizza," he said. "But the little guys were in such a mood, we couldn't leave Shira to handle them by herself. It wouldn't have been right."

"You're such a good guy," I said, not meaning to be sarcastic, but feeling a little sarcastic anyway.

"I try," he said.

"I can't tell when you're kidding."

"I'm never kidding," he said, with a lightness to his voice, as if he were smiling at someone.

Shira came back on the phone after some sort of scuffle. "The boys dragged him back to the playroom."

"Oh."

"Can I call you tomorrow?"

"Sure."

Shira said goodbye and I let her go. She was busy, and David was busy, and it's not like they knew what was going on with me. They didn't know that I needed them, because I refused to say so. My fault.

Sunday morning services at Grandpa's synagogue were shorter and held in the small sanctuary. Grandpa was still bitter about the wall of windows at the back of the newly renovated small sanctuary, and the unnecessary etched glass partitions between each short aisle, and each time he looked around his whole mouth tensed up, no matter which prayer he was in the middle of chanting.

There was a communal breakfast after the service and an argument broke out among a number of the older men, Grandpa included, over which numbskull had actually okayed the architect's design. It was nice, for once, to be surrounded by screaming that had nothing to do with me.

Grandpa dropped me off at home after that so he could go on to his study group with the cantor and the head of the Hebrew school. I was pretty sure there would be debates on drink preferences rather than on matters of Talmudic importance, so I didn't feel bad about being left out, but I wasn't sure how to fill my time. I thought about calling Shira, but with nothing boy-related to report I was afraid to bother her.

The bookshelves in the living room were filled with hefty volumes and I chose *The Portable Nietzsche*, because that's what Jake would have read. David would be hurt that I wasn't searching for books that would remind me of him. Or maybe he wouldn't care.

After an hour of trying to read Nietzsche over the loud nasty voices in my head calling me stupid, Grandma came out of her room. She walked along the hallway towards me, gripping the handrail Grandpa had installed himself, and she sat in her special chair in the living room, across the room from me.

"Would you like to watch a movie?" she asked in her little girl voice. I wasn't sure how to answer her. I thought she meant to watch TV, *Matlock* or *Murder, She Wrote,* and she couldn't tell the difference. She lost patience with me and her voice switched back to gruff and aggravated. "In the cabinet next to the TV, Isabel. Video tapes."

I left my *Portable Nietzsche* face down on the couch and walked over to the cabinet, which I had assumed was filled with old, dust-covered tchochkes that would make me sneeze. Instead there were dust-covered videotapes that made me sneeze, and a VCR. The way it all was hidden made me worry about what kinds of movies might be kept in there.

136

"Ignore the top shelf, those are the movies your grandfather likes." I looked at the box for one of the movies on that shelf, worried, but it was a documentary about gardening. "Try the musicals, bottom shelf." My grandmother was pointing the TV remote at me. I'd been wondering where they kept it. She clearly believed it had wider uses than just controlling the TV.

We watched *Singin' in the Rain*, because she wanted to watch Gene Kelly dance. I made sandwiches for both of us, and coffee for her, during one of her bathroom breaks, which took a while because she walked with such difficulty up and down the hall. I'd always assumed she was faking it, putting on a show, probably because that's what my father said about her.

When we settled back into our seats, she picked out the pieces of lettuce and turkey from her sandwich and wrapped them in her handkerchief, then she ate tiny bites of what was left and slurped her coffee. Then Cyd Charisse came on screen in her slinky green dress.

"She's sexy," my grandmother said, and pressed the pause button on the remote control. "Don't you think so, Isabel dear?" Her voice was girlish again. I chewed the last of my sandwich, aware of the turkey and mayonnaise squishing on my tongue. "You can finish chewing, but then answer," she said, holding the remote in my direction again.

"She's a good dancer, I guess."

"More than that, Isabel. She's languid and sensual. She's the kind of dancer I would have been."

I tried to picture Grandma pointing her toe at Gene Kelly: her arthritic, blue veined, bent-to-the-side big toe. But then I looked into her opaque brown eyes and had a flash of understanding. She used to be someone else, someone stronger and sexier, and more menacing. There were good reasons why my mother could not say no to this woman.

"I hate all of this Israeli dancing," Grandma went on. "Folk dancing, girls dancing with girls, what a waste."

That was the way we danced at school every month for Rosh Chodesh in the gym, barely even touching the other girls, and with an invisible but impenetrable wall separating us from the boys. I felt safe with that kind of dancing. I was afraid of the seductive power Cyd Charisse had over Gene Kelly in the movie. I couldn't live in my body if I thought it was capable of that kind of power. Poor David. I was just stealing time from him and it wasn't fair.

"Isabel, you must speak up more," Grandma said. "Tell me what you're thinking."

I'm thinking, Grandma, that in your brown sweater, green polyester pants, and thick grey slipper socks, you have no business complaining about how other women do or do not express their sensuality. "Can we watch the rest of the movie?" I asked. "Cyd Charisse has to be tired standing in that position for so long."

"No need to be snippy." She gripped her armrest and turned a half an inch further in my direction. "I worry about you, Isabel, with that father of yours up to such nonsense," she said, and then pressed the "play" button on the remote control and focused her attention back on the movie, as if she hadn't lobbed a firecracker right at me.

Mom came by after dinner but she didn't drink the coffee I'd put so much effort into learning how to make. I was sent to my room to do homework but sat on the rug instead and listened through my half open door.

First there was a lot of shuffling, probably Grandma's slippers, then a snort and some whispers, and then Grandpa's voice, low but not impossible to hear. "You should listen to your lawyer."

Grandpa paused but then must have been given the okay to continue. He would have waited for that. "Best case scenario," he said, "if he's guilty of the crime he's been accused of committing, and he is convicted, that would make it easier for you to get a judge to grant your terms in a divorce."

Lots of mumbling.

Grandpa again. "But, if he's convicted, he may lose his pension, and the money he has already paid into his pension account could be claimed by his victims in a civil case."

I slumped against the open door and then worried that my slump had made too much noise, so I scooted back a few inches, which made the rest of the conversation more difficult to hear. There was some mention of "abandonment" and "you could win the lottery." That one was Grandma's suggestion.

"The lawyer's advice," Grandpa said, sounding deflated but full of authority, "was to stay where you are."

"If I didn't have to worry about Izzy," Mom said, too loud, "I could leave right now."

My mother's voice could really carry when she let it. There was no other sound to block her out, no shuffling or snorting from Grandma or whispering from Grandpa. I imagined Mom in a boat with her old friends from art school, going out into the ocean and sailing as far away from me as possible. No one came to my room to say good night, or goodbye, but even if they had, I was invisible, hiding under the bed. Grandma had a penchant for bed ruffles that hung to the floor and gathered dust and hid teenagers from the outside world. I didn't sleep much, even after I'd rolled myself out onto the rug for fresh air. I kept thinking about how much I missed my dog. And I imagined my mother sitting in the kitchen at home, thinking about how she didn't miss me at all.

Jake called the next day. "Are you bored out of your mind?" he asked when I picked up the hall extension. I waited while Grandpa retreated back into the bedroom to check on Grandma for the fiftieth time.

"Izzy? You have to speak into that device in your hand," Jake said after too much silence from me.

"You've never called me before," I said finally. I leaned my back against the wall, because my legs were shaking. "How did you get this number?"

"Should I hang up so things in your world can get back to normal?"

"No."

There was too much silence but I didn't know how to fill it.

"Shira gave me your number. I decided to skip the family ski trip and stay with some of the guys from school."

"Were your parents upset?"

"Oh please," he said. "As if they'd notice."

I didn't know if I should ask more about that. Talking about our families couldn't lead to much good, for me.

"So, Shira said you're staying with your grandparents."

"Don't laugh. I like it here."

"I'm not laughing. My grandparents are too far away for visits like that."

"Saturn?"

"Israel."

"I've never been."

He was quiet, as if he was waiting for me to say something more intelligent, but I was stumped. "When did you speak to Shira?" I asked instead.

"Shabbos party at her house. I keep trying to submerge myself in the orthodoxy thing. And your David was there," he said, in a tone I couldn't place.

140

"He spends a lot of time there."

"Okay."

"Okay." It was easier to talk to him on paper, when I could erase the stupid parts.

"Do you know what book we're supposed to read for Mrs. Sturm und Drang's class?" he asked in his bravado voice.

"Heart of Darkness."

"That's the one where they eat the beating heart?"

"I haven't gotten that far yet," I said. "I've been reading Jane Austen books instead." I didn't want to tell him about the Nietzsche, or about how desperate I was for him to think well of me.

"You read that girly stuff?" he asked.

"Yes. I'm a girl."

Silence again.

"I just wanted to know the English homework."

"Is that your exit line?" I asked.

"I'll see you in school, Izzy."

I waited for Grandpa to talk to me about my parents, or to suggest that I get a job to cover room and board, or maybe move into a halfway house, because Grandma couldn't stand me. Instead he taught me how to make challah rolls, and shovel snow from the slate walkway without putting undo strain on your lower back. He made a list of the books he thought I should have read by now and collected copies of each from his shelves for me. Grandma had her own educational program for me. She made sure to introduce me to black and white musicals, including a lot where Fred Astaire was wearing too much make up and had his pants hitched up too high.

David finally called on Tuesday to tell me that the rabbis were keeping them busy at school to keep them from ogling the

141

Christmas lights. And he was working on college applications too, though he didn't mention which ones.

"I'll be more communicative when the work rush slows down."

I mumbled something in response.

"So, why are you at your grandparents' house?"

"Because they invited me."

"That's nice."

"Yeah."

"I'll talk to you soon, okay?"

"Sure."

I hung up the phone and fell into a pit. It felt like there were three miles of dirt over my head and what right did I have to be dating a boy who was two years older and so far ahead of me. A boy who needed me to be ready for the future. A boy who would be better off with a religious girl, like Shira.

My mother came by that night, and almost every night, but she spent most of her time sitting with Grandma or whispering with Grandpa in the kitchen.

And then my father showed up. Well, first, Delilah came rushing into the house, galloping and hyperventilating, as if she'd been trapped in a cage all week. She ran around me in circles and then smelled behind my knees and under my bare toes to collect the exotic new aromas.

"She missed you," my father said. He looked worn, as if he hadn't changed his shirt in a while, and he was wearing slippers and no socks despite the cold. My heart hurt looking at him. I wanted to not miss him, to not love him, but he was my Daddy and when he reached out to hug me, I let him.

"Delilah was in the mood for an excursion," he said. "So get your shoes and let's not keep her waiting."

He grabbed her leash when she tried to follow me to the guest room. I really did feel like I had to hurry or I would miss something, lose something I needed in order to survive.

Delilah jumped into the back seat and panted in my ear as I buckled my seat belt. My father was babbling and I didn't know how to interrupt him to ask where we were going, or if it was okay with Grandpa for me to leave just like that. My father was saying something about a family vacation "after the trial is over," and maybe we'll even move, so we can be closer to your school friends, or maybe we'll go to Israel. He started to spin a fairytale about how I could go to cooking school in Israel and we'd open a restaurant together and Mom could paint the walls. "We need to stay together," he said.

I wondered where he was taking me, and if Mom knew where I was. What if he was abducting me? There was a momentary thrill at the idea that he loved me so much he would kidnap me so that he would never have to lose me. But I didn't believe in it, that was just another story, like my father's stories.

I'd pushed my father out of my head for a week and it was as if the peanut butter jar incident and the memories it triggered had never happened, or had buried themselves in a part of my brain I couldn't, and didn't want to, access.

We pulled into an alcove with only a few parking spots, but I could see water in the distance.

"It's a hidden beach the locals don't want you to know about," he said. It looked deserted. Delilah scratched at her window and I obeyed, opening her door, and caught her leash at the last second before she raced to the sand.

We used to go to the beach a lot, as a family. My mother would bring her sketchbook and try to capture the seagulls in flight. My father brought stale bread so he could coax the birds wherever he wanted them to go, usually in the opposite direction of where my mother needed them to be.

I would pick up shells and rocks, but I never collected them. I always put them back when they didn't get Mom's attention.

We stopped going to the beach at some point, maybe when Mom went to work for the accountant. But maybe also because the last time we went, my father threw me in the water. We were walking in circles, waiting for Mom to finish a sketch. She forgot about us when she was drawing. I was wearing the orange jeans she'd found on sale, and my father was talking to me about his first shady incident at school. He told me every detail of how the girl's mother spit at him, and how the spit landed on the floor two centimeters from his shoe. He had stopped touching me, even in the most casual way, a few years earlier, so I was surprised when he picked me up, mid-sentence, without even complaining about how big I'd gotten. For just a moment, I was on his side. My dad loved me. Clearly that girl and her mother were crazy to say mean things about him and get him in trouble. I rested my head against his polo shirt and closed my eyes. And then I was in the water. I'd heard his feet splashing the waves, but it was a restful sound. He had to grip my upper arm and my thigh hard in order to get enough traction to throw me even a few feet. There was never an explanation given. He just laughed while I blew water from my nose and mouth. Mom said she didn't see what happened, but said it was probably just an accident.

At the alcove beach, Delilah walked right up to the edge of the water and let it touch her toes and then she looked shocked. She didn't understand that the water would be cold this time of year and it took a few seconds for her to process the information and back up.

"Silly mutt," my father said, struggling through the sand in his terry cloth slippers. Delilah ran up to him and pressed her wet paws on his belly. She didn't wink at me, but I knew she wanted to.

We walked for a while, Delilah in the lead, my father too far back for conversation. I wondered what my mother would have chosen to draw if she'd been there. I wanted her to draw Delilah feeling the water for the first time, or trying to scamper up the big rocks, but she didn't draw dogs, or people.

I didn't consciously intend to torture my father's feet or give him frost bite, but I didn't rush back to the car either. Delilah and I were enjoying our power, just for a little while.

When we did go back, we had to sit in the car and warm up for a while before his feet were defrosted enough for driving.

"Your mother and I have been talking about extending your stay with your grandparents," he said. "She thinks you'd be better off there for a while."

"Uh huh." I didn't look at him. Mom hadn't said anything to me. Grandpa either.

"Of course, I'd rather have you at home, with us."

Delilah nosed me from the back seat, adding her own opinion. I didn't want to lose my whole family at once, just to live in a house where I was clearly an interloper, intruding on Grandma and Grandpa's intimate little world.

"You don't have to decide now," he said, as he started the car. "I just thought you should know what's been going on."

We stopped for ice cream on the way back to Grandpa's house and my father gave the rest of his chocolate waffle cone to Delilah, even though I told him she wasn't supposed to eat chocolate.

"Oh, let her enjoy it," he said.

I didn't want to be the bad guy who took her treat away, and I didn't want to get my hand bitten for trying, so I left it.

My father dropped me off in the driveway and then left before Grandpa came to the door to meet me. He stared after the car and held the front door of the house open for me without a word.

Mom came to pick me up the next day. My father had convinced her that I was desperate to come home and couldn't last another day. I told her that I hadn't said that, and I think she believed me, but she was too tired to fight. That's what she said as she helped me pack my things.

When we got home, Delilah led the way up to my room, with Mom carrying the bag of books and videotapes from Grandma and Grandpa. She helped with the unpacking and sort of dusted my shelves with her hands once there was nothing else to do.

"Are you okay Mom?"

She looked up at me and rubbed her eyes, from tears or dust, I couldn't tell. "I was worried you'd be lonely there. That they wouldn't know what to do with you."

"It was fine, Mom. I was fine."

I spent the last few days of vacation at home, in my room for the most part, and alone. I talked to Shira a few times, but not for too long, and she had too much to do at home to plan a get together. Which was a relief.

Chapter Fourteen

THE HEARING

My father prepared for his hearing by making long speeches at dinner about how children can't tell fact from fantasy and therefore shouldn't be trusted to give testimony. I did my best to argue with him, but he acted like I was playing devil's advocate to help him sharpen his argument. Mom just sat there pushing peas across her plate.

The morning the hearing was scheduled to take place, I woke up in the crawl space in the attic listening to mice, or rats, rubbing their paws together and practicing their ballroom dancing skills across the wooden slats of the floor. I'd gone there in the middle of the night, turning on every light in the attic as the rooms got smaller: the main room of the attic where my mother used to paint, the storage room where she kept her folded easel and old canvases and sketchbooks, and then the crawl space where we kept garbage bags full of my baby clothes and dolls and stuffed animals. My father rarely came up to the attic and never lowered his head to fit through the door of the storage room. The dog had refused to follow me into the tunnel-like space, probably because she could smell the mouse droppings. Dog shit she would rub into her neck like expensive French perfume, but mice were diseased creatures. And scary.

I'd opened one bag of baby clothes overnight and looked at the ugly orange knit dress my mother thought looked cute on me when I was bald and my eyes took up half of my face. I wasn't a naked baby, like those babies in diaper commercials or the little boy I tried to baby-sit for who thought running around with his penis in his hand was the most fun thing ever. The one time my mother found me crawling around diaper-less, because my father said he couldn't make me hold still, my mother was furious. She told me that story all the time to explain why, of course, she would never leave me alone with my father after that.

I could hear my father's footsteps on the second floor and then going down the stairs and then to the kitchen. That's probably what woke me up. I left the crawl space, but I wasn't ready to leave the attic, even after I heard his car drive off to morning services.

My mother hadn't been up in the attic in a long time, as far as I could tell. Her sketchbooks were warped with age and slathered in dust, but still intact. I remembered hating those books, hating the sound of charcoal scratching against the thick paper when all I wanted was for her to play with me. She wanted me to sit still and draw pictures while I sat next to her with my crayons, but I didn't know what to draw, and when I tried to color her black and white sketches she didn't like it.

I opened one of the spiral bound books and there were so many birds. The most ordinary birds. They barely even looked like they were flying.

I had to close the book to stop the meanness from pouring out of me like water. I was filled with it, almost entirely, like a balloon ready to pop. I also had to wash the dust and mouse shit out of my hair before dressing for school, but even three rounds of shampoo didn't seem like enough.

Our Jewish History teacher decided that, given her utter failure to inspire interest in her subject, we were better off having an open notebook test. Parents had complained bitterly when the average grades on her previous test were in the 30's. Tova told me all about it because her mother was one of the parents who'd complained. She said that parents, and college admissions committees, only care if you get good grades, they don't care if you get early onset arthritis from copying over your notes endlessly (like me) or if you read the answers off of your wrist (like Tova) as long as you do well on the test.

"I'll pay for the copies," she said.

"Of what?"

"Your Jewish History notes. Weren't you listening to the lady with the plastic hair?"

We were sitting in the English classroom that afternoon, waiting for Mrs. Sturman and her scent to arrive. Jake leaned forward, nose almost touching my hair, listening in, and I tried to pretend he wasn't breathing on my neck.

"Why would I let you copy my notes, Tova? Don't you have any of your own?" I knew the boy she bought notes from in our afternoon classes, but she'd never tried to buy mine before.

Tova tried again during math, while the teacher was droning on at the front of the room and Jake was doodling on the back of his textbook.

"How about I give you a makeover," Tova said, wrapping a few strands of her long, curly black hair around her index finger, as if she was trying to sell me some.

"I don't need a makeover."

Tova sucked in her bottom lip and chewed on it. "Yes, you do."

149

I tried to ignore her but it took more energy than I had available.

Jake handed me a sketch on my way out of class that was clearly meant to be Tova, with Medusa-like snakes for hair. Just in case I didn't get it, he'd written "Tova" with an arrow pointing at the snakes. But he didn't stop to talk to me.

My mother was in her car, parked in front of our house, when the bus dropped me off after school.

"Why are you sitting out here in the dark?" I asked, leaning into the car, noticing that she didn't have the heat on, despite the pre-snow chill in the air.

"I lost track of time, just thinking."

"About what?"

"The hearing was today."

"Uh huh."

She was lost in her own thoughts, unaware of me, unaware of my need to know what had happened. I couldn't figure out if she was in a haze because my father had gotten away with everything and she didn't want him to, or because my father had been punished and she didn't think he should be.

"There was something between the judge and your father's lawyer," she said, as if she was continuing a thought mid-sentence, as if I could hear everything that was going on in her head. "I think they were friends."

Blood was rushing to my head, getting ready to pour out of my eyes. "So what happened, was he acquitted?"

"They lost the girl's testimony, and some other paperwork the prosecutor needed to make the case."

"Lost it?"

She nodded, looking straight ahead at nothing.

"What happens now?"

"They set a new date so that the Assistant District Attorney can try to find the paperwork or retake the deposition."

My right arm was balanced on the top of her open car window and beginning to ache in one long line down to my wrist. I stepped away from the car to stretch.

"I don't understand. How do you lose something like that?"

"I don't know."

"What does it mean that the judge and Dad's lawyer are friendly?"

"While The ADA was trying to convince the judge that your father is a monster who should never be allowed in a classroom again, the judge didn't seem to be listening. She checked her watch a few times, and then she said that she didn't see any danger, since your father isn't in the classroom currently."

"The judge was a woman?"

"The judge and the ADA both." She shook her head like an etch-a-sketch, clearing the picture on the screen. "I'm going to sit with Grandma tonight while Grandpa's working with his students. He doesn't like her to be alone."

"I don't like to be alone either," I said, but Mom was already driving away.

I gave in to Tova's demands for class notes the next morning, because of Shira. She handed me half of her powdered donut – which most days she knew I hated – and asked me for my notes. Tova stood a few desks away, listening.

I rubbed the sugar off the donut, making a mess. "Do you really need my notes? Couldn't we just study together?"

"I don't have time for that," Shira said. "I have to make dinner when I get home from school, and start on the laundry, and I still have homework in every other subject. Not everyone has as much free time as you do, Izzy."

I handed her my spiral notebook.

Tova ran with it and spent the break between classes making photocopies, with Shira and a handful of other girls keeping watch for the secretary to return from her morning smoke. When Shira came back into the classroom, she was smiling, and out of breath, and she told me that they were able to make thirteen copies before the secretary came back and started screaming at them.

By the time we took the test a few days later, more copies of my notes must have been made because most of the class had my handwriting in front of them. Tova threw a pencil at me to get my attention, so I could tell her on which page to find the answer to question three. The teacher didn't seem to notice.

Tova came over to my desk afterwards and pounded on my shoulder blade. "See, that didn't hurt."

I rolled my shoulders. "Everything hurts."

She blinked, stumped for a second. "You know Isabel, you have the handwriting of a crazy person." She whipped her hair over one shoulder and walked away.

I called David that night. He talked about his college application essays, but I didn't really listen. I pictured us sitting at the center of the ice at the skating rink, where I could keep him cold and keep myself safe. When he paused in his recitation of SAT scores I asked him, "Are we breaking up?"

I didn't realize I'd been thinking about it until the words came out.

"Is that what you want, Isabel?" He didn't sound surprised.

"I think I'm hurting you," I said, meaning that he was hurting me.

"You're not."

"I don't want to start hating you."

He just breathed in response.

"Shira will be mad at me if I can't make this work," I said, as if Shira was the reason I'd liked him in the first place, as if the feelings were never mine.

"Shira has more important things on her mind."

That rankled.

"Why did you like me in the first place?" I asked, dragging my phone cord across the floor so I could squash myself into the back of my closet, behind the hanging clothes.

David sighed to let me know how patient he was trying to be with me. "Do you want the honest truth?"

"Yes," I said, but, no, I didn't want the truth.

"I liked the fierce way you listened to me," he said, "as if every word had an impact. You made me feel important."

I pulled my knees to my chest, brushing against the hem of a green corduroy skirt I never wore. I wanted him to be the one who listened. I wanted to tell him about the time when I was seven years old and my father took me fishing and we were so good together, quiet and focused, and my father told me stories about a little girl fish in the lake who looked just like me. And then he said I had to learn how to kill a fish. I couldn't expect to keep my hands clean forever, he said. Then finally, because I was crouched in the dirt and crying, he did it himself. And when my mother came to pick us up he slipped the dirty knife into my hand and told her, with pride, that I had done it myself.

"Isabel?" David's voice was high and thin. "I don't understand you. You've been telling me that all along, and you're right. Okay?"

"Okay David. I guess we're saying goodbye then." I waited for him to hang up, but he didn't.

"Let's talk about something else," he said, and for the next two hours he told me about the colleges he was looking into, wondering aloud if he should spend a year in Israel first or wait until junior year of college. I was happy to listen.

Chapter Fifteen

HOW TO BE GOOD

"There's more to being a good person than simply not doing the wrong thing," Mrs. Lichtman said, pacing the front of the classroom. She seemed smaller walking around. When she sat on top of her desk there was the appearance of height.

Shira stared at the door. Tova unscrewed and re-closed the cap of her water bottle. We were moving on from Family Purity to other sorts of Jewish Law that could be applied to women, and without chance utterings of the word "penis" on her side, Mrs. Lichtman was having trouble keeping our attention focused on the topic of the day. I found myself looking through the small square window in the classroom door, wondering if today would be one of Jake's skipping school days, or skipping Izzy days. I wanted to know which shirt he was wearing and if it was a glasses on or off day. I wanted to know if today would be one of the days when he reached out to me and said something heartfelt so I wouldn't have to feel so alone.

"Isn't it interesting," the teacher said to our blank faces, "that we tend to use the word Mitzvah in casual conversation to mean a kind act, like holding open a door for an old woman, or visiting the

155

sick, but the word really means 'commandment,' because we are commanded to act in these ways.

"Huh." That's all the teacher got from us, an anonymous response that suggested one of us might be listening, or had something stuck in her throat.

"I would like you to consider this question." Mrs. Lichtman raised her voice a few levels. "With so much of what we consider 'good' behavior already required by Jewish Law, what would you girls need to do in order to feel like good people? How could you go beyond being obedient and become generous, or compassionate. To be a mensch."

"You want us to be men?" Tova asked.

"I'm using the word in its colloquial sense, not literally men, but good people."

Tova muttered to herself, not so quietly.

"Does anyone want to hazard a guess as to what else you'd need to do in order to be a good person?" Mrs. Lichtman asked, pulling her beret on one side, and then on the other, exposing loose brown hairs. I couldn't understand why she went to the expense of buying a wig, a very ugly, fake looking wig, and then rarely bothered to wear it. Not very charitable thoughts, bad me.

"You could give money to the poor," Brooke, a girl in the back of the room, said. I didn't know her well. She was only in a few of my classes and had enough friends without seeking out a weirdo like me.

"We're required to give ten percent of our money to charity," the teacher said. "But the question I'm asking is: is it enough just to do what we're told to do?"

Shira raised her hand, which was out of character for her, especially when she hadn't seemed to be listening to the conversation in the first place. "Giving money is easier for some people than for

156

others," she said. "Rich people shouldn't be given more credit because they have more money to give away. Should they?"

"This isn't a competition," Mrs. Lichtman said.

"Of course it is," Tova said, tapping her water bottle against her desk.

Mrs. Lichtman rubbed her eyes, pulling the skin in a way that reminded me of a movie where aliens wore human skin and were revealed as their true selves when the skin was peeled off.

"For homework," Mrs. Lichtman said. "I want a list of ten things each of you could do, positive actions, to make yourselves better people. And I don't mean losing five pounds or studying for the SAT's."

I tried to think of things for my list during Jewish History class. I could tutor Shira. I could tone down my sarcasm, especially the stuff I didn't say out loud, because, of course, God was listening. But that was the point of thinking the sarcastic thoughts in the first place, to let God know where he was going off track.

Number one on my How-To-Be-A-Better-Person list would be to pray more often.

I had two ideas for the next spot on my list. One, I could be nicer to my father. My mother was always telling me that he'd had a tough childhood and I should have compassion for him, and then maybe he'd be nicer to me in return.

The second idea was to stand up to my father. I liked that one better. But it would probably mean breaking one of the big commandments, either honor your mother and father, or do not kill.

Be more helpful to Mom, because she lives a martyr's life. She goes to a job she hates and lives with a bad man and an ungrateful daughter.

Listen to Shira more, instead of pretending to listen as she warbles on about her little brother Yossie and how she has to do the laundry and deal with the "railroad tracks" on his underwear. I didn't understand the reference at first, imagined he was using magic marker in an odd way after running out of paper, until Shira explained that little boys are not great at wiping their own butts.

Do better in math, could be on my list, and don't draw geometric designs on the sides of my textbook while the teacher is trying to explain obtuse angles.

Become a lawyer and fight for the rights of abused women.

Become a divorce lawyer and get Mom a good settlement before my father loses all of his money in civil suits.

Become a doctor. For what? To heal Grandma? Can you really heal arthritis and a critical temperament?

Become a rabbi or a teacher. No. Too close to being like my father.

Tell the truth.

When I wrote to Jake about the assignment, he was intrigued.

Izzy,

It sounds like this teacher actually wants you to think for yourselves. It's a novel approach. But I don't think I have any advice to give you on this topic. I could recite rabbinical answers, or be snide, but I'm just not an expert on goodness. I think I should leave that to you.

Jake

I fell asleep on my bedroom floor with my notebook open and when I woke up and saw my list I ripped the pages out and tore them into tiny pieces. I knew better than to try and flush them down the toilet where they might float back up to the surface. I chewed a few pieces of gum and stuck it all together with another piece of paper on the outside and shoved the whole mess into the jumbo garbage can at the edge of our driveway the next morning.

I wrote a new list on the bus on the way to school.

1. Pray more.

2. Find compassion for people who don't deserve it.
3. Eat the oatmeal Mom makes for breakfast.
4. Listen to friends more closely.
5. Listen to teachers and assume they know something I don't know.
6. Don't lie.
7. Don't tell the truth too much.
8. Don't tell the truth just because it'll make you feel better.
9. Figure out the rules of each new environment.
10. Follow the rules.

I fell asleep in the little rabbi's class and had a dream that I was an alien and people kept pulling at my human skin to prove that it was a mask.

Shira woke me for the break between classes, so I could accompany her to the bathroom. I followed dutifully and leaned against the sinks while she peed and told me about her father's latest attempt to cook.

"Crunchy scrambled eggs," she said through the stall door. "He said the shells add texture."

"Hmm." I decided to wash my face with one of the rough brown paper towels. I scrubbed hard but no skin peeled off. I pulled extra hard at the hairline, just to be sure. Shira came out of the stall just in time to see me pull my bottom lip out as far as it would go.

"Are you even listening to me?"

I nodded, yes, and she chose to believe me.

There was a note on my desk when we got back to the classroom, telling me to come to the secretary's office. My mother was waiting for me.

"Why?" Shira asked, reading the note over my shoulder.

I must have forgotten about a doctor's appointment, I said. Probably Mom wanted to make use of my father's generous health insurance coverage before he lost it.

Shira had to stay in class and take notes so I went up to the office alone. My mother was sitting across from the school secretary, listening politely to something or other with her fake "that's fascinating" smile.

"Ready to go to your dentist appointment?" she asked as soon as she saw me in the doorway.

I nodded and stepped back out into the hall.

My figure skates were in the front seat of the car and I had to shove them onto the floor with my book bag to make room for me to actually sit.

"What's going on?"

"I thought you could teach me how to skate backwards, finally," Mom said. "The rink shouldn't be crowded today."

"How come you don't have to be at work? I thought it was tax season or something."

She didn't answer, just started the car and didn't even wait for me to buckle my seatbelt before driving out of the parking lot.

Mom used to take me skating when I was a kid, when she was only working part time and she didn't mind if I missed a day of school here and there. But it was out of character for her now, to risk breaking the rules and upsetting my father. He was the one who had decided that she needed a more practical job to help pay for private school, because I needed a Jewish education, and he needed to pay synagogue dues, and then he needed to buy black hats and black suits and the second set of dishes to separate meat from milk, and it was all for me, he said, so how could Mom argue and selfishly think only of her own need to pursue her art at the expense of her little girl.

160

Not many people were on the ice mid-morning. The music wasn't even on yet. I couldn't help but see David on the benches and then holding onto the railing. I missed him. But not the same way I missed my daily dose of Jake. There was relief in not having the pressure anymore to be normal for David, but a sort of hopelessness had set in. All I could have was this longing for Jake, and nothing more. I couldn't do better, or feel better. I'd made the effort to be normal and now I knew my limits.

Mom and I sat on the bench together, struggling with our skates in silence, and I watched a large, older woman in jeans do a spin center ice. She was mesmerizing, and so fast, and came out of the spin in a sharp stop, with her arms wide, presenting herself to the world.

"I quit my job," Mom said, holding onto my elbow for support as we carefully stepped onto the ice together.

Then she wouldn't be leaving my father anytime soon, I thought. "What happens now?" I asked, keeping my arm steady for her to lean on.

"Pop said he'd pay your tuition for now, until I get a new job."

"I thought my father was paying for school. With his salary."

"He says he can't afford it. The lawyer he chose is expensive."

I wanted to scream but couldn't see how it would help. I thought about the girl who had accused my father. I couldn't understand what had made her brave enough to do that. She was younger than me. And she was telling her story to police officers and lawyers, under oath, maybe into a tape recorder or on videotape, however that worked. I wondered if she was telling her whole story or leaving out the more embarrassing things. Like maybe she told them that he touched her right buttock through the thin fabric of her

161

skirt, or stuck his hand into the back pocket of her jeans. But she didn't tell them about how he took her to lunch and listened to her complain about her mom's new boyfriend. Maybe it didn't even happen that way. Maybe he used different tactics with each girl. Maybe he ran out of tactics and he just didn't think she'd notice if he just once brushed his thumb against the breast pocket of her polo shirt.

The cold rink was supposed to freeze out those kinds of thoughts, but I brought my own heat everywhere I went. I could see my father so clearly in his classroom, wrapping his arm around the waist of a girl with thick glasses who never got as much attention as she needed from her own father. I could see her inching away from him but not knowing what to think about the way his fingers dug into her hip before he let her return to her seat. I couldn't imagine the same girl each time. One minute she was a shy dark-haired girl, the next she had flaming red hair cut short over her ears, then she had tight cornrow braids. She was tall, then short, then fat. Though maybe not fat. Maybe being fat would be the one thing a girl could do to discourage my father.

I stared at the ice with its squiggled cuts from all the different blades.

"His mother was disturbed," Mom was saying, because after admitting some of my father's flaws she always had to excuse them. "Do you remember her? The way she looked at him…"

I dropped her elbow for a second and she lost her balance and tripped forward on her toe pick and I had to grab her under the arms before she could hit the ice.

We kept skating.

I remembered that kitchen with the peeling orange wallpaper and the smell of boiled chicken and Lysol. My father's mother was almost bald when I met her, not long before she died. She wore a dressing gown and her breasts rested on the kitchen table in front of her. We'd brought her cold cuts from a deli nearby: Olive loaf, salami, liverwurst and rye bread. She held my father's hand and smoothed it like a wrinkled shirt. When he stood up to get her teapot from the stove, she rubbed the back of his leg and he, slowly, poured the tea past her empty cup onto her forearm. The tea was steaming. It had to have hurt when the water hit her crepey skin, but she kept smiling at him and rubbing the fabric on his thigh.

When I returned to school the next day Mrs. Lichtman was finishing up the discussion of how to be good and she sounded frustrated. She said we were just saying what we thought she wanted to hear instead of thinking for ourselves. Tova mumbled, loud enough for all of us to hear, that our teachers had put a lot of time into brainwashing us, and it would be rude to forget our lessons so soon.

Mrs. Lichtman stood and started pacing the front of the room. "How about, what makes a good wife?"

"Beauty," Brooke said. I turned to look at her and she was busy brushing her dark hair with her fingers.

"And sexual skill," Tova said.

Mrs. Lichtman raised an eyebrow. "And a big dowry and the ability to hem a pair of pants, yes, fine. Is anyone going to take me seriously?"

"Loyalty," Shira said, staring down at her desk, "Being faithful no matter how hard it gets to live with someone."

"Good, Shira," the teacher said, perking up.

"But you're *required* to be faithful," Tova said. "Women were stoned for cheating on their husbands."

"What about a man who's unfaithful to his wife?" Brooke asked. There were rumors going around about her eleventh grade boyfriend and a public school girl.

"More is expected of women," the teacher said. She'd turned her face towards the blackboard, so I couldn't see how she felt about that.

"But," I asked, to the back of her brown sweater, "how did they get the women to stand still and allow themselves to be stoned?"

Mrs. Lichtman literally spun back around to see who'd spoken. Graceful.

"Maybe they tied her to a tree," the girl sitting next to Tova said, spit collecting in the corners of her mouth.

"Or the guy she did it with has to hold her in place." Brooke.

"Or," I said. "Maybe the society has so convinced her of her own guilt, teaching her what it means to be a good wife and teaching her how much God hates her, that she just stands there and lets them kill her."

The whole class was quiet for a good long time after that.

Chapter Sixteen

AFTERMATH

Shira sat next to me on the floor during gym. She'd stopped talking about boys. I noticed because it meant we spent a lot more time being quiet and watching the other girls play volleyball. Tova screamed at her teammates because they didn't know how to set the ball for her. Instead of boys, Shira talked about her father's therapist and her mother's extra hours at work and the loan from her mother's brother that made them all feel like poor relations. I kept my thoughts to myself. Mom was at another job interview for another stupid job she would resent as much as the last one. My father was probably wandering around the five boroughs looking for girls to molest. I much preferred watching Tova spike the ball at the heads of my classmates to making small talk.

Tova and Jake and I had a surprise math test right after gym. The teacher handed a pile of blurry copies to the girl in the front row to pass out, so he wouldn't have to stand up. The papers fanned out across the room and I picked one up from the floor where the boy in front of me had dropped it over his shoulder.

I looked at the five problems on the test sheet and I had no idea what they meant. My father had only helped me with math once, when

165

I was struggling with a workbook he'd brought home for me. He got frustrated when he realized that I didn't understand basic algebra. He expected that by third grade I would have absorbed something as obvious as that.

I stared at the incomprehensible word problems on the page and then around the room. Tova was in the next row, bent over her test, and carefully erasing one thing and writing in something else. Even Tova knew this stuff without having to cheat. I considered turning the paper over and writing to Jake on it instead. Every piece of paper seemed to offer this potential. I could write to him about my father and ask him why he wasn't close to his parents.

But Jake was busy scribbling on his own test paper and wasn't even thinking of me and my empty, stupid, useless brain. Tears started to press at the back of my eyes and I had to get out of that room, so I wrote a big fat zero at the top right corner of my test paper, and then gave it a percent sign so it wouldn't be lonely. The teacher didn't even blink when I handed my paper in and walked out of class. I started to hyperventilate on my way down the hall into the girls' bathroom, and then the serious crying kicked in. I crouched against the bathroom wall, out of the way of the stalls, thinking the words, "I'm an idiot," over and over like one of the repetitive songs on the radio that stopped meaning anything after the first minute. I ended up trying to figure out what a "nidiot" might be.

Tova came in a while later, when I was at the hiccup stage, and squatted down next to me, unwilling to let her flower patterned silk skirt pick up germs from the bathroom floor.

"Are you OK?" She had to lean a few fingertips against the wall for support and I focused on how gingerly she did that.

"The teacher asked me to find you," she said. "He told me to take you to the guidance counselor. Moron. What kind of school does he think this is?"

"I think we do have a lady who comes in once a week," I said.

166

"Whatever." Tova checked under the stalls, no feet were showing. "Are you, like, losing your mind or something?"

I shrugged.

"Do you want to go back to class, or just sit here and moan? Moaning can be fun." She blushed. "I didn't mean that in the sex way."

"I didn't even consider it, Tova."

"Okay then." She pushed herself up, using the wall, so of course she had to wash her hands with the pink liquid soap and then, since she was in front of a mirror, check her hair. "You shouldn't sit there too long, you'll get some incurable disease," she said, and walked out.

I stayed in my corner until the door opened again and a bunch of seventh grade girls came in. I had to stand up and move away so that they could get into the stalls. I washed my face and dried it with a brown, scratchy paper towel and when I left the bathroom Tova was waiting for me out in the hall, holding my books.

"One more minute and I was gonna drop these on the floor," she said.

I took my books from her. "Thank you."

"Whatever." She walked ahead of me, pretending she wasn't slowing her pace so I could keep up.

Rabbi Gottlieb called me to his office the next afternoon.

Two boys wearing jeans – not allowed in the dress code – were sitting in the chairs outside of his office. The door was open, but I wasn't sure if I should just walk in, or if I was supposed to find a chair and wait my turn. I leaned towards the doorway, until the top of my head was in the office.

"Get back in your seat until your mother arrives!" Rabbi Gottlieb did not look up, until I lost my balance and had to brace myself on a filing cabinet.

"Isabel?" His voice softened. I had assumed that he spoke to everyone in the same tone he spoke to me.

"Do you have any cookies?" I asked from the doorway.

He opened a drawer in his desk and handed me an unopened box of soft baked cookies. Chocolate chip. I ripped off the closure on the box and then sat down across from him, with the box open on my lap.

"So what happened with this math test?"

"I don't know," I said.

"Are we failing you?"

I wanted to say yes. I wanted to tell him that my brain was leaking out of my eyes and if he didn't do something to help me soon, I'd be left with nothing. Instead, I shrugged.

"Maybe a tutor would help?" He spun his rolling chair a half turn away from me and looked into the eyes of his Chihuahua for a moment before turning back to me. "I'm surprised your parents haven't called me, to complain about our teaching methods or the strain of the long school day." He winked at me.

"Do parents really do that? Blame you, I mean, instead of blaming their kids?" I put the box of cookies back on his desk.

Rabbi Gottlieb had a perplexed look on his face. "Would it be all right with you if I called your parents, to see if we can problem solve together?"

"Could you really do that?"

He nodded. "And please, take some cookies. I'd like to see you smile."

He held the box open and I took two cookies and closed my hand around them.

"Off you go."

Jake was standing in the hall as I left the office, talking to one of the boys in the chairs. Seeing him face to face was strange. I was used to feeling his breath on my neck, hearing his voice, reading his slanty handwriting, but looking him in the eye felt like...more.

"What are you doing here?" he asked, pushing his newfound glasses back up on his nose.

I took a step backwards, even though he was more than a body length away, and managed to step on Rabbi Gottlieb's foot, which led to leg-to-leg contact and immediate humiliation. The Rabbi blushed and then quickly grabbed one of the boys by the sleeve and dragged him into the office.

"You too," he said to the other boy, the one Jake had been talking to. Then I was left alone in the hall with Jake, who was supposed to be in Gym class, which explained why his button down shirt was untucked and his white undershirt showed through at his neck.

"Can you really eat those things once you've bent them in half and sweated all over them?" he asked, directing his gaze at my chocolate-covered fist.

"Want them?" I opened my hand. I was being obnoxious because I was so unbelievably uncomfortable staring at the open button at his neck and remembering the moment when my hip touched Rabbi Gottlieb's pant leg. I didn't expect Jake to come over to me and take a piece of cookie from my palm and put it in his mouth. But he did. And then he raised his eyebrows and made a humming sound and walked backwards until he knocked into a seventh grade girl. He had to turn around then in order to see where he was going.

I dropped the rest of the cookie pieces into the garbage on my way to Hebrew language class, and then I licked the melted chocolate off my hand, and I think that's when everything in my head really went to shit.

I missed the bus for school the next morning because I'd only closed my eyes at around Six AM and Mom was unwilling to force me to get up before she went over to sit with Grandma My father was gone, to morning services and then, somewhere.

I napped on and off with game shows and soap operas for company. Delilah avoided me. I thought I heard the phone ring and the door slam a few times, but I was too exhausted to move.

Mom knocked on my bedroom door sometime in the afternoon, carrying a bowl of soup and a folded paper towel that had already dipped into the broth without her noticing.

"I thought you might be hungry," she said, and then must have seen how wrong she was, because she left to deposit the bowl out of view and then returned. "Are you feeling sick?"

I rolled my head from side to side on the pillow and mumbled.

"Headache?"

"Grrmmm," I think is what I said.

"Stomach?"

"Hrrmmm."

"So articulate." She smiled at me and then took a deep steadying breath and leaned against my wall. "Rabbi Gottlieb called."

I pulled the blanket over my head. "Mad at me."

"No," she said. "If anything, he's mad at *me*."

"For what?"

"He was very diplomatic. He suggested a tutor, for math, and then casually mentioned a psychotherapy clinic in Brooklyn that works with Orthodox families."

I pushed the blanket off my head and sat up. "Really?"

"He's worried about you."

"What did he say exactly?"

"I don't remember, exactly. He did say that this clinic charges on a sliding scale. But your father would never let you go for therapy, so what was I supposed to say?" Her voice raised up a notch. "It's so simple for him, sitting in his office and giving advice I can't possibly take."

"But..." I tried to interrupt but she couldn't hear me, or see me. She was in another place. I wanted to ask her why it mattered what my father wanted me to do. Why couldn't she find me a psycho-therapist who *didn't* work with orthodox families and just take me there behind my father's back. Or send me away to a hospital where he could never find me. But Mom couldn't hear my thoughts, or even remember that I was in the room. She was still ranting.

"What the hell am I supposed to do?" she asked. "I mean, if Pop thinks it's so easy, why doesn't *he* fix it?"

"Rabbi Gottlieb, you mean," I muttered.

"He expects too much from me," she said, clearly not hearing me. She sounded like a little girl. A whiny little girl. And that was supposed to be my job. I was supposed to be the one complaining to her and getting her help.

"You don't even try!" I screamed at her, surprising myself. "You're supposed to be the mother!"

She shrunk back from me, surprised, and the squirrelly look on her face made me want to throw knives at her instead of protecting her, the way I usually wanted to do. And that thought wiped me out.

"You didn't protect me," I said, my voice barely above a whisper now.

The look in her eyes changed from surprise to confusion. "From what?" she asked.

"He gave me food," I said, eyes on my blanket.

171

"Rabbi Gottlieb?"

"No. Daddy."

She relaxed her arms and sucked in air through her nose and blew it out through her mouth. "I keep telling him not to bring you all that junk food, but he never listens to me."

"You're not listening, Mom. Why can't you listen?"

I rubbed my head against the paneling on my wall, feeling for the grooves with the sore parts of my scalp. I could see the late night feasts we used to eat together: banana pancakes, sausage and cheese omelets, long before we became kosher. The buttery smell still seemed to hang in the air.

"I could never sleep, even when I was little," I said.

Mom touched my elbow and smiled. "I remember, you came in and woke me up and I let you snuggle with me."

"And you fell asleep again, and I didn't."

Mom stared at the tall windows next to my bed. "Do you remember those drapes I made on the old sewing machine, with vertical stripes in blue and green? Whatever happened to those?"

I banged my head against the wall and my hair gathered static and spread out and I was about to hit my head again when Mom ran over and stuck her hand in the way. I didn't want to break her hand. "You're not listening to me, Mom. You're changing the subject."

"I'm listening. You're upset because your father gave you food in the middle of the night."

"No!" I shoved her hand away.

"Then what?"

"You don't care," I said.

"Yes, I do." She knelt down on my bed and waited.

"How come no one ever cared that he abused *me*?"

Her eyes popped open and the tears just fell out, big drops that sort of fascinated me.

She tried to tuck me into my bed, but I was still sitting up, so the blanket kept falling down. "I didn't know, baby."

"You knew something, Mom. You had to."

She shook her head until dark hair covered her face. "I didn't know it was *that*. I thought, I was just jealous, you know?"

"No idea."

She took a deep breath and tried to explain. "I thought I was like my mother. I thought I was jealous that my husband loved my daughter, loved someone else, more than me. Your father told me I was imagining things, seeing things that weren't there because I was so insecure. He said I just didn't know what a good father looked like."

"But you believe me?" I asked. "You believe that my father molested me when I was little?"

"Yes."

She had to leave again, to feed Grandma and keep her company for a few hours while Grandpa was away, but she came back, after dinner, and spread a blanket on the floor next to my bed and spent the night in my room. I don't know if she slept, but I did.

Chapter Seventeen

THE RAPE OF DINAH

My father brought me a marzipan-covered cake from a kosher bakery for my sixteenth birthday in February. I'd hoped Grandpa would come over, or we'd go over there, but my father said no, without explanation. I thought Grandma was probably punishing me for how much time Mom was spending at home now, keeping *me* company, at least in the evenings. But my father said we were better off just the three of us. Grandpa called to wish me a happy birthday, and said something about how he was sorry I wasn't able to spend a weekend with them. I tried to ask what he was talking about, but he had to cut the call short to take Grandma to the hip doctor or the lung specialist or some alternative medicine practitioner to figure out why her left eye twitched and her littlest toe had turned red. When I hung up the phone, my father said, Grandpa just doesn't love you anymore, and then he offered me more cake.

My bed was covered with new clothes, including a sapphire blue sweater that Mom had been knitting for me during her visits with Grandma. I'd told Jake and Shira about my birthday and Jake brought me a book his parents had bought for his little sister, about how to be a good orthodox girl. Which started us on a long letter writing campaign throughout the afternoon, with Jake advocating for the rules on touch and modesty from my family purity class. "Men need women to cover their collar bones and other provocative parts, or better yet to leave the room entirely, or else the desire to touch is constant and distracting."

I wasn't sure if he was playing games with me or trying to tell the truth and when I asked if he was following the no touch rules with his public school girlfriend he stopped writing back. At the end of the day I returned his little sister's book, which I'd been carrying with me all day, and he took it without saying anything. I couldn't read his expression clearly, but instead of being angry, which is what I'd assumed he was, he seemed almost embarrassed.

I was sixteen now; almost an adult, my father said. I ate my marzipan cake, piece by piece, from the freezer in the middle of the night for the rest of the week. I made sure to schedule my kitchen raids not to coincide with my father's three AM panic omelets. I couldn't look at him without seeing flashes, literally like flashbulbs going off so that I couldn't make out what was behind the lights. And then there was the smell; like shit, with a metallic something added. When I closed my eyes the smell of shit was pervasive and I could feel some phantom wetness dripping on my legs. Clearly I was better off with my eyes open. Even at school.

The little rabbi read through the biblical passage quickly. "And Dinah the daughter of Leah and Jacob went out to see the daughters of the land and Shechem, the prince, saw her."

That's as far as he would translate.

"You get the idea," he said. "I won't test you on this part."

He jumped ahead to the blood and guts scenes where Dinah's brothers plan and execute the slaughter of the whole town by convincing Shechem's father that Dinah would be handed over in marriage if all of the men in the town agreed to be circumcised. In their weakened state the townsmen were unable to fight when the brothers attacked, killing them easily. Retribution. That's what we discussed. Whether the story is there to tell us that retribution is righteous or wrong.

There's only one line describing the rape itself and I couldn't translate it.

I sat through the rest of my morning classes distracted, trying to do the translation myself. "And he took her," the line starts, which could mean he wrapped her in a passionate embrace, or grabbed her by the hair, or pulled her by the hand out of the middle of the street.

Mrs. Lichtman collected our permission slips for the upcoming girls only Shabbaton at her husband's shul. I thought about asking her for a translation of the Bible passage but she was on a roll with a discussion of the modesty laws, using Brooke's sheer blouse as a demonstration of fitting the letter but not the spirit of the law.

"Yes, your elbows are covered," the teacher said, standing next to Brooke, who had her arms crossed in front of her clearly visible black bra. "And the skirt is as modest as any rabbi's wife could hope to wear." She pointed at the floor length hem of Brooke's denim skirt. "But THESE," one finger pointed at each offending breast, "need more camouflage before you leave your bedroom."

Even Shira laughed, though she didn't turn towards me to see if I was laughing too.

I called David that night. I could hear him asking his brother, "Are you sure she said 'Isabel?'" and then there was scuffling and muttering and "I'm not stupid!" and "Give me the damn phone," and then there was David, a little out of breath but still David.

"Are you okay?" he asked me. "I mean, why are you calling me?"

I held the phone to my ear but I didn't know how to answer.

"Sorry," he said. "That was rude. What I should have said was, 'Hello Isabel, it's so nice to hear from you.'"

"But you're not a liar," I said.

"It wouldn't be a lie. I miss our talks."

"I have a biblical question for you."

He waited a second before speaking. I loved the sound of his brain whirring. "Do you mean Biblical as a measurement of the operatic quality of the question, or do you mean a question from Torah?"

"The rape of Dinah."

"Oh boy."

I explained the morning's class with the little rabbi and how he'd raced past the rape itself, barely looking up from his desk, and my difficulty coming up with a translation of my own. He took a moment to find the passage and reread it, though he seemed to know it all by heart.

"There are people," David started in his Talmudic drone, "who question whether it was rape or seduction." I had missed the reassuring rhythm of his voice and the confidence that came so naturally to him. Listening to him made me calmer. He continued. "Shechem takes her and lays with her and then the text says he humbles her. What does that sequence of events mean?"

"That's my question," I whispered, because I'd just heard the front door slam, which meant my father was home.

David didn't seem to notice. "In modern parlance, when Shechem lays with Dinah that would mean that he has sex with her, right? So why add the humbling part? Is it force right from the beginning when he takes her, or only at the end when he humbles her? Why describe it three ways?"

"Did you study this already?" I asked, crawling into the corner of my bed, as far as I could get from my unlocked door.

"You never finish studying," he said and then paused. "Why did you want help with this section in particular?"

I took a deep breath, wondering if I could really tell him what I was thinking. But I had to. Someone had to know me.

"The three parts of the rape confused me," I said, and my voice kept going. "First he takes her, by force I'd assume. He grabs her because he wants her and who cares what she wants. But then he lies with her. It sounds so gentle. He's seducing her now. She doesn't know how to react. Should she still be afraid of him or is he safe now because he's being nice to her? Maybe he's telling her how beautiful she is and how smart and special and how he just wants to be with her forever. And it seems real. Maybe he really loves her and values her. But then he humbles her. It was a trap all along. She was the only one who forgot that. For a moment she forgot that he was a rapist and started to believe she had a choice and that's when he gets her. Because not only has he raped her but she thinks it's her own fault."

David's silence was filled with deep breaths, the way I breathed when I tried and failed to keep calm.

"David?"

"I don't know what to say to you Isabel. I'm afraid of where your mind goes."

"But it makes sense, doesn't it, David? The rape is written in three parts because that's how it is done."

"Yes," he said. "It makes sense."

I held the phone with both hands. "Thank you."

"You're welcome. But now I have to go."

"I know."

He hung up and I listened to the dial tone for a long time.

Chapter Eighteen

THE SECOND SHABBATON

As a special gift for me to wear to Mrs. Lichtman's Shabbaton, Mom bought me a shiny red button down shirt that I could wear untucked. She needed me to love my present, so I kept my sarcastic comments for private conversations with the dog. Mom was sleeping in the guestroom, and avoiding meals with my father, but other than that, my life at home seemed horribly the same. I had hopes that a change of scene for the weekend would do me some good, but not very high hopes.

I needed something bigger than my bookbag in order to bring my clothes and toiletries and an extra pair of shoes with me to school on Friday morning, so I raided the room of mismatched luggage (the attic bathroom) for a collapsible nylon bag that would hold it all, but I forgot to take into account the size of my locker, and had to spend an extra five minutes shoving the bag in piece by piece until the door could just barely close, but not lock. I wasn't especially worried. We'd only had one thief in the school since I'd been there: someone with a desperate longing for pens. One of the rabbis had found the stash of pens behind a garbage can in the stairway. We were all more curious

about why the rabbi was looking behind the garbage can in the stairway than about who stole the pens. I discovered after morning prayers that most of the other girls had stored their garment bags and suitcases in the secretary's office.

Jake wrote to me all through English class. We were back to normal, whatever that was. He told me how his older sister thought orthodoxy was another phase their parents were going through, like vegetarianism, or the martini fixation. He refused to take notes on how to diagram a sentence, he said, because proper grammar would prevent him from spewing the meaningless drivel that flowed so naturally from him. I took notes, but I also kept track of the sheet of paper with his meaningless drivel on it, and my responses scattered in every corner. I shoved the paper into my skirt pocket at the end of class as he walked out of the room ahead of me. He'd only been telling me about Yitzchak, who had left our class in favor of non-honors English, where he'd hoped to get away from the sex-filled godless fictions Mrs. Sturman had us reading. He was now reading non-fiction, about the evolution of women's rights. Poor Yitz.

But in the bottom right corner of the page, after the third time passing the paper back and forth under his desk and next to my left hip, Jake had written, "Are you busy this weekend?"

That's why I kept the note.

Shira was waiting for me at my locker, after the last class of the day, with her jacket on and her garment bag over her arm.

"Aren't you excited?" she asked.

"Don't I look excited?" I wrestled my overfilled bag out of the locker, and my coat and books and random pieces of paper fell out of it in a cascade. Shira picked up my prayerbook and kissed it and placed it on the upper shelf, where it was supposed to be in the first place, out of harm's way. I had to get down on the floor to gather the battered paperbacks, heavy Biology textbook, ripped and crumpled English papers, notes from Jake, notes from Shira, official class schedules, tests that had gone well (a 98 in Jewish Law) and not so well (a 55 in social studies). I was usually more organized than this, but lately I didn't know where anything belonged, and couldn't even try to decide which papers mattered to me and which ones didn't. I saw Shira pick up a note with her purple handwriting all over it, stuck to a Jewish History test by a kind of glue I didn't recognize, and noticed her quick grimace as she recognized the paper, from one of the days when she'd been venting to me about her father's joblessness. She rubbed the stickiness off on her skirt and pocketed the note without saying a word to me about it.

By the time my locker was closeable, the front of her skirt was covered in a layer of dust from the floor. She swiped at it a few times and then shrugged.

"Dirt comes off."

"Nice philosophy," I said, and didn't even bother to clean myself off. I wanted her to look better than I did. It would only be fair.

Mrs. Lichtman walked in through the front door of the building and clapped her hands. "The bus is here. Anyone not on the bus in two minutes will have to spend the weekend in this building."

"Would that be so awful?" I asked Shira as she gripped her garment bag and led me down the hall. "I mean, we could hang out with the caretaker and his family, eat candy bars from the kitchen, sneak into the boys' bathroom to see what that's all about, and raid the teacher's lounge. I wonder what they keep in there anyway. Is there a fridge? Folders on each one of us?"

I kept yammering as we found seats together on the bus and shoved our bags in between us and on top of our feet, wherever they'd fit.

"There's a pay phone at school, Izzy. Your Mom could pick you up if you really don't want to come." Shira's tone was more abrupt than usual and I didn't try to argue the point or tell her that I wouldn't want to go home. I'd rather hide in the small library where the boys had afternoon prayers. I'd rather sleep between the dusty stacks of books than go to this Shabbaton, or go home.

Tova took the seat across from us and placed her suitcase on the seat next to her so that no one could sit down.

The frizzy-haired teacher, who guarded us during morning prayers, and the Jewish History teacher, with helmet hair, sat in the two front seats and ignored all of us.

Mrs. Lichtman was not on the bus. She drove ahead of us in her little blue car, and watching her drive became the entertainment for the trip. She switched lanes for no obvious reason, tried to nose in between cars that were only a few feet apart, and never slowed down at yellow lights. She had to pull over a bunch of times to wait for our driver to catch up.

He finally parked the bus in front of a big, plain, sand colored building, and Mrs. Lichtman came onto the bus to talk to us. "My husband's congregants have volunteered to house you, sight unseen, and I expect you to behave." She glanced at Tova, who just stared out of the window. "We'll be eating at the shul. Don't let your hosts feed you: first, because I don't want you to make a burden of yourselves; second, because I can't guarantee their degree of Kashrus. But they will have beds, and bathrooms, and you won't freeze to death."

Shira pulled her puffy black coat closer around her body, even though the heater on the bus was stifling.

"Shira and Brooke, you'll be staying in that Brown house over there," Mrs. Lichtman said and pointed at it, but kept her eyes on her paper.

The list paired us alphabetically even though in our Judaic Studies classes we tended to sit by cliques. I wondered if Mrs.

Lichtman was intentionally splitting us up. I also wondered if she would admit to it, or if anyone would have the guts to ask her. Tova and I were assigned to a pink house three blocks over.

"I can't point to it from here, but you'll know it when you see it."

Tova had trouble negotiating her suitcase down the stairs of the bus and around the patches of ice on the sidewalk, but she refused my help. Shira followed Brooke over to the Brown house without looking back or saying goodbye.

As we walked down the sidewalk together Tova was uncomfortably silent, until she stopped on the sidewalk in front of the Pink house. "Is Mrs. Lichtman trying to teach us tolerance for the color blind?"

"Like bubble gum," I said, trying to chat, something I had no apparent facility in. "My grandfather took me to an ice cream shop once, where they had ice cream exactly that color, with pieces of bubble gum in it, and I ate too much of it and threw up pink."

"That's sad, Izzy. You shouldn't repeat that story to regular people."

An older woman with an immaculate poof of white hair stepped out from behind the screen door at the front of the house. She held her long ivory coat closed with one hand and used the other to wave us inside, where she immediately took her coat off, draped it over a wooden hanger and carefully pressed it between two coats of the same style, one in black and one in a soft grey. She didn't ask to take our jackets.

"The room is upstairs," she said. It's possible that she smiled, but she was ahead of us on the stairs so I couldn't tell. Tova held her shoulders high and smoothed the back of her skirt every few seconds, in imitation of our hostess, all the way up to the second floor.

"This is it," the woman said, pushing open the door of a room at the end of the hall. The walls were yellow. The carpet was a lighter yellow. The curtains were gold. The bed was queen-sized and there was only one in the room.

"For both of us?" I squeaked.

"I only have one guestroom available at the moment. If the rebbetzen wanted better accommodations for you girls she should have given me more warning."

It was strange to hear Mrs. Lichtman referred to as the rabbi's wife.

Tova wandered into the connected bathroom while the woman remained out in the hallway with her hand on the doorknob.

"Pink soap," Tova called out.

"My grandchildren used up the yellow guest soaps on their last visit," the woman whispered to me. "I don't know what they did with all of them. The pink ones are from the downstairs bathroom."

In her public voice, the woman said, "The back door remains open throughout Shabbos so you don't need to bother my husband or myself. Let me know if you need anything else." She shut the door and I listened to her steps receding down the uncarpeted stairs.

"She gone?" Tova asked. She came out of the bathroom and held out a pink piece of soap. "Fetal pig."

I changed into my shiny red shirt and a black skirt, and then sat on the edge of the bed and waited for Tova. I thought about the woman's grandchildren and how they must have felt in this perfectly blinding yellow room with no TV and no books to read. The yellow soaps might have been their only entertainment; something to throw at each other, or float in the toilet, or carve into new shapes. I held the fetal pig soap in my hands and as it melted the flowery smelling scum coated my skin. We didn't have special bathroom soaps at my house; we just had white soap. My father tried to make me eat the white soap when I was little, because he said I used words he didn't think a girl should use. He also told me the soap would taste just like butter. It did not.

Tova brought another animal-shaped pink soap from the bathroom and set it on the dresser. An elephant. "This one's for you," she said.

She had on a fitted black dress, flared at the hem, and sheer black stockings. I put my fetal pig soap on the dresser next to the elephant while Tova found her high heels and her Shabbos coat in her suitcase.

Once we reached Mrs. Lichtman's shul, I searched for Shira right away amidst the mass of girls from our class. They looked like strangers all dressed up. I didn't even recognize Shira until she turned around. She was dressed like one of them, in her black and white fitted dress, and black pumps, and she was huddled with Brooke in the corner. She waved to me and I practically ran to her.

My shiny shirt and flat shoes, my puffy jacket, my everything made me self-conscious. I didn't have a long wool coat for dressing up, and I refused to wear stockings, and I couldn't walk in heels without feeling like I was going to fall on my face. I wanted to hide behind Shira, but she was backed against the wall, and I couldn't think of anything to say in front of Brooke, with her dangling crystal earrings, and gossamer thin white blouse, and plum-colored lips, but luckily she left quickly, grabbing Shira's arm for a quick squeeze before going off to find her friends.

"Brooke is so nice," Shira said. "But she can't stop talking about her boyfriend."

"Hmm." I wasn't sure whether that was a criticism or not in Shira-speak.

"He plays guitar, and he eats non-kosher potato chips, and his hair is down to his shoulders. She showed me a picture."

"Rabbi Gottlieb would attack him with those scissors he keeps on the shelf in his office if he ever walked into our school," I said, remembering one of Jake's stories about an attempted shearing.

"Her boyfriend goes to a not-so-observant school. Like the one you went to before," Shira said.

The use of the word "observant" as a synonym for "religious" always bothered me. They meant observant of Jewish law, but it felt like they were presuming to actually be more observant of the world around them. Which they were not. But there was a kind of Big Brother quality to our school that had never existed at my old, less religious school, where they taught bible stories as literature instead of as life lessons, and they didn't really care how religious we were at home. At yeshiva we were watched and judged for every variation from the accepted norm, so maybe that's what they meant when they called themselves observant.

I scanned around the room for Tova but she'd already disappeared. She had her admirers and she certainly didn't need me for comfort. Even the thought that Tova might need another person surprised me, and seemed unlikely.

Shira continued chattering about Brooke and her jewelry and her clothes and makeup as we followed the other girls up the stairs to the women's balcony, where Mrs. Lichtman was waiting for us. She was shined up for the occasion with a blondish wig set in soft waves to her shoulders, and a dark purple cotton dress cinched at the waist. She actually had a waist.

"I wanted you here a few minutes early so you can appreciate the sanctuary in silence. We're here to make Shabbos holy, not ordinary," she said. "Tonight, I want you to listen to the words of the prayers as you say them. No pretending to pray and mumbling and shuckling back and forth just to fool me."

A few of the girls giggled, but Mrs. Lichtman stared them down.

"Men are given so many opportunities to argue with the written word, and with each other, while women are expected just to take it all in by rote. And we accept that, because it's comfortable. We like to be comfortable. We like to chat and not to challenge each other too deeply. We like to be polite, and avoid any confrontation that might upset us. I include myself in all of this. I'm human."

She raised an eyebrow and waited for a laugh that no one was willing to give her.

"Anyway. Take this opportunity to listen and read and speak more carefully. Allow yourself to be uncomfortable and to rediscover your religion and your classmates. I want this Shabbos to be a turning point in your life so that you will be able to create more turning points in your lives when you need them most."

A woman in a big white hat walked in on the other side of the balcony and Mrs. Lichtman crouched down to whisper her final instructions. "One more thing. I want you to pretend that the men are not even here. They are only a distraction."

So of course all eyes focused down below on the men's section.

I hadn't been to Friday night services on a regular basis in a while. We used to go every week, when we were still members of the Conservative synagogue in our neighborhood. They held services at 8:30 every Friday night no matter what the season and we had a cantor in a black robe to lead the services who stretched each word out until it had no meaning. Sometimes it got so bad that I had to hide under my seat, trying not to laugh, while my father pinched my arm, supposedly to help. There was a seriousness to those occasions and a melodrama that radiated from the stained glass windows and the high-arched ceiling and the richness of the embroidered fabrics all around the sanctuary. I grew up with millionaires donating whole rooms to the synagogue, which I knew I would never be able to do. I knew I would never feel any ownership over the building, no matter how much time I spent there, no matter how often I spoke to God.

Mrs. Lichtman's shul was more humble, with regular-sized windows and a man in a tan suit mumbling from the podium trying to lead the prayers. Everyone mumbled here and I *had* to read each word carefully in order to keep track of where we were in the service.

One theme jumped out at me. God is great, and God is our God in particular, and therefore we, the Jewish people, are great. It seemed dangerous, given the tendency for Jews to be targeted for annihilation, to exaggerate the us-versus-them rhetoric. But what really bothered me was the logic that it is only because God is great that we, his people, are great. Therefore, if my father is an asshole, pedophile, all around bad guy, then as his daughter, so am I. If the court found my father guilty, then not only would he lose his job and maybe spend more than one night in jail, he would also be *known* as a criminal. My teachers would know. My classmates' parents would find out. No one would ever offer me a babysitting job again; not that I wanted to wipe snotty noses just for the chance to raid a new fridge, but still. And I couldn't wish for him to be exonerated, because that would mean that the adults believed him instead of the girl. He would keep his job and his pride and, more than ever, he would know that he could get away with *anything*.

Paying attention to the words of the prayers was turning against me. I would have been better off with the thirty syllable distortions of the cantor at my old synagogue, or with David leading the services in his calm, peaceful voice.

Once the congregation began to file out, Mrs. Lichtman led us down to a large white room in the basement with a horseshoe of tables covered with white paper tablecloths, paper plates, and plastic utensils, for our first meal together as a group.

My red shirt made a vivid contrast to the room, and the mostly black outfits of my peers. One of the girls who had borrowed my notes for the open book test put her hand over her face after staring at me and squealed, "My eyes, my eyes," loud enough for every one to hear.

Shira pulled me away. "We don't have to sit near her."

"My mother bought the shirt," I said.

Shira chose our seats. "Shiny."

Mrs. Lichtman's husband said the blessings over the wine, or in our case, grape juice, and then over the two challahs on the breadboard. Then his wife pushed him out of the room as he tried to grab an extra piece of bread.

"But you know the kind of food Mrs. Baum is going to serve for dinner," he whimpered. "I'll starve!"

Mrs. Lichtman laughed and swatted the back of his suit. Lower back. And pushed him out the door. When he poked his head back into the room and winked at his wife she said, "Go away. No men allowed."

"Good Shabbos, girls!" he called out and then slipped out the door again.

Mrs. Lichtman sat at the head table and slowly lifted a piece of gefilte fish on her plastic fork with beet red horseradish dripping off the side, as if she was trying to teach us how to eat. I tried not to picture the fish being ground into a paste and molded into logs, and failed.

"David doesn't like gefilte fish," Shira said. But she said it in the same exaggerated way Mrs. Lichtman was eating, to teach me something.

"He spends a lot of time at your house, now." I said. I'm not sure what my intention was, certainly not to invite confidences, even about things I kind of knew already.

"How did you know?" Shira asked, her cheeks as red as the beets in the horseradish.

"I just assumed," I said, and loaded my piece of fish with horseradish to cover the fish smell, not to eat it.

"Do you still like David?" Shira asked me and I noticed Brooke, on her other side, leaning in to listen.

"Sure," I said. "There's something about his rabbi-in-training voice that's reassuring."

"But he doesn't love you anymore. He loves me," Shira said, fist clenched around her fork. That had to hurt. "You shouldn't be talking to him anymore."

It would be disingenuous to say I was surprised at the news of their relationship, but in a way I was shocked, because I didn't expect her to ever tell me the truth. I expected her to go on with the lie. That's the way my family would have handled it.

I leaned back in my flimsy folding chair and felt, suddenly, so tired. David had never actually loved me. He liked me, yes, and he found me fascinating, and worthy of study. Shira stabbed her fork into her fish, making holes in the paper plate underneath, clearly a violation of Shabbos, but I wasn't going to mention it. She stuffed the fish into her mouth and practically choked on it. I worried that the horseradish would hit her pretty soon.

"Are you alright?" I asked.

She swallowed, with difficulty, and then turned to me, plastic fork still in hand. I thought about my father's fork-through-the-hand story, just for a second, and was glad my hands were down at my sides instead of on the table within her reach. She took an exaggerated deep breath and exhaled in my face. "I am sick of you being such a bad friend to me that I've had no one to talk to about David, or my father's lost job. Brooke barely knows me and she's already a better friend than you've been all year. You're so wrapped up in being depressed and weird. You never ask me how I feel. You're selfish!"

Her eye sockets were red, as if the anger was seeping out of her brain and into her skin. I thought I was surviving her tirade pretty well, keeping my mouth shut to avoid spewing at her in return. I wanted to rip her hair out and slap her around. I felt like an animal was living under my skin and trying to get out. But I held still. Until Brooke, sitting on Shira's other side, chimed in.

"You've been a real bitch, Izzy."

I knocked my chair over trying to stand up and my feet tangled in the legs of the chair, trapping me at the table. I wanted to get away before I started to scream, but I couldn't.

"You can go to hell!"

I was finally able to extricate myself from the chair and I ran out of the room, but then I didn't know where to go. I went towards the women's bathroom, then changed my mind and turned towards the staircase, then turned around, and again and again. I couldn't think of a safe place to escape to, so I stood in the middle of the hallway, shoulders and head slumped forward to find some kind of privacy and I started to cry.

Tova snuck up on me. I'm not saying she meant to do that, but my peripheral vision was shot and I didn't see her standing next to me until she clapped her hands in front of my face.

"Anyone in there?"

I looked down at my red shirt, and there were deeper red marks that looked like blood stains covering my chest. I shook my head.

"Should I get Mrs. Lichtman?"

I stared at the gold bracelet on Tova's wrist, chain links that looked too big for her. I wanted to warn her that if she lost any more weight the bracelet would fall off, but I couldn't speak.

When Tova disappeared, I lifted my head and tried to locate where I was: near a stairway, in a synagogue, and so far away from my mother that I couldn't fathom the amount of walking it would take to reach her. The hard wood floor under my feet had little dark spots on it, like the ones on my shirt, and I wondered about the physics of that: how much force did I have to cry with, and at what angle, to make certain tears reach the floor?

The frizzy-haired teacher came out to see me, except that her hair wasn't frizzy, it was all done up in perfect curls, as if she'd shellacked each circle into place.

"Is something wrong, Isabel?" She approached slowly, in that exaggeratedly careful way you approach someone who is holding a gun.

"I'm fine," I said.

"Are you sure?"

I stared at her in her perfect size six dress and tiny shoes and that stupid look on her face. "I was being sarcastic."

"You can't be that upset if you can make jokes." She smiled at me.

"Whatever you say."

"Why don't we find somewhere to sit down, in private, so you can catch your breath." She led me up the stairs and I thought we would sit in the main sanctuary, where the men prayed. Even in my off kilter state, I was curious how it would feel to sit where only men were allowed. Instead she led me up the second staircase, to the women's balcony, where the lights had been turned off by the janitor. A non-Jew. There were all kinds of rules for how to break the rules correctly. You could give the Shabbos Goy a schedule of services before hand, but if it got hot on Shabbos or you needed an extra light you couldn't ask him to turn things on. You'd have to hint. Something like, "Oh, it would be so much nicer in here with a little more air and a bissel light to see by." And hopefully the Janitor wouldn't wink too obviously at the subterfuge, but just go ahead and do the things the righteous Jews were not allowed to do for themselves.

The teacher directed me to sit in one of the seats closest to the stairway of the women's section, where there was a little pool of light. I would have preferred the full dark, actually, somewhere to curl up and not be seen, but I just sat down where she pointed.

"How's school going for you, Isabel?" She leaned away from me and rubbed her hands down the sides of her skirt.

"You don't want to know about me."

"Of course I want to know," she said. "I wouldn't have asked otherwise."

She was, maybe, five years older than me, and reminded me too much of the girls in my class; the kind of people who asked a question because it made them sound good, not because they cared about the answer.

"School sucks," I said.

"Why do you think that?"

"Because all of the people in that school are full of shit," I said.

I didn't have to dwell too long on the shocked look on her diamond-shaped face, because Mrs. Lichtman came up the stairs at that point.

"Found you," she said, catching her breath.

"I wasn't hiding her," the girl said, backing away from me. "I thought she needed to be away from the other girls."

"Thank you," Mrs. Lichtman said. "I need you to go downstairs and keep an eye on them, prevent food fights with the chicken legs."

I listened to the clip clop of her heels as she rushed down the steps.

Mrs. Lichtman sat next to me in the dark. "You were double teamed, so I hear."

"You talked to Shira?"

193

"Shira, Brooke, Tova, and several eavesdroppers who were eager to share."

"Are you mad at me?" I asked. I expected to be blamed. At home it would have been my fault, for provoking the attack, for responding to it, for making life at our house even more trouble than it already had to be.

"Why would I be angry at you for fighting back?" Mrs. Lichtman asked. "You didn't do anything wrong, Isabel."

I didn't believe her. There was going to be a "but" coming up; a reason to expel me from the Shabbaton. I *wanted* to be excommunicated. I wanted her to get so angry that she would send me out into the cold to find my own way home. I needed an apocalyptic event to change the direction of my life. Her little turning points from reading the prayers more carefully were not going to be enough to blast through the crap and make me into someone new. She put a hand on my fidgety fingers and modeled a few deep breaths, because I was suddenly breathing was too fast.

"I was surprised though," she said to me, when I was somewhat calmer. "Usually you are very careful with what you say."

I wondered if she was going to give me a lecture about how Jews don't believe in hell, but she didn't.

"Did Shira tell you what she said to me?"

"I got the gist of it. She already regrets it, though I wouldn't test her right now if I were you. People say some extraordinary things in the heat of the moment."

"People always blame the heat of the moment when they want to get away with what they've done."

Mrs. Lichtman chewed on her bottom lip and focused on the light from the stairway. "Is there something else you need to talk to me about?"

I wanted her to know the truth already. I was tired of having to censor every word out of my mouth so carefully, just so I wouldn't burden anyone with the weight of my life. I wanted to tell her that I got these flash pictures in my head of my father's penis, but how could I be so arrogant as to believe that I mattered to her enough that she'd even care. I was one of the naked plastic dolls at the cheapskate store, with the head popped off, and the toes stuck between the wall and the shelf. I wasn't one of the pretty dolls that everyone loved.

"You can talk to me, Isabel. I'm not the thought police. I may not agree with your opinion, but I'm willing to hear it."

I noticed that I was scraping the armrest with my fingernails. She thought I wanted to argue with her about religion. That's as much as she could imagine about me. But I'd never given her a chance to know more.

"My father," I said and took a breath, not sure how much she could stand to hear.

"He brought you to yeshiva against your will," she said. "Rabbi Gottlieb told me the story. But is it really such a bad place now that you're here?"

"No," I said. I meant no, you picked the wrong problem with my father.

"All you need is a chance to express yourself. You'll see that there are a lot of people who will respect what you have to say." She patted my knee and then used me as ballast to help her stand up. "Let's see what the maniacs are up to downstairs."

She walked ahead of me down two flights of stairs to the basement and found me a new seat near the teachers at the head of the horseshoe. The other girls looked over, but didn't approach. I pulled the skin off my chicken leg and tiny sticks of rosemary glued themselves to my fingers. I didn't want food for comfort; I wanted something bigger than comfort. I wanted there to be a force more powerful than my father. I wanted God to be on my side, instead of his. But praying to God for the big things was not working out, so I closed my eyes and prayed we'd have brownies for dessert. When I opened my eyes, the frizzy-haired teacher passed me a paper plate filled with dry Italian cookies covered in hard purple icing.

"Sorry," she said, as if she knew what I'd been praying for.

Chapter Nineteen

THE TEACHERS

After Friday night dinner at the Shabbaton, we dragged our folding chairs away from the horseshoe and sat in a half circle with Mrs. Lichtman filling the rest of the space, filling the whole room with her voice so that we barely noticed the neighborhood volunteers cleaning up around us.

"I want to give you a few things to think about tonight when you go back to your temporary homes," she began. She didn't shift her clothes or her hair or seem hemmed in the way she sometimes did in the classroom. This was her territory.

"I don't need to be a teacher to make a living," she said. "I could be a social worker or a nurse. I could be a doctor if I were willing to break Shabbos just to be seen as an important figure by people in the outside world, but I'm not willing. Shabbos is too precious to me."

I was sitting between two girls I never talked to in school and they were listening intently. It bothered me that everyone was as affected by Mrs. Lichtman as I was. I wanted to be special.

She continued. "I wanted to be your teacher because I know something about the struggle to do the right thing. The desire to do wrong. And it bothers me how little you are taught about how to

197

govern your bodies and your lives as women. These essential things are ignored in favor of lessons in how to slaughter a cow. I'm pretty sure you will not be called on to slaughter a cow."

She pulled herself up and sat on the window ledge, looking down on us. "You need to be taught how to treat your desires with respect, not with neglect or shame. And you need to take my word for it that this has everything to do with leading a righteous, Jewish life." She stared around the circle. I thought she stopped on me longer than she really had to, but I wasn't sure. "Your sexuality is an essential part of who you are and if you don't learn how to manage it and take ownership of it then your other attempts to be righteous will be at risk. You won't realize how often you may use your body to seduce or deflect other people. Your body and your spirit will be two separate creatures, unable to come to an understanding with one another. You will be, if you will pardon me, too much like a man." She jumped down to the floor and her dress parachuted out like one of the tulips in my grandfather's garden turned upside down.

"Sleep well, girls," she said abruptly, and it took all of us a moment to realize that was the end of the evening. I was still in my chair as she passed by on her way out and she patted my head, but I was too slow to turn around and see what look was on her face. She didn't touch anyone else that I noticed, except for her husband who was waiting for her at the door.

Tova and I walked back to our house with a group of girls going in the same direction. I missed my dog. Not because she would have been any use if a dangerous person approached, just because it would have been nice to have someone to talk to. Tova and I were the last ones in our group and once we dropped off the other girls at the house on the corner, we glanced at each other and silently agreed to run the rest of the way.

The pink house looked white in the dark, more inviting than the house next door with the brown shingles and the eerie stone statue on the lawn. The back door was unlocked as promised and all of the downstairs lights were on and the rooms were spotless and silent. It was too quiet. The woman and her husband were supposed to be there, somewhere. But we couldn't hear anyone talking or rustling the pages of a book or gulping down pints of vodka. I worried that we were alone in the house with the back door unlocked. I worried that there was no husband and the poofy haired lady was going to haunt the halls and shriek all night long.

The lights were on in the kitchen, but the hallways were mostly dark and the stairs creaked and the temptation to break the Sabbath and call home, or watch TV or at least turn the lights on was enormous. But I couldn't do that in a stranger's house. I couldn't even do it at home.

Once we reached the guest room, Tova dragged her suitcase into the bathroom where the light had been left on, and I stood next to the closed but unlockable bedroom door and listened for noises in the hallway. Still nothing. I managed to find my pajamas because I'd folded them under my pillow before we left. I dropped my red shirt and the rest of my clothes on the rocking chair in the corner after I'd changed and then took the extra blanket off the bed and wrapped myself in it. The blanket was crocheted, and felt like a big piece of Swiss cheese, not much to keep me warm, but I didn't want to share the quilt or the sheets on the bed with Tova. Sharing the bed itself made me uncomfortable enough, especially after Mrs. Lichtman's sexuality-athon. It's not that I thought I was going to roll over onto Tova in the middle of the night and molest her. But I was afraid she would accuse me of wanting to.

By the time Tova came out of the bathroom, I was wrapped in my blanket and curled in a ball on the edge of my side of the bed.

"Don't you have to brush your teeth, or at least pee?" she asked.

I struggled out of my blanket and into the bathroom. The fluorescent light was a shock after the total darkness of the bedroom. I don't know what order things happened in; I was crying; I stepped into the cold bathtub and pressed my face against the tile wall; I think I brushed my teeth; but then I was standing in front of the bathroom mirror, staring at my blotchy face. I wanted to press the fast forward button and get to the end of the Shabbaton, but that wouldn't be enough; the end of the school year; the end of high school; the end.

I stayed there for such a long time, making no noise, Tova finally knocked on the door.

"You're scaring me," she said, in a more childlike voice than I'd heard from her before. I let her in. "I thought something bad was happening in here." She rubbed her arms, pushing on the sleeves of her flannel pajamas. She had matching plaid slippers, not her usual style. In fact, I'd never seen her wear pants before.

"I don't like the dark out there," I said, because I couldn't explain the strange loop I'd fallen into, staring at my face.

"I didn't think to bring a night light," Tova said, snapping back to her normal voice.

I looked at her full in the face, the same way I'd examined myself in the mirror. Her jaw line was sharper than I remembered. Unhealthy. "Sometimes, Tova, sarcasm is the wrong thing."

"You're gonna pick on me now?" She stared at the sink, anywhere but at me. Her gold link bracelet dangled off her wrist, touching the middle of her palm. She looked fragile, and small.

"This is boring." She walked out, leaving the bathroom door wide open, and I realized that she didn't want to be out there alone in the dark. She was afraid too.

In the morning, I packed my clothes while Tova took her turn in the bathroom. She took a lot longer to pack. By the time she had finished and set her suitcase next to my bag we were late for services. Of course, almost all of the other girls were late too. Mrs. Lichtman was guarding our section of seats, deflecting the ladies of the congregation without much sympathy for their desire to sit with their usual views of the men below.

This was a shul, I discovered, where most of the women wore hats to cover their hair instead of wigs. It was a subtle distinction, but it meant that Mrs. Lichtman was more religious than her husband's congregation. She didn't fit in with them. If she'd worn a hat it would have covered all of her hair, for modesty. These women wore their hats to draw more attention to the silky hair flowing down past their shoulders or curling around the small velvety grey cap perched above their ears.

The frizzy haired teacher patted the seat next to her and I felt obliged to sit down. Tova tried to sneak away to the bathroom, but Mrs. Lichtman was guarding the door and scaring people into sticking around.

I forced myself to pray, to fill my brain with noise so that my own thoughts wouldn't have a chance to bubble up.

When Shira arrived especially late and then stood in the back to pray silently, I muttered, "Hypocrite," and the teacher looked at me sharply, but said nothing.

I sat near the teachers again at lunch. Tova found her group of admirers on the other side of the horseshoe of tables and didn't even bother to look in my direction. Shira sat down next to me.

The rabbi said the blessings for us again, and when Mrs. Lichtman walked out of the room to say goodbye to him, I thought I felt an ant crawling up my arm and worried I was getting some mental illness that makes a person imagine bugs are crawling on her skin. But it was just Shira, tapping insistently on my upper arm with her stubby index finger.

"What do you want?" I asked, and then of course felt guilty for the bitchiness in my tone.

She took her finger back and batted her eyelashes. I couldn't believe David fell for that shit.

"I'm sorry," she said.

"For what?"

"I don't know." She licked her lips. "I feel like you're testing me. I don't do well on tests."

"Let's try multiple choice," I said, hearing the edge in my voice and pushing forward anyway. "Are you sorry for yelling at me last night? Or sorry for going after David? Or for encouraging me to date him when you really wanted him for yourself?"

One of the volunteers from the shul was handing out bowls of chulent. The traditional stew had to be simmered overnight, starting before Shabbos began, because the heat couldn't be turned on or off on the Sabbath. I couldn't imagine the size of the Crockpot they must have had in that kitchen.

Shira politely thanked the volunteer who, in surprise at actual kindness from a student, almost dropped the hot stew on my blue sweater.

"I *did* like David the whole time," Shira said. "I thought you would make him happy, but you didn't."

I contemplated the pearls of barley embedded in the disturbing gloss on top of the chulent and said nothing.

"But he told me that you helped him see how much orthodoxy means to him," she said quickly.

"So I wasn't a complete waste of his time?" I asked, and she looked away from me. I didn't understand why Shira was even bothering to talk to me. She could have easily been sitting with Brooke instead. She didn't need me. "I thought forgiveness wasn't really a Jewish thing anyway," I said, moving stew around with my fork until the gravy started dripping over the side of the bowl.

"Why are you so unhappy, Izzy? For months I've been trying to figure it out."

"Why bother wondering about me?" I asked. "You don't really care."

Her face turned red again, just like the night before. "Don't tell me what I care about! My parents are always telling me who I am and what I feel and what I should want. You didn't do that. You always listened to me." Her eyes were just like my dog with that wet-but-not-crying look.

"Why isn't that enough then?" I asked her. "Why can't I just listen to you and not talk, for now."

"But that wouldn't be fair to you. I want to be a good person, Izzy. I want to be a good friend."

I did believe her. It just didn't change anything.

"I like your sweater," she said. "Sapphire is a good color for your skin tone."

"How's your father?" I asked, and she was more than ready to be listened to again. She told me about the antidepressants he'd been taking and how they kept him up all night so he learned how to bake seven layer cakes with complicated flower designs but he still couldn't figure out how to use the washing machine or keep track of all of the kids' schedules and . . . I kept asking her questions until her spine relaxed into the back of her chair and she could finally take a deep breath.

After lunch, the two younger teachers talked to us about their *Shidduch* dates, matchmaking dates set up by friends, family, and sometimes professional matchmakers, in order to find a man to marry.

The frizzy haired teacher had been on fifty set ups already, but none had been "right."

"How did you know?" Brooke asked. She seemed like the least likely candidate to need a matchmaker, but she was leaning forward in her seat, looking fascinated.

The Jewish History teacher spoke up. "It's about finding your *Beshert*, your destiny, the man who was ordained by God to be your perfect mate."

"Oh please," Tova muttered, loud enough for everyone to hear.

The frizzy haired teacher coughed and straightened her already perfectly straight skirt. "To answer Brooke's question," she said, with another cough in the Jewish History teacher's direction. "You go on these dates and, at least for me, there is a list of questions I ask them. To see if our values are compatible and our goals are similar. And I'm human, just like you," she glanced at Tova. "I want to feel a spark, an attraction."

"Do you believe in finding your *Beshert*?" Tova asked her.

She took a long time answering. "I want to believe in it. I try to believe in it."

In the late afternoon, after egg salad and tuna fish, and study groups and sing alongs, we were back in our chair circle in the basement of the shul and the Jewish History teacher was leading a group bonding exercise. Mrs. Lichtman stood off to the side with her husband. She looked exhausted.

The Jewish History teacher sat up so straight in her chair I expected to hear her tailbone crack at any moment. "I think… wouldn't it be interesting…how about we go around the circle and everyone says where she wants to be, or thinks she's going to be ten years from now." She nodded at us with such a mix of eagerness and terror that even Tova held back what must have been an over-whelming urge to snort. Brooke volunteered to go first, which was a relief because she was on the other side of the circle from me.

"I'm going to have a house in Cedarhurst and a second house up in the mountains or maybe on an island. No, I'll have three houses and . . ." She went on to describe the suits her husband was going to wear and all of the adorable shoes she would buy for her daughter.

The next two girls, friends of hers, continued in the same vein, describing the interior design possibilities of a house with two kitchens, one for regular and one for Passover, and threw in a few lines about how they would be so proud to send their children to the same school they themselves had loved so much.

Tova was shifting in her seat by the time her turn came. "I'm going to law school. And then I'm going to make Aliyah and study politics in Israel and then I'm going to completely overhaul the Knesset. Brooke can do the decorating if she wants."

"But what about marriage? Or children?" the Jewish History teacher asked. It was her first interruption of the whole exercise. She didn't mind the twenty-minute explorations of fabric patterns but this blew her mind.

Tova stared at her. "I'm not worried about finding a husband. I know how attractive I am. He'll find me."

The next few girls rushed through their more humble plans, trying to ignore the hateful expression on the teacher's face.

Shira said, quietly, that she wanted to be a teacher, "for the slower kids. Because teachers always make me feel like I don't deserve to learn because I'm too stupid." The teacher tried to interrupt, maybe to defend herself against another slight, but Shira raised her voice and kept going. "I want to marry a smart man, a rabbi, or a man who could be a rabbi if he chose. I want my children to be lucky and loved." She blushed then, and didn't look at me because we both knew which smart husband she had in mind.

When it was my turn I stalled. "I can't think ten years ahead."

Mrs. Lichtman turned from the conversation she was having with her husband by the kitchen door. "How far ahead can you think?"

"A few months?" Anything beyond that point was a black void in my mind, rainy cold and dark. After that, God would bring another big flood, but this one wouldn't end after forty days and forty nights, like Noah's, this one would last my whole life.

Mrs. Lichtman persisted. "Where will you be in a few months?"

The other girls shifted in their seats. I couldn't blame them. The folding chairs were terrible.

"I think I'll be trapped in the same place," I said. "Or I'll be dead."

Brooke gasped. The melodramatic kind of gasp they do on soap operas.

Mrs. Lichtman watched my face and I'm not sure what she saw there. Shira grabbed my elbow and squeezed hard. I think this was supposed to give me comfort.

"Your turn," I said to the girl on my other side who had already moved her chair about a foot away from me so that she was practically sitting in her best friend's lap.

"Not yet," Mrs. Lichtman said. "You don't get away that easily, little girl."

She thought I was a kid. I liked the idea of that. I liked that maybe she could see how helpless I really felt. The Jewish History teacher, hair immovable, did not look all that sympathetic towards me. I was ruining her beautiful bonding exercise. The room was really quiet, no giggling or shifting around.

"Try again, Isabel. What do you *want* to see in your future?" Mrs. Lichtman had taken her seat in the circle, feet planted wide on the floor, fight stance. Shira was practically breaking my arm.

"I want my father to disappear," I said. "My mother will have her own art studio. And I'll be the rabbi of a shul and my grandfather can sit in the front row every week and help me with my sermons on the torah portion of the week."

"A rabbi?" Tova called out from across the circle. "You can't even stay awake during Chumash class!"

The rest of the girls laughed, because my naps in bible class were the thing everybody knew about me. Mrs. Lichtman didn't ask for more elaboration from me, so we continued on to the next girl in the circle.

YESHIVA GIRL

Chapter Twenty

THE SACRED AND THE PROFANE

Rabbi Lichtman led us into the main sanctuary after sundown for Havdallah. Shabbat was over but we now had to officially usher it out, to separate the holy day from the secular week, or the sacred from the profane, which made me think of curses and sin and animals torn apart and bleeding on the floor, for some reason. Evening services had ended and the congregants were gone and we were allowed to not only enter the men's lair, but to swarm onto the podium. The overhead lights were then turned off and we could hear the match strike and the wicks of the long braided candle hiss into one flame.

Tova whispered to me, "and people say *I'm* melodramatic." The Rabbi looked up in our direction, raised an eyebrow, and then returned to his task, pouring wine into the silver Kiddush cup until it overflowed.

"Havdallah is a ritual we perform in order to make a distinction between the holiness of the Sabbath and the secular nature of the rest of our week. But it represents other distinctions we learn to make in our lives, between the light of love or God, and the

darkness of evil or a life without God. We try to use all of our senses
– to taste the wine, smell the spices, see the flame of the candle, feel
the heat and hear the blessings, to make this transition as vivid as
possible."

He broke into the Hebrew blessings and each word was
articulated and chanted rather than mumbled. He held his fingernails
up to the light of the flame and smelled the spice box with relish and
drank the wine and doused the candle in the leftover wine so that the
sizzle was the last sound we heard before the overhead lights came
back on.

We were still under his spell even while Mrs. Lichtman dried
the wicks and wiped the spilled wine from the metal tray. He looked
around at us.

"There is only so much joy you can absorb before you *need* to
take a breath and return to normal life, or else you won't be able to
appreciate the sacred moments when they arrive. I want to thank all
of you for giving my wife your full attention this Shabbos. You have
given her a great gift and we both cherish it."

"Shavuah Tov," he said. "Have a good week."

Mrs. Lichtman's cheeks were bright red and she waved at us
with both hands. "Enough! Shabbos is over. Go to your guest houses
and pick up your luggage and we'll meet at my house in half an
hour." She organized us into groups and gave directions and then
shooed us out of the sanctuary still blushing.

"They always take us bowling," Tova said with authority,
though it was dampened by the way she kept smacking her suitcase
into the backs of her legs as we walked towards the teacher's house.

"Why?" I'd gone bowling once for a birthday party and I
wasn't any good at it. I wanted to throw the ball at the mean kids
instead of at the harmless white pins.

"What do you think we should do instead?" Tova asked. "Go to a nightclub?"

I didn't bother to answer her.

A van picked us up at Mrs. Lichtman's house and drove to the local skating rink, where we had the ice to ourselves for an hour. I didn't have my pretty white skates and I was annoyed at the way the blue plastic ones made my ankles cave in, but then I stepped onto the ice.

There were so few places where I felt at home; certainly not in my own home; maybe at Grandpa's house, but only with him there. On the ice, for some reason, I felt safe.

Shira stood on the rubber mat and couldn't get herself to put a skate on the ice. For two minutes she stood there, until Tova pushed her out of the way and proceeded to stomp about flat-footed. Brooke and a few of the other girls in her group circled around the teenage skate guard in his yellow jacket and followed him on his circular route. Mrs. Lichtman and the Jewish History teacher stood off to the side in street shoes watching us and clearly finding much amusement in what they saw.

There is a ritual to skating. The rhythm from right foot to left. I felt separated from the other girls who couldn't find the rhythm. I thought about the blades on my skates. How sharp they were. How they could be weapons, if I needed weapons.

Shira clunked her way over to the pay phone in her skates. I could hear David's voice in my mind, but she may have been calling home to make sure someone would pick her up. Tova sped past me, digging her toe picks into the ice like a pole-vaulter. The frizzy haired teacher took over the center circle. Her hair was frizzy again somehow, despite all of the spray and gel and other junk she'd put in it. She had on a wide cotton skirt, not what she'd been wearing all day, as if she knew we were going skating and this was her skating outfit. But the skirt was down to her ankles, not her upper thighs like the girls on TV. She started to skate backwards in a circle, one foot crossing the other with control. She hypnotized me. I stood still in no man's land, nowhere near her or the railings. She went around and around at a constant speed and at a constant angle. I couldn't see what her legs were doing under the skirt to make the whole thing work. I wanted her to teach me this. I wanted so much for her to teach me how to do this magical thing, and to spin as if my body had found its niche and was perfectly aligned with the universe. I watched her, studied her feet, and wondered at the newness of wanting something specific.

And then Tova knocked me down.

"What are you doing just standing there in my way?" she screamed. "I don't know how to move on these skates!"

"Tova!" Mrs. Lichtman called out. "Leave Izzy alone!"

"Fine!" Tova yelled back and crawled a few feet away from me. "Better?"

I couldn't quite breathe because Tova's elbow had hit my chest in the fall, but I didn't like that the answer was to leave me alone. I didn't like being alone. I wanted to call out to the frizzy haired girl and tell her she was beautiful and ask her to please teach me how to get to the place where she was. But I just coughed and coughed, and then it was time for pizza.

There were only eight of us left at Mrs. Lichtman's house when Shira's Mom showed up. We were sitting in a circle on the living room floor listening to the Jewish History teacher as she played her guitar and sang Israeli songs in a surprisingly lyrical soprano. I still hated her, though now I felt crummy for it, with her pretty voice and romantic ideas about love. Shira jumped up to greet her Mom and then waved me over and before I knew it I was being hugged.

"Do you need a lift home?" Shira's mother asked me. "Or would you two girls want to have a sleepover?"

Shira looked uncomfortable.

"My Mom will be here soon," I said. "She's usually late, that's all."

"Yes, Mothers, we make your lives so difficult. I don't know how you manage."

Shira had her garment bag and her book bag and her jacket on and seemed to be trying to propel her mother towards the door with the power of her mind. But it wasn't working. I had to agree to visit again soon, and to promise to eat, and even then, Shira's mom was looking back and forth between Shira and me, as if she was studying something invisible in the air between us. Finally, Mrs. Lichtman broke the stalemate by coming over to say goodbye to Shira, so I was able to escape.

I found my spot in the circle again while the frizzy haired teacher was answering questions about her skating background. It turned out that I wasn't the only one who'd noticed her out on the ice.

"Skating is like meditation," she said. "You discover all of these small details about how your muscles work that you never noticed before. And you feel like you're in a cocoon, protected, even in such a public place."

We were a little mesmerized by her, and then the doorbell rang again and broke the spell. Everyone jumped a little, but something about the bell or the duration of the ring or newfound ESP told me that danger was coming. I watched Rabbi Lichtman shake my father's hand as I ducked into the bathroom at the end of the hall. I stayed in there, breathing vanilla scented air and trying not to think about why my father was there instead of my mother.

Someone knocked on the door.

"Is that you, Izzy?" Tova tried to whisper but her voice naturally came out very loud.

I opened the door and she scooted into the room with me and leaned her back against the door. "What are we hiding from?"

"I'm hiding from the man in the black suit and black hat out there who isn't a rabbi," I said. I was backed up against the shower curtain, which was covered in brightly colored fish and offered no actual support.

"What's wrong with him?" Tova asked, checking her lipstick in the mirror and wiping the edges of her lips with the knuckle of her pinky.

"He's my father."

She watched my reflection in the mirror and for a few long seconds we stared at each other that way.

"I need to pee," she said. "Sorry."

She stepped away from the door so I could get out. Mrs. Lichtman was wandering in the otherwise deserted hallway holding a two-liter bottle of diet soda to her chest. "There you are, Isabel. Your father's looking for you."

She nudged me with her shoulder towards the living room where he was waiting, with the girls. He was only leaning against the wall listening to the guitar; all singing had ceased as soon as the doorbell rang. I wanted to pull Mrs. Lichtman aside and ask for asylum, but she was so used to melodrama, she wouldn't have taken me seriously. Or I didn't trust her to, anyway.

I grabbed my jacket and bag and said quick goodbyes at the front door.

"Let me take that," my father said, crushing my thumb between the straps of the bag as he took it from me. It was cold outside and I had to stop to put my jacket on before following him to the car along the icy sidewalk.

"Where's Mom?" I asked when I caught up to him.

He opened the trunk and deposited my bag before answering me. "She's at the hospital."

He'd taken my pretty white skates out of my closet and bashed mommy over the head and then calmly took her to the hospital and found the directions to Mrs. Lichtman's house in her pocket book.

"She's with Grandpa in the hospital," he said. "Your grandfather had a heart attack this morning." He opened the passenger door for me and grabbed my shoulder for a moment, offering comfort.

He drove directly to the hospital, parking illegally in the emergency lot and then ignoring the lady at the visitors' desk who asked where we were going.

When I saw my grandfather in his hospital bed, under a thin white blanket that outlined his skinny legs, I backed out of the room and tripped over my father's feet. He took my arm and pulled me into the room. Grandma was in a chair at the end of the bed, looking drugged, with Mom next to her holding a plastic cup of water and petting her arm.

"I wanted to come and get you myself," she said, dripping water from the cup as she stood and reached for me, but I moved out of the way and she sat back down.

She drove me home after an hour of sitting and watching Grandpa sleep. My father was already home and barricaded in their bedroom with the volume on the TV as high as it could go. I stood in the kitchen, waiting for the dog to greet me, knowing that the only reason she wouldn't come to see me was because she was behind the closed door of my parents' bedroom with no way out. I opened the refrigerator and held the cold door as if it were a very large, very stiff, teddy bear. Mom pressed the play button on the answering machine and suddenly Grandma was shrieking.

"He's going to die! The only person who ever loved me, and God is taking him away! You have to fix it. Where are you Robin? Why aren't you here where you belong? This is your fault!" She stayed on the line, moaning, or keening, for a few more moments before the sound cut off.

I looked at my mother and her eyes were red rimmed and deeper in her face than I remembered, as if every time she pressed away tears the clay of her face shifted.

"What is she talking about?" I asked. "What's your fault?"

"I told them about the abuse, about what your father did, to you."

"And she thinks that's what caused Grandpa's heart attack?"

Mom pressed her eyes closed with her thumbs. "Yes."

"Do you agree with her?"

"I don't know," she said and then walked away from me, up the stairs to the guest room, and closed the door.

Chapter Twenty-One

THE KISS,
OR HELL IS OTHER PEOPLE

Jake wrote me a note in his spidery half-script during English class on Monday.

So after my fifth beer (oh, and the stuff we found in the liquor cabinet, unidentified, mixed with cranberry juice because that's all they had left in the fridge) and after I fell over the couch and hit my head on the glass coffee table, I felt like Moses on the mountaintop. God was in the air. *Every breath, I was gulping God. God is right here in this paper, in your hair, available and infinite.*

He wrote more. He filled more pages writing to me about God than I'd ever seen him fill with notes about, say, Sylvia Plath.

I feel like the rabbis are trying to bottle up my soul, he wrote, *and sell it back to me piecemeal because they are afraid of what I will do if I breathe God without their guidance on how to use the resulting power. They are scared of me, and you, especially you. They are scared of what women would do with power, how women would break through the bottle and become an uncontrollable force, a chaos. They are afraid of the Godness of you.*

To a certain extent, I figured he hadn't gotten all of the alcohol out of his system. He had the craziness of the prophets who claimed to see the face of God; the drunk with hope voice of every sacred book I'd ever read. I wanted to feel that. I wanted the words to rub off the page and onto my fingertips. And I wanted to believe he really meant to be telling *me* and not just anyone who would listen.

I couldn't write back to him. I tried five times but only got as far as *Dear Ja* before I ran out of words. I didn't look at him when we left the classroom, so I couldn't know if he was angry or if he didn't care either way.

Mom picked me up from school, so we could visit Grandpa in the hospital. He was having surgery the next morning, so this was my last chance to see him and wish him well. Mom had been babysitting Grandma all day and we had to race back before one of Grandma's needs could go unmet. We didn't talk about Grandma's theory of heart attacks being caused by too much honesty. Partly, I was afraid Mom regretted telling Grandpa about the abuse, but mostly, I was afraid that Grandma was right and this was my fault.

When I entered the hospital room I found Grandma on her cot, with Grandpa's water pitcher, Jello, and TV remote surrounding her. I ignored the spectacle and walked around to the other side of his bed and kissed his stubble-covered cheek. He was still warm, alive. His hands were waxy but when he reached one out to me and I took it, I could feel his energy just under the surface. I sat on the edge of a white plastic chair Mom had dragged in for me while the nurses weren't looking.

"How are you, little bell?" Grandpa asked, still holding my hand.

"I feel like I'm about to be cut open," I said, and he smiled at me as if he was about to cry.

"Distract me," he said, squinching his eyes shut and rubbing my thumb.

I sat in the chair and told him a censored version of my weekend of prayer and contemplation. I told him about the pearls of barley in the chulent and the mysterious gloss. He told me it was the fat from the meat they used, it needed to be extra fatty to withstand all of the extra cooking since they had to start it before Shabbos on Friday and we didn't eat it until Saturday afternoon. A lean piece of meat would be like a rock by then, he said.

Grandpa held my hand tighter when we both ran out of things to say.

"Will you be okay while I'm asleep?" he asked me.

"I don't know."

We waited in silence for Mom to come back into the room and take me home.

After Mom dropped me off, she continued on to Grandpa's house, Grandma's house, whatever, with Grandma in the passenger seat. I thought about calling Shira, to see if she was planning to move to Israel to get as far away from my poisonous life as possible, but I wasn't up to actual conversation, especially with Mom giving up her protect-Izzy vigil in order to stay with Grandma overnight, as if she believed that, left alone, Grandma would end up running through the streets naked.

I crawled into my closet with a notebook and a pen to write to Jake, but I fell asleep before anything appeared on paper. I woke up to the feeling of my pen, cap off, drawing lines on my cheek. The clock on the VCR said it was nine pm but it felt a lot later. And I was hungry. Delilah had her nose pressed into the small opening between my bedroom door and the door jamb, pretending to be a watchdog, except that she was twitching through one of her squirrel chasing dreams. I had to nudge her aside to squeeze out of the room.

"Buy her a damn night light and come home!" My father screamed. He was downstairs, but his voice carried well.

"You're my wife and you belong here with me!"

I inched toward the stairs, but Delilah was too chicken to inch with me. There were a few moments of silence and I tried to imagine Mom's side of the phone conversation. Was she screaming? Trying to mollify him with sweet nothings? Or just staying quiet and waiting for him to get the ranting over with?

"What kind of mother would even think of moving out of her home to take care of a selfish old harpy? Let her hire a nurse!"

He threw something; I could almost see his fuzzy slippers as he paced through the hall, away from whatever had shattered on the kitchen floor. I could hear him wandering around downstairs, shuffling his feet on the hardwood floor. His voice was softer when he spoke again, and then the crying started.

"I can't live right without you," he said, and cried some more.

I tiptoed back into my room and curled into the closet again. It was hard to decide which would be worse, if my father was able to use me as bait to get Mom home, or if the really successful argument wasn't that her daughter needed her, but that *he* did. Either way, he would win.

I picked up my notebook.

Dear Jake,
God is a jackass.
                    Love,
                    Jezebel

219

YESHIVA GIRL

One of Jake's theories was that the school's alarm system was put in place in order to keep the students in, rather than to keep the terrorists out. But on good weather days the chained doors were left open during lunch and we were allowed to wander the grounds during lunch.

I had my heretical note to Jake in my pocket, but I wasn't ready to give it to him. I wasn't up to communicating with anyone, so I walked out into the yard. I tried to sit on one of the black rubber swings and dangle my feet, but my legs were too long. The swing set and jungle gym were meant for the little kids who came for camp in the summer, and I was supposed to be an almost adult with no need to rock back and forth.

I walked across the wet soccer field towards the fence at the far end. My loafers made a squelching sound as they lifted out of the muddy spots and the sound hypnotized me. I liked the idea that I could leave footprints behind. By the time I reached the fence, though, I had no idea how long I'd been out there. It felt like years. I started to run back towards the school building and had to stop when I reached the empty pool, because all of those days of not participating in gym meant I had no endurance whatsoever. I was doubled over for a moment staring at the grass, so I didn't see Tova and Jake right away. And when I did finally see them, everything blurred together so that I couldn't put the events in order. I know that I fell down and mashed my right knee into the mud. I know that I started making this funny sound, half choking, and half crying. I also know that Jake and Tova, before they were interrupted by the spectacle of me, were kissing pretty seriously against the brick wall behind the pool.

Tova rushed over to me and knelt down in the grass to help me up. She kept saying, "Are you choking?" and I couldn't answer. I

220

was so impressed that she was willing to get her pale yellow skirt dirty, for me.

Jake stayed back. I wiped the tears from my eyes so I could see him clearly. He kept hitting his head against the wire fence and all I could think was, hey, there's a brick wall not so far away, try that.

Tova led me back into the school building and into the bathroom where she wet a clump of brown paper towels and proceeded to wash my face.

She didn't say anything more and I couldn't read her mind. I couldn't understand why she was taking care of me. She stayed until I was able to breathe again and then she ran her fingers through my hair to straighten it out and said, "I'm sorry," and then, suddenly awkward, she ran out into the hall.

I hid behind a big garbage can in the stairwell at the back of the school building, instead of going to English class, because they would both be in there. The alcove behind the garbage can didn't smell too bad, kind of like bubble gum and pencil shavings. I imagined my grandfather, tubes in his nose and arm and wherever else, saying, "I'm disappointed in you, Isabel. I wouldn't expect you to skip class for something as commonplace as a broken heart."

I was surprised at how few people seemed to use the back staircase. I had only avoided it for most of the year because of an unfortunate encounter with a tuna fish sandwich on the handrail. But mostly I was surprised that my imaginary Grandpa would call what I felt a heartbreak. As if I had a heart.

My legs ached. I was sitting with one knee touching my nose and the other perpendicular and pressed into the wall. I was a pretzel instead of a girl and I liked the change. When I stood up after more than an hour in that position I fell back down. The dizziness seemed appropriate. I stood again and started climbing the stairs, slowly, not wanting to tumble backwards.

"Isabel, what are you doing out of class?" Rabbi Gottlieb turned to me from his perch on the windowsill.

"I was hiding behind a garbage can in the back stairwell," I blurted at him.

"And why is that?" He looked at me with a sort of smile on his face.

"Because I saw Jake kissing Tova, out there." I pointed out the window to the empty pool, because the location seemed important. "And my grandfather is having heart surgery, and my father has been accused of molesting one of his students and he should go to jail and stay there but I don't know if I can survive that. So I had some things to think about."

Rabbi Gottlieb stopped smiling.

"I've been trying to tell people what's going on with me, but I don't know how to say it right. I thought Mrs. Lichtman would understand but she can't even imagine how shitty my life is. She thinks if I just pray more I'll feel better."

I caught myself when I realized that I had just said "shitty" to a rabbi. I thought he might be angry with me for that, or for any of the other things I'd said. I was afraid of what he would say to me, but excited too that he might answer me at all. That someone would finally have heard me.

He stared back out the window and was quiet for a long time. "I think the best thing for you to do right now is to go back to class," he said. So I went.

Chapter Twenty-Two

CONVICTION

My father was home for dinner that night; my mother was not. I wanted to tell her the way Jake couldn't look at me anymore, the way he seemed to stop breathing each time I moved in my seat, the way he kept scribbling and then crumpling paper behind my head.

But she'd left a message on the machine that Grandpa was recovering from surgery and Grandma refused to leave the hospital.

"They *do* have good coffee there," Dad said after he played the message for me.

I was torn. I wanted to laugh. I wanted to make fun of Grandma and make light of the surgery and just hang out with my Dad. But I also wanted to, I don't know, do something apocalyptic.

"Were there any other messages?" I was hoping for and dreading a call from Rabbi Gottlieb and a knock on the door from the child welfare people.

"There *was* one special phone call today," he said.

"Yeah?" Pins and needles.

"My lawyer called." He opened the freezer and started unloading blank white ice cream containers. The good kind.

I lifted the caps on each pint: pistachio; Rocky Road; something very white that could be coconut; chocolate chocolate chip; cherry vanilla swirl.

He'd gone to the dairy utensil drawer for the big spoons and they clanked in his hand.

I made the hurry up motion. "Nu?"

"My case has been dismissed."

We ate all of the ice cream. ALL of it.

"What does 'not enough evidence' mean?" I asked as I watched a piece of frozen pizza heat in the microwave.

"You remember that the file for the case went missing," he said, leaning back in his chair and rubbing his belly.

"And there were no copies," I said, meaning to sound sarcastic but coming across, even to my own ears, resigned.

The microwave beeped and I put the next piece of pizza in to heat. Next up on my menu would be the value-size bag of rippled potato chips in the top of the pantry.

"They asked the girl for her testimony again, but her parents decided not to go through with it," he said. "They probably realized she wouldn't be able to lie the same way twice and were afraid they'd get in trouble. They must have thought there was money in this, originally."

The pizza was almost too hot for me to touch, but my father was made of asbestos and wolfed his piece down.

"I don't understand why the Assistant District Attorney would let it go so easily. Does *she* believe the girl was making it up?"

"I don't know what that bitch believes, but she has no case."

"Huh." Time to eat my piece of pizza, no matter how badly it scorched the top of my mouth. What I really needed was a pound of twizzlers to chew on, to keep me from talking. "But, I still don't understand how the file went missing?"

He ripped off a piece of crust and fed it to Delilah who was resting at his feet. "It's good to have friends," he said and winked at me.

"File clerk friends?"

"Police officer friends."

"Oh."

After he and Delilah traipsed upstairs for the evening TV shows, I camped out in front of the fridge wondering what I could eat next. Certain foods brought up more nausea than others; more cheese, for instance, was unthinkable.

I didn't wind up on the bathroom floor until around midnight. I couldn't throw up, but the cool tile around the toilet was refreshing. I remembered nights like this. There were a lot of them when I was little. A lot of middle of the night tea parties with my father, and then hours of hiding in the bathroom, or under my bed, waiting for my mother to wake up.

I saw Shira at the lockers the next morning, whispering with Brooke, and I turned and walked in the other direction. I couldn't deal with her, not now, not with my father gloating and indestructible and my mom always somewhere else.

I was so sure that Shira was going to ignore me, that I didn't know what to do when she came to sit next to me in our little classroom after she finished saying her morning prayers.

"I heard," she said, leaning her head close to me, so she could whisper.

"What did you hear?" I asked, afraid to look at her.

225

"Tova's a reptile."

I shrugged, remembering the way Tova washed my face.

"No, really, Izzy," Shira said, touching my arm. "Tova knows how Jake feels about you. Everyone with a pulse knows. She was jealous."

"There's nothing to be jealous about."

"Of course there is. I mean, I'm jealous."

"Why?"

"Because he listens to you. Boys listen to you."

I felt the walls closing in and tried really hard not to raise my voice. "Can we skip the part where you say mean things to me about David? I can't. Really." And all of a sudden I was crying.

Shira had to hustle me out of the classroom, into the empty hallway, and away from prying eyes. I slid down the wall to the floor and couldn't lift my head back up for the longest time. She put her arm around my shoulder and held on even when I tried to duck away.

"I wish I could call my mom," Shira said. "She'd know what to say. She was so angry at me after the Shabbaton. She saw something was wrong and I had to tell her and she said I was the one who was a bad friend for not noticing you were in so much pain."

I could picture Shira's mother standing there in Mrs. Lichtman's house, watching me, caring about me. My whole body hurt with the ache of wanting her to fix everything for me.

Shira knelt down next to me and leaned her head against the wall. "I spoke to David. He told me he thought we were good friends, but not dating. So I got that wrong, too. He doesn't want to make any commitments when he knows he's going to Israel next year. And I thought he was being really religious and that's why he didn't touch me."

I mumbled, "I'm sorry," and she turned me to face her.

226

"It was my fault. I was so jealous of you," she said. "I kept thinking how you were just like my sister, smart and pretty and you don't have to help take care of the younger kids because you're away in Israel."

I finally lifted my head to squint at her. "I'm in Israel?"

"It's my aunt's theory. She's a social worker, and she thinks I'm taking my anger at my sister, and my mom, out on you, because you're here. And something about how you're a blank screen, because you're so quiet, and I imagined all this stuff to fill in the blanks."

She was quiet, too, for a while, and I blurted out, "My grandfather had a heart attack."

"What? When?"

"Saturday. He had to have surgery."

"Oh my God. Is he okay? Are you okay?"

I shook my head. "I'm scared. Things at home are bad, and if he dies..." I couldn't finish the sentence. "And my grandmother blames me."

Shira stared at me with the oddest look. "Your grandmother blames you, for what?"

"For the heart attack."

"But, why?"

I could feel my internal wall building back up to stop me from telling her about my father. I could barely even see her over that wall, and I couldn't think of anything else to say.

Shira seemed to get that. "You don't have to tell me if you don't want to. But if something is wrong, and you need a place to stay, you could stay at my house and take the bus with me. My mom loves you, really."

I was tempted to say yes, to escape to her house and sleep in her sister's empty bed and hide from my family. But I couldn't leave my mom behind. I couldn't leave the possibility of Mommy behind.

And my father wouldn't accept it. He'd come to get me and bring his poison with him to Shira's house.

The rest of the girls spilled into the hallways before I could think of something neutral to say and we almost got trampled sitting there on the floor. But I felt better. For the rest of the school day I felt better, as if the weight of the world was hovering, instead of sitting right on top of me.

When we were waiting for our buses at the end of the day, Shira made a point of dropping her book bag on the sidewalk to give me a hug, and it felt good. I felt connected to her, and comforted. She promised to call me after dinner, to check in and see how I was doing, and I realized how much I wanted her to call. Knowing she cared about me would be my Teflon, to protect me from the bad stuff in the air at home. And then maybe I could breathe, and sleep through the night.

Chapter Twenty-Three

THE LITTLE RABBI AND FRIENDS

I was awake during the little rabbi's class on Friday morning because Shira and I were passing notes back and forth about home nursing – which was what her Mom did for a living and Grandpa would need – and we were both excited to have something not-David-related to talk about. I hadn't told her about my father's case, or the anti-climactic ending, or the abuse, or my fear that Mom had forgotten about the abuse. But at least we were talking. I hadn't spoken to Jake since before the Tova debacle.

We were discussing the Book of Esther in class, because Purim was coming up soon. It was a holiday where you were supposed to get so drunk that you couldn't tell the difference between the hero and the villain of the story. But I didn't need the loud noises and alcohol and strange costumes to get me to that place. I was already there. I'd been reading the *Book of Esther* every night lately when I couldn't sleep, and it bothered me that it all seemed to be about celebrating a Jewish girl who won a beauty contest. Very Long Island.

"I have a question," I said, to the wall.

The rabbi raised his head from his hands where he'd been mumbling about...I don't think even he knew what.

229

"Isabel?" he asked, surprised.

"Why are we supposed to admire Esther for basically prostituting herself to the king just because Mordechai told her to do it?"

"Are you suggesting that you've actually been *listening*?"

"This isn't funny," I said and I could hear the righteous indignation in my voice and knew I would have rolled my eyes if it had come from anyone else, and so, automatically, I rolled my eyes. "This guy Mordechai sends his dependant niece out to a beauty contest so she can become *one* of many wives. Even if you believe that he did this to save the Jewish people rather than simply to forward his own political career, doesn't that make him a pimp? And therefore, you know, icky?"

"Good question," the rabbi said, no longer mumbling. "And why do mothers dress their little girls as Esther for Purim without a second thought?"

I noticed that Shira was listening and even Tova, with her head resting on her elbow so that her hair could trail down the side of her desk like a coal black waterfall, even she was listening to the little rabbi. "We study Torah every day, and in these stories women are used over and over again for the sake of their families' desires, righteous or otherwise. Have you noticed that? You sit here and I wonder if you hear any of the words you read out loud."

The little rabbi had built up so much steam that there was a moment when I almost thought he was going to stand up. But he stopped himself. "What do *you* want to learn from Esther?" He asked me. "Do you want to live as she lived?" He slapped the desk and then shook off the pain for a second. "My point is: these are not lessons to be followed *as is*. More often than not we're reading stories about the pitfalls our forefathers, and foremothers, fell into because of their human weaknesses. They were jealous or lonely or selfish or just plain stupid. You are adults, or you will be. If something sounds wrong to you then maybe you're the one who's right."

He looked over at me. "Not *you* in particular, but eh…"

He stared at me and I stared back. "Now," he said, his head back in his hands. "Can I expect that you will, at the very least, remain awake for the rest of the class?"

I nodded.

"Good. Read the next passage."

I was still thinking about *The Book of Esther*, while Mrs. Lichtman was giving us a speech about modesty in Purim costumes. She was building into a rant about the girls at her shul who showed up each year dressed "like streetwalkers" when Tova interrupted her.

"What do you think about Mordechai prostituting Esther to the king?"

Mrs. Lichtman's eyebrows popped up like toast. "Excuse me?"

Shira jumped in to explain the back story and Mrs. Lichtman's eyebrows slowly lowered back to a more moderate level of curiosity. A few of the other girls added bits and pieces: Is Mordechai an uncle or cousin or guardian? Does he have the right to tell Esther what to do? If he were her real father would he be so quick to send her to the king? Are parents really supposed to do that sort of crap?

That last question was mine. We were creating pandemonium and I was really enjoying it.

Tova sat up and coiled her hair behind her back, which quieted the rest of us for a moment and gave her a chance to speak. "How come we're learning about how to be good wives, and when and what to wash, and eat, and wear, but no one talks to us about how to be good parents?" She dropped her hands to her desk and kept her eyes down, not making eye contact with anyone. "If we're not supposed to use birth control but we *are* supposed to marry young and we *shouldn't* say no to sex, don't we need to know how to raise the children that pop out?" Her fingers were turning white from pressing them down on the desk top. "Or are we supposed to raise our kids the way we were raised and mess up a whole new generation?"

Her face was red, not just her cheeks, and she was breathing hard, almost hyperventilating.

"You want a class in how to be a good parent?" Mrs. Lichtman asked in her gentlest voice.

"Yes," Tova whispered.

"I'm not the right teacher to ask."

Shira, who must have been listening as carefully as I was, raised her voice. "Why not?"

The teacher smoothed her skirt. "Because I don't have children."

"Why not?" Brooke.

"Three miscarriages. And a still birth."

Everyone was quiet and very still.

Except Tova. "You still must have an opinion," she said, and Mrs. Lichtman started to laugh so hard she couldn't keep her balance and had to lean against her desk.

"You're right," she said, gasping for air. "I have an opinion about everything."

We all laughed, because it was true and because she didn't seem to mind that we were laughing. When we finally calmed down she sat on her desk and folded her hands in her lap.

"Raising kids is the hardest thing to do right. Keeping kosher is easy, praying is easy, charity is easy. That said, if I had a daughter and my righteous husband tried to offer her to the king, even to save all of the Jewish people, I'd shoot my husband in the head. Period. Now, where were we?"

Mrs. Lichtman stopped me after class, waving Shira out into the hall with the other girls.

"Rabbi Gottlieb spoke to me," she said. She wasn't whispering, but she wasn't in full voice either. I was very aware of Shira's face looking through the small window in the door to the classroom, and so was Mrs. Lichtman, so we were both quiet for a while.

"He's concerned about you," she finally said.

My brain filled with sludge. He wanted to get rid of me and never speak to me or see me again. He wanted to throw me out of his school because I was tainted with my father's slime, or because I was dangerous to be around, or because he thought I was a liar. Mrs. Lichtman watched me as if she could hear the content of my brain and found it fascinating.

"Izzy, you're not alone," she said, putting her hands on either side of my head. "You have people here who care about you."

"My head hurts," I said, and she let go, which made my head hurt even more.

"I can't force you to confide in me, Isabel. But how about we plan to sit down together next week, and stare awkwardly at the walls if need be. And we can just keep doing that until something changes. Okay?"

I nodded, but not intentionally. I felt like my whole body was shaking and my head was just going along for the ride.

"Okay then," she said, and picked up her bag at the side of the desk. I watched her leave the room, but I couldn't move myself. The shaking was still happening at a deep cellular level, as if something inside of me was shifting.

Shira walked me to my next class. She said she was afraid I would have stayed stuck in that spot for hours, without her help. And she was probably right.

Chapter Twenty-Four

THE RUN AWAY, PART TWO

Jake called that night, after Shabbos had already started and my Shabbos candles were blinking at me from the counter. I was alone downstairs, pacing, waiting for my mother to come home while my father waited upstairs. I wanted to tell Mom about Mrs. Lichtman and Shira and the strange buzzing in my body that wouldn't go away.

Jake's voice on the answering machine was too loud, because I'd left the volume high hoping to hear my mother's voice over the sounds of my father's blasting TV upstairs. He'd taken to leaving the TV on for all of Shabbos, so as not to break the Sabbath by turning it off.

"I shouldn't have called," Jake said. "I'm sorry." His voice was shakier and less confident than I'd ever heard it. "Of course you won't answer the phone on Shabbos. Shira's right. I'm an idiot. I'm not worth God's wrath."

I almost picked up the phone, to ask what Shira had to do with it, and to tell him he was worth it, even though I wasn't sure if he was. But then I heard my father's bedroom door open to announce that we would be starting dinner, with or without my mother, and I couldn't move and Jake's voice disappeared.

234

My father woke me up Saturday morning to walk to shul. Mom had made it home halfway through Friday night dinner, but now she was at the hospital again, getting Grandpa ready to come home. Or go home. To his house. There had been no discussion about me walking to shul with my father. But there he was, standing over my bed, clapping his hands and telling me to hurry up.

Delilah followed me to the bathroom and then nosed my bare feet all the way back to my room. She was doing her best to keep an eye on me while Mom was away, but the turmoil in the family was stressing my poor doggy out. She helped me choose an appropriately modest outfit and then chewed on a pair of socks so I'd have her scent with me on the long walk. I made sure to give her the larger half of my piece of challah with chopped liver before I left, because, well, food is love.

I wore my winter jacket even though there wasn't much of a chill left in the air. All of the ice had melted into sloshy puddles and there were only occasional mini-mountains of snow on the grass. My father had on a new black suit, new black sneakers, and a new black hat, with a feather stuffed into the band. He'd been shopping.

"Maybe we'll visit Grandpa at home after Shabbos," he said as he closed the front door. He didn't lock it, as if he believed Delilah could protect the house with her ferocious bark, and she didn't need to be protected herself.

"Maybe Grandpa doesn't want visitors," I said.

"That's certainly possible."

The only chance I'd had to speak to my grandfather since the surgery was a short phone call when he sounded a bit out of his mind. He told me about the pretty pills the nurses gave him, and the rabbits hopping across his ceiling, and he gave me his theory behind bypass surgery: "There are blockages that you may have ignored, or

235

long believed could be healed, with hard work and compassion, but eventually your only choice is to find an alternate route around the blockage so that healthy blood can finally reach your heart." Or something to that effect. As I said, he was pretty loopy. But if my father was the metaphorical blockage in question, he probably shouldn't be allowed to visit the patient at home.

"Oh," my father said as we passed the library. "Rabbi Gottlieb called some time during the week. Actually, he called my rabbi, to talk about you. Did he tell you he was going to do that?"

"No."

"He said that I have a brilliant daughter, as if I didn't already know that. How could you be anything but brilliant?"

I didn't answer.

"He also expressed some concern about your school work and your inability to concentrate in class." He rubbed my shoulder, but only managed to massage the thick filler in the shoulder of my jacket rather than me. "I think you were right," he said. "You never belonged at that school."

"But," I said, shifting away from his hand, "didn't Rabbi Gottlieb say anything else?"

He ignored the question. "I've been looking into that all girls yeshiva for next year. I probably should have sent you there in the first place," he said and then laughed. "Never thought you'd hear me say I made a mistake, huh?"

His face lit up and he gazed at me with what he thought was love. And I wasn't sure if he was wrong about that. His love was twisted, certainly, and controlling and destructive, but it was all he had.

"A new school will be good for you. We all need a fresh start."

"I don't want to switch schools again, not now," I said, surprising at myself. I wanted to see Shira, and Jake. I wanted to sit

236

in Mrs. Lichtman's class and listen to her explain Judaism to me in a way that made more sense than whatever my father had patched together.

"You've never liked the Yeshiva," my father said. "Isn't that what you've been telling me all year?"

He put his arm around me and squeezed my elbow with his thumb and index finger, hard. I stepped on his foot and jerked away.

"You don't know what's best for you, Jezebel. When you're the Daddy you can make the decisions."

We walked the rest of the way in silence, because I couldn't think of anything else to say.

The rabbi's daughter ran up and down the aisle of the women's section of the synagogue until she finally ran out of breath and squeezed herself onto the rim of my chair.

"You wear ugly shoes," she said, pointing at my scuffed loafers.

I glanced at her red Mary Janes. One buckle was undone and I leaned down to fix it.

"Imma says you're coming to my house for lunch." She dangled her legs off the side of the chair and I tried to catch her left foot to tighten that buckle too.

She lifted her butt up onto my lap and clapped her hands against my knees in her own peculiar rhythm.

She was so little. So unafraid. She didn't care that her knees were showing and that some man might see her naked legs and think... what? I was afraid that if I could imagine the contents of their slinky, spiky minds then I would become one of them. I had to protect her from ever thinking that when she danced in the kitchen or kissed her father's cheek or sat on my lap, she was the cause of all evil.

"I need you to do something for me," I said and she seemed to recognize my seriousness and sat very still and only nodded once. "If my father tries to touch you this Shabbos, or at any time, scream."

She didn't ask me why or ask me to repeat myself she just nodded her head, five times in a row. She had no idea what I was talking about. And, really, why was I pretending that a five-year old girl could protect *herself.*

She leaned against me and went back to clapping her rhythm on my legs. She clearly thought she was hilarious. And then she giggled and pulled at the bottom of my sapphire sweater and her hand brushed my stomach before I knew what was happening.

I didn't want to hurt her. I didn't want to rip her little girl hand off. So I stood up and excused myself and ran to the bathroom. How could I be afraid of Rivky's hands? I found an empty stall and closed the door and rested my head on the cool metal. I would never be okay. Never be able to kiss Jake the way Tova did. Never be able to feel safe in my own body.

The outer bathroom door opened and closed and then Rivky's head appeared under the stall door.

"I see your shoes."

"Hi."

"You're not peeing," she said and I had to admit that I was not.

"Come out here." She pulled at my shoe under the door. "Now."

I opened the door, careful not to let it hit her as it swung over her head.

"You have to wash your hands," she said as she straightened up. Then she stood on her tiptoes and turned on the cold water in the sink. I let her shove my hands under the faucet and then blow on my fingers until she was satisfied that they were dry enough, despite the water still dripping on the floor. She held one of my hands and walked me out of the bathroom.

"Come see my baby," she said, and dragged me to the back of the shul where her mother had just come in pushing the baby carriage.

"See?" Rivky leaned over the baby and grabbed a hand to show me the tiny fingers. "She's dressed up as a boy baby." Sure enough, there was a little black beard drawn on the baby's chin.

The rabbi's wife sighed. "Magic marker." And then she laughed.

I tried to smile but my jaw ached. Another little girl.

"Congratulations, by the way," she said.

I forgot I was supposed to say that to her, and I was utterly confused that she was saying it to me.

"The case was dismissed against your father, yes?" she asked. "I've been so busy with the baby and hormones I may have misunderstood?"

"It was dismissed on a technicality," I said.

"But at least it's over, right?" She reached down and tucked the baby's blanket under her chin. "It's unbelievable the way people will persecute someone who is different from them."

"Excuse me?"

"He's being targeted because he's orthodox. That's what he said."

I looked into her eyes and she really seemed to believe what she was saying, and that scared me. For Rivky's sake. For the new baby. "My father is guilty, whatever he may have told you."

"But I thought..." she glanced automatically over to the men's side, at her husband's swaying back. Rivky was busy chewing on her little sister's thumb.

"He lied to you," I said.

The Rabbi's wife stared at me and I watched the words sink in. Rivky thought we were having a lovely conversation and decided to lift my hand and swing it back and forth. But with each second that passed, I began to realize what I had just done. I had outed my father to the people he most wanted to impress. He would be furious. Even if they didn't believe a word I said, it was enough that I had said something so horrible about my own father. As soon as he found out, and by the look on her face that could be very soon, he would come after me.

I placed Rivky's hand firmly on the side of the carriage, turned for the door, and walked out, and then, I ran.

Chapter Twenty-Five

TO GRANDFATHER'S HOUSE

I didn't know where I was running to at first. All I could think about was running away, like my mother. I had always believed, at least in part, that she was running away from me: because I was so difficult; because I needed too much of her; and I was such a disappointment; and I always required feeding and washing and talking to. But maybe, and I could feel this in my lungs as the air scraped across the raw red skin, maybe she simply ran away because she was afraid of my father and what he might do to *her*. She only escaped after the fights became so loud that I was afraid he would kill her. The moment after something crashed onto the kitchen tile or clattered against the Formica counter tops, that's when I would hear the front door slam and watch the car race down the street.

I slowed to a walk only when I could glance behind me and not see even a brick of the shul building in the distance.

Mom had tried to stand up for herself over the years. I remembered pressing my ear to the conjoining wall of our rooms, listening through the clothes in her closet, the yellowed wedding dress she'd kept for me. She could never convince him: that her friends were not out to get him; that her art was not more important to her than he was; that his flirtations were humiliating; that his religion was not going to help.

I had to sit down and take off my shoes and stop thinking. It was all of that damned thinking that was wearing me out, not the walking to nowhere. I was suffocating in my winter jacket and there was a pain like splinters through my toes. There was a bench for me to sit on in front of a building that turned out to be a library, and I wondered if there would be a water fountain in there. Water was good. There was probably a pay phone in there too, but I had no money and no one to call. Mom wasn't home, and even if she were, if she came to get me she would only take me home and that was not the place for me.

The water from the water fountain was cool and dripped in and then out of my mouth and down the little circles in the drain, separating out the puddle of water into sections, making it manageable. There were comfy chairs in the library and I sat in one, with a magazine open on my lap, but I couldn't read. My eyes were fuzzy and I'd forgotten how to put letters together into words. There was something peaceful about not making sense. You can just breathe and sit and wait while the noise swirls around you. I wondered if that's how Jake felt when he was drinking, and maybe he needed to drink, or kiss Tova, because his thoughts were as painful as mine and he needed a way out of the center of the pain, off to the side where things wouldn't hurt so much.

I closed my eyes and tried to find the dizzy place again.

Mom wouldn't be worried about me. She thought I was at the rabbi's house for the afternoon, eating chicken soup and helping Rivky dress her dolls. She had so many dolls. The women in the congregation brought her all of their hand me down dolls and the dolls' wardrobes. There were flight attendants and punk rockers and doctors and horseback riders and they drove cars and wore roller skates and draped feather boas around their necks. Those dolls were so damned intimidating. I could never live up to all of the things they could do.

The next thing I remember, I was walking again, passing the duck pond, not the usual one near home. There were stone bridges and slate walking trails and goose families walking flat-footed, just like me.

Even Delilah would think this was too much walking. She would be drooling by now, long ropes of saliva twisting together under her chin.

I rubbed my face a bit but kept going, following my true north, or west, to my grandfather's house. I must have been headed there all along but I only realized it when I passed the ice cream shop. I couldn't feel my toes anymore and there was a rasp in my chest that grew louder with every step. I knew, theoretically, that I was scared and angry and hungry and exhausted, but I was almost there and I had to keep going.

The driveway appeared in front of me with its craggy rocks marking each side and the black asphalt radiating heat. I stepped out of my loafers and just stood still, watching Grandpa's house spin in slow circles.

"There you are!" Grandma stomped her slipper-socked feet in the open doorway. "Your mother has lost her mind worrying about you."

"Why?" I asked. The whole world was tilting, or I was. I couldn't fathom walking even the last few steps into the house.

"Your father came home without you. And when she asked where you were, he wouldn't answer."

"Hmm," I said. The idea floated in my head that it didn't make sense for my father to already be home. It was late in the day, but not dark yet, not time for Shabbos to be over.

"Get inside before I freeze to death standing here in the doorway!"

She liked to scream, my grandmother. I stretched my arms wide and felt pins and needles start in my toes. I couldn't lift my feet off the ground, but I managed to shuffle forward up the stone walk and into the house.

"Why didn't you call home? How can you be so selfish?!"

Still screaming.

"Is Grandpa home yet?" I asked, leaning against the nearest book case as she closed the door behind me.

"Yes, and he's sleeping, so keep your voice down."

"Grandma?"

She stopped her march into the living room and turned to me. "What?"

"You are a freakin' lunatic."

Her cheeks reddened and her eyes narrowed. "Watch yourself, Isabel."

"Why? Why does everyone have to be so careful with you when you are such a screaming bitch?"

"How dare you?! I don't care how you talk to your parents, but I am your grandmother and you will treat me with the respect I deserve."

"You don't deserve anything from me," I said, holding onto the bookcase with whitened knuckles. "You could have fixed this. You could have loved my mother and taught her how to protect me. You could have seen what was happening and stepped in when I needed you. My father is a child molester and you couldn't care less."

I had to sit down. My legs were like cotton candy and I was filled with rivers of pee, but I didn't have the energy to walk the rest of the way to the bathroom. All I could do was collapse into the rocking chair and hope for the best.

"How could I have known what he did? If he really did any such thing, to you." She had to hold her self upright with one hand while her other hand gestured around the room like an errant feather duster.

"I have to pee," I said.

"I'm not stopping you."

I staggered a bit and then grabbed the handrail made especially for Grandma's arthritic hands and started down the hall. "If my mother calls, tell her I am drowning in a sea of urine. Let her guess who it belongs to."

"You're not as funny as you think you are, missy."

"Of course not," I said, and then focused my energy on getting away from her, one tiny footstep at a time.

Chapter Twenty-Six

THE BOOK OF ISABEL

I huddled in the bathroom for what felt like hours after the Grandma debacle. I'd wrapped a soft blue towel around me, but it couldn't stop the shaking in my legs. I imagined Grandma rooting through the attic, looking for a shotgun. She would run me out of the house, or, okay, stumble me out, and Mom would stay with my father and I would have no safe place to go. And Delilah would think I'd left her behind on purpose, but I didn't. Really, Delilah, I didn't mean to abandon you in that place.

"Izzy? Where are you?" My mother's voice ricocheted around the small house as if she was running from side to side and top to bottom. I had locked the bathroom door at some point, when I heard Grandma's asthmatic cough coming down the hallway, and now I was afraid to reach up and risk letting the maelstrom back in.

"Sweetheart?" Mom's voice was close by. "It's okay to come out now."

"I don't think that's true, Mom."

"She won't leave that room," Grandma said, then wheezed. "She's being a little brat."

"Shut up, mother! Just shut up about my daughter and my husband and whatever else you were about to say!"

Go Mom! I did a little seated dance with the towel I'd wrapped around my legs and then waited to see how Grandma would respond.

"Now I see where she gets that mouth of hers, Robin. You've spoiled that girl. Rotten."

"What would you know about raising a child, Mom?" My mother had been successfully distracted from her search for me. Grandma always knew how to shift attention away from other people and on to her.

"Are you going to start this again, Robin? Blaming your childhood for every mistake you've ever made?" Grandma snorted. "I don't need to hear any more of this."

"Yes you do. You have *never* listened to me."

I leaned toward the door to hear better.

"I did my best," Grandma said, without much conviction, I thought.

"And your best efforts weren't enough because your daughter was such a needy, stupid, deformed creature, right?"

"I never said that!" Grandma was huffing and puffing, either from outrage or asthma, I couldn't tell.

"You *did* say those things, Mom. Every time you ran away from home to stay at your brother's house or with one of your protégé's, you made sure to tell me I was the reason you needed to leave."

"Well, you should have known I didn't mean it. I was just letting off steam."

"At a child."

"A child whose every whim was filled, by her father and the housekeeper and whoever else happened to stop by and feel bad for the poor, mopey, silent thing in the corner. How long are you going to punish me for this?"

"You think I've been punishing you?"

I wanted to unlock the door and pull my mother inside where she would be safe, but then there was such a long silence, I wondered if Grandma was even out there anymore. Maybe there was some crucial body language going on and I was missing it. Some relenting from Grandma once she realized how much pain her daughter was in, and had always been in. When my father saw someone in pain, he reveled in it, but I didn't think Grandma was the same way.

"Let me in now, Izzy." Mom.

"Is she still out there?"

"No."

I unlocked the door and Mom slipped into the room and sat across from me, on the edge of the bathtub.

"Is she okay?" I asked, tucking the blue towel under my feet for protection from stray Grandma vibes.

"She's not my concern right now, sweetheart, you are." She gave me a steady gaze. "What happened today?"

"Didn't the bad man tell you when he got home?"

"The bad man," she repeated, and her lips turned up at the corners. "He started to tell me some story about the rabbi's wife but I couldn't concentrate on that. I was too worried."

"About me?"

"Of course." She slipped down to the floor and leaned her back against the vanity, next to me.

"I had to get away from there," I said, resting my head on her shoulder. "I told the rabbi's wife that Daddy really did molest that girl, and I was afraid he would come after me."

"So he wasn't completely lying," she muttered into my hair.

I tensed up. "What do you mean?"

"Your father said that the rabbi's wife had gone into a hormonal rage and lashed out at him for no reason and told him to get out of her house. She must have confronted him with what you said."

"She believed me?"

Mom stretched her legs out and I could hear her knees crackle. "I guess she did."

"Grandma doesn't believe my father molested me," I whispered.

My mother dug her fingers into the bathmat. "I should have known what he was doing, Izzy. I love you so much; I should have felt it the way I felt the pain every time you scraped your knee."

"I wasn't much of a knee scraper," I said, chin pressed into my chest to muffle the sound.

She didn't seem to hear me and just started to shake her head, as if she was arguing with herself. "But even if I had known, I don't think I would have had the strength to confront him. Not the way you do." She started crying and I gave her a corner of my towel to wipe her eyes, so of course she blew her nose with it. "You deserved a better mother than me, Isabel. A mother who would have known how to protect you."

"You're the mother I have," I said. "And you can learn."

We sat on the floor a little while longer, but I was starving. Really, desperate for a pizza. And my butt was numb.

"I can't go back there, Mom," I said, as we both tried to stand up with our various numb and creaking body parts. "Even if you need to stay with him, because you love him or he needs you or he has all the money. I can't do it anymore."

"I know," she said and then didn't say anymore.

Grandpa wasn't up to eating real food yet, just dry toast and Jell-O. Mom and I ate in the living room, and Grandma sulked with her slice of pizza in their bedroom, so I was left with half of a cold pizza when I woke up on the couch at midnight. Mom must have stayed until I conked out and then written her goodbye note on a spare napkin.

Dear Izzy,
Delilah needs dinner. Will bring your clothes tomorrow. Sleep well.
Love,
Mom

That was my mother, never one to tell the whole story when cryptic fragments would do. No mention of my father, or the possibility that he was waiting at home with a dull knife in his hand.

My legs ached from the long walk, and now my neck refused to turn to the left because couch cushions are not pillows and should not be used as substitutes. I needed to wander a bit, and even though this house was on the small side for walking trips, I'd be damned if I would go outside to stretch my legs. It was dark and spooky out there, and surprisingly, not so scary inside.

I checked the fridge first, of course. It's important to know the food supplies available in any environment. Mom had emptied the kitchen down to bare bones for Grandpa's new low-fat, low taste diet. Even the secret stash of chocolate behind the coffee cans was missing. All of the regular bread had been replaced with sawdust bread, and the egg shelf wobbled with little cartons of eggs whites. Worst of all, the ice cream was gone.

Next stop, the guest room, which was usually mine, except that Grandma was sleeping on the bed with a grey shawl draped over her and pajamas that looked suspiciously like the clothes she'd been wearing all day.

A pit stop in the bathroom again. Then a light tip toe down the hall past the master bedroom to examine the sewing room to see if I could sleep there, but I must not have tiptoed well because Grandpa heard me.

"Isabel?" His voice was breathier than usual, but still his.

I knocked on the open door to his room.

"Come in," he said, in his pretend formal voice, which was only slightly different from his casual voice.

I stayed in the doorway for a second, assessing the new invalid's room. He was ensconced on his own side of the bed, not even a finger encroaching on Grandma's side.

"Why is she in the guestroom?" I asked him, nodding to the empty space.

He glanced at the white pillow next to him, but didn't answer.

"Sorry, not my business," I said, feeling my cheeks burn. I dragged the hard backed chair over to the bed.

"I needed to rest," he said, finally. "The medications they gave me are potent." He paused and stared at something over my head. "And I've been thinking, which Grandma doesn't appreciate from me." He grinned, just a little, and caught my eye. Those sparkly eyes of his made everything seem better. I couldn't explain why; just a natural wonder of the world.

"The kitchen has been denuded of all good things," I said, pulling my legs up onto my chair, using my skirt as a sort of tent.

He gave a long, dramatic sigh. "Yes. No more chopped liver, for a while anyway. But when I'm feeling more myself, I'll teach you how to make ice milk, and egg white omelets, and if you're really good, maybe we'll explore the wonderful world of bran muffins."

Meaning, he wanted me to stay. I wondered if that was one of the things he'd needed to think about without Grandma's interference.

"So, once I've learned the art of oatmeal and jam will I have to go back to my father's house?"

"Never," he said, teeth gritted.

"But..."

"He will never get his hands on you again, even if I have to cut off those hands myself."

Grandpa didn't scream, or even raise his voice, really, but all the tentativeness was gone. My legs started to tremble and I couldn't make them stop.

He stared over my head again and seemed to be talking to himself. "I've always loved challenges too much. I gave my attention to the students who resisted learning, and resisted me, instead of the kids who wanted what I was offering them. I believed that the eager students could take care of themselves, but the rebels – oh – they really *needed* me."

His breathing was labored, and too fast. I reached out to touch his arm. "It's okay, Grandpa."

"No, it's not." He shook off my fingers. "I always knew that part of Grandma's charm, for me, was how difficult she could be. She presented so many unique problems. She was never boring. And when Robin chose your father, I actually *approved.* I thought, my daughter is just like me, she takes on the tough cases."

I reached for him again. "Please, just breathe normal for a while."

But he couldn't calm down. "I should have known what he was, Isabel. But I am so foolish. So arrogant." He rested his head more heavily on his pillow, running out of breath and energy at the same time.

"You didn't know what he was doing, Grandpa. You couldn't have imagined that." I leaned over to cover his chest with the blanket, but he turned away from me. I thought he didn't want me there anymore, but I was afraid to leave him alone with his bad breathing.

"When does the nurse come to check on you?"

"Tomorrow morning." He looked back at me and there were little tear puddles on his cheeks. I wiped them away with the handkerchief he kept on the bedside table.

He fell asleep so fast that I had to stay for a few more minutes to make sure his chest still rose and fell. When I went to put the handkerchief back, I noticed there was a notebook open on the bedside table. I recognized his handwriting from before the heart attack and then, halfway down the page, it got shakier. It was a list: find math tutor; call Rabbi Gottlieb; convince the lawyer she has to leave now; redo the guestroom; plead with her; tell Izzy how much I love her, because she doesn't seem to know.

I placed the handkerchief on top of the notebook and left the room, careful not to wake him as I made my way down the hall.

I hadn't been in the sewing room in a long time, not since Grandpa built the shelving unit and I stood next to him holding a can of nails. This was the dustiest room in the house, by far. The sewing machine cover had started out as a rose patterned fabric, but now it was just grey. The single bed in the corner was covered with piles of quilting scraps Grandma had collected for projects that, with her arthritis, she could no longer finish. I'd been in fabric stores with her, watching her touch the fat quarters with her eyes closed, as if she was mentally putting the quilt together, as if knowing it could exist in her mind was enough.

The shelving unit was floor to ceiling and held her collection of yarns, including the sapphire blue Mom had used for my sweater. Then there were open boxes filled with knitting needles and stitch holders and Velcro and buttons and a huge clear bag full of white stuffing.

If I was going to sleep in this room, it would need cleaning, organizing, and some judicious throwing out of unnecessary crap. But first I had a call to make.

I knew Jake's phone number, but I'd never called it before. I worried that one of his parents would answer, but figured I could handle a screaming adult. One more wouldn't matter at this point. The rotary phone on the bedside table looked ancient, but it still gave me a dial tone, and a dusty surface to draw on while I waited through five long rings.

"Hmm, uh," someone answered.

"Can I speak to Jake, please?" Even after midnight it seemed like a good idea to be polite.

"Izzy." His voice was muffled but recognizable.

"How'd you know it was me?"

"Hoped," he said, and my heart ached with the way he said it.

"I just wanted to tell you," I said, holding the receiver with both hands. "I want you to know that it's okay. The Tova thing."

"No, it is not okay." I heard rustling in the background and footsteps and a door closing. "I don't wanna wake my little sister," he whispered, and then more footsteps.

I waited.

"The thing is," he said, and his voice was more clear, wherever he was now. "You should expect more of me. My parents should care if I'm a good person. I care if I'm good or not, and I want you to care."

"I care."

"Good."

"So then, why did you do it?"

"Because I'm an idiot. Shira was right."

"What does Shira have to do with it?"

"She said I was making things worse, hiding from you. She said especially now, I should be trying harder not to be an asshole."

"Huh." I couldn't picture Shira using that word, but then, she'd been surprising me in a lot of ways. I'd have to take care not to make assumptions about her from now on.

"What's so special about right now?" Jake asked, reminding me that he was there.

"It's a long story."

"I'm up. Tell me a story."

"No."

"Why did you call me so late at night?"

"That's part of the story."

"Oh."

"I'll see you on Monday."

"You will."

"Then good night, Jake."

"Don't go."

"Go back to sleep."

He didn't answer, just stayed on the line, and I listened to him breathe for a while before I hung up the phone.

I couldn't call Shira at this hour, but I wanted to and that wasn't like me. I'd call her in the morning and at least tell her that I wasn't at home anymore. That I was safe.

Very odd.

I started organizing the piles of fabric on the bed, and making an imaginary list of the tasks to be done during daytime hours: vacuum; run sewing machine cover through the wash; throw sewing notions at Grandma's head.

It was strange to think of my intellectual snob of a grandmother being so devoted to craft work, something so feminine, and so often ignored by men. I wondered where she'd learned how to sew, if there was a story behind it that she'd be willing to tell me, and if it would help me understand her enough to figure out how to live in her house without going crazy.

There was a closet in the back of the room. I'd already gone through every open drawer and shelf in the room by then, and checked under the bed and behind the yarn. This was the last frontier. Mom's artwork. Her old sketch books were segregated by periods in her life: before me, and after me, for the most part. I hadn't realized they'd been moved here from the attic in our house, where they'd lived for most of my life. There were loose sketches, new ones I hadn't seen before, so many pictures of me, with birds. Birds at my shoulders, birds lifting me up, a thousands birds surrounding me, acting as two glorious wings to carry me. I couldn't stop looking at this new version of me, wondering if this was really how Mom saw me, wishing I could feel the wings on my back.

I heard a car outside and then the front door opened and there was a tap tap on the hardwood floors and then scraping in the hall before Delilah rushed in and started licking my face and my fingers and then she was gone again, with a piece of paper in her mouth.

"What have you got there?" Mom whispered, not too far away.

I put the rest of the loose sketches back in one of the notebooks and placed it on the bed next to me.

"Mom?"

"I'll be right there, when Delilah lets go."

I chose a skein of thick red yarn and threw it out to the dog and she gave up her prize and immediately started to unravel her new toy.

"What are you doing in here?" Mom asked, folding her slightly chewed but mostly intact artwork and hiding it behind the sewing machine.

"Grandma stole my room. I am making do."

"Ah." She looked around. The room was much messier than when I'd started cleaning.

"There was a message on the answering machine at home, from the rabbi's wife," Mom said, clearing off a seat for herself on the small bed. "She wanted to know if you were all right."

"Huh."

"Your father was asleep when I got back, or else I'm sure he would have erased the message."

She leaned against a pile of fabric and it held her up pretty well. "I went to a lawyer, you know, a while ago," she said. "And he told me that I shouldn't move out because I would lose my share of the house, and his pension. I wouldn't be able to support you."

"You didn't tell me," I said, even though I'd overheard snippets.

"I wanted to leave months ago, but the lawyer said I should wait, because I wasn't in any immediate danger."

"You wanted to leave without me," I said, thinking of her sailing away. That image had stuck with me.

"God, no!" she said, thoroughly surprised. "I was afraid you wouldn't come with me. I thought you might choose to stay with your father."

"Why would you think that?" I said.

"Because, I would have chosen my father."

I leaned back against another pile of scraps and lost my balance. "Communication skills are sadly lacking in this family," I said, trying to sit back up.

Mom smiled and lightly slapped my knee. "Ahem."

"I saw Grandpa's list."

"Yes, I saw that too."

"I thought no one cared about me," I said. "I thought Grandpa was so busy with Grandma that he didn't have time for me."

"Oh no, that's not true at all. He wanted you to spend weekends here, and Grandma said okay, but your father refused. There was no negotiating, no way to move him."

"No one told me."

"I was hoping a guilty verdict would change things, and then you wouldn't have had to deal with any more bad news. I only wanted to tell you good things."

"But he got away with it, Mom. He got away with everything."

"No," she said, "That's not true."

"Yes it is."

"No. I found another lawyer, and I trust her. We're going to be alright."

Delilah stumbled in with yarn wrapped around both front paws, through her mouth and over one ear. Mom reached forward to untangle her. "I couldn't sleep in that house," she said, "knowing he was there and you weren't." One paw came free. "I could never sleep those nights when you stayed with Shira or went to a Shabbaton. The house seemed so dark without you. The summers you spent in camp were unbearable."

Two paws free, but somehow the yarn had migrated towards my poor dog's belly and I had to scoot down to the floor, with a pair of scissors, and stop her from cutting off blood flow to her internal organs.

"Maybe you'd be able to sleep here," I said. "I mean, I sleep alright when I'm here. Maybe it's the air quality."

"I'm sure that's what it is," Mom said, kindly ignoring the dust wafting up from the carpet. But she couldn't ignore it for long, because Delilah was scratching at the floor, kicking up more dust as she tried to free herself from a whole new set of knots around her back paws. The red yarn would have been striking on her, if it had been in sweater form. Alas. Mom found a sharper pair of scissors and we set to work cutting through the knots and untangling the mess while Delilah sighed with what I choose to believe was happiness.

YESHIVA GIRL

Made in the USA
Middletown, DE
05 March 2019